T0196869

The Simulation

PHILLIP J. WATT

BALBOA.
PRESS
A DIVISION OF HAY HOUSE

Balboa Press books may be ordered through booksellers or by contacting:

Balboa Press
A Division of Hay House
1663 Liberty Drive
Bloomington, IN 47403
www.balboapress.com.au
1 (877) 407-4847

Because of the dynamic nature of the Internet, any web addresses or
links contained in this book may have changed since publication and
may no longer be valid. The views expressed in this work are solely those
of the author and do not necessarily reflect the views of the publisher,
and the publisher hereby disclaims any responsibility for them.

The author of this book does not dispense medical advice or prescribe the use
of any technique as a form of treatment for physical, emotional, or medical
problems without the advice of a physician, either directly or indirectly. The
intent of the author is only to offer information of a general nature to help
you in your quest for emotional and spiritual well-being. In the event you use
any of the information in this book for yourself, which is your constitutional
right, the author and the publisher assume no responsibility for your actions.

Any people depicted in stock imagery provided by Thinkstock are
models, and such images are being used for illustrative purposes only.
Certain stock imagery © Thinkstock.

Print information available on the last page.

ISBN: 978-1-5043-1142-7 (sc)
ISBN: 978-1-5043-1143-4 (e)

Balboa Press rev. date: 11/27/2017

Dedication

This work is dedicated to the re-enchantment of our individual and collective consciousness, as well as the rebirth of our social system so that it truly benefits earth's ecology, including our human family.

CONTENTS

CHAPTER 1

Beginner

G ary and Elle were on holiday. They'd been travelling for just over a week, taking a much needed break from their daily grind back home. They had been doing the usual tourist circuit, such as losing their breath in the natural sights, exploring the wilderness, playing at the theme parks and really letting loose on the club strip.

They were trying to hold onto their youth as long as they could, given Gary was 33 and Elle was 29.

It was well after 1am on Tuesday night. They'd been at a nightclub not far from their hotel, when Elle started feeling a bit overwhelmed by the many drinks she'd consumed since going out for lunch.

"I'm really glad I got this fresh air", she told Gary. "I feel much better already. Want to go home and get a bit naughty?", she continued, seductively.

"Fuck yes I do", replied Gary with a slightly cheeky tone, whilst putting his arm around her shoulders, down her back and onto her bum. "You know I do", he continued, giving her a sexual squeeze.

The street they were walking along was filled with neon lighting that penetrated deep into their sensory tapestry. Bright greens, pinks, purples and blues were the dominant colours, although a yellow flashing signage caught Gary's attention.

"Meet Your Master?", Gary asked in an interested tone. "What is that meant to mean?"

"I don't know Gaz; who cares", replied Elle. She was too obsessed with stroking Gary's chest, whilst thinking about taking their clothes off when they get back to the hotel, to properly focus on what he had said.

Given his vision was slightly fuzzy due to the long drinking session, it took him just a little longer to realize that on the top left of the sign it read 'New Arrival'. He then looked for the store name, which he was eventually able to process as 'Adventure Games'.

"Hmm, it must be a new game", Gary uttered under his breath. "I've always wanted to try one of those new virtual reality things", he continued, just after he noticed the 'open 24 hours' blue flashing sign. "Let's go have a look baby".

"Oh really, hell no", Elle replied with a fake tone of anger. "I want to make love and lust honey", she said in a persuasive fashion.

"What, you're not happy with the three orgasms you've already had today?", he responded cheekily.

"Actually, it's four", she smirked. "I fucked myself in the shower before we came out".

"Then it's settled", Gary concluded. "Let's just take a quick look and then I'll take you home so you can satisfy me", he said with a faint giggle.

"Alright baby".

They looked to the right to make sure no cars were coming, even though the street was only littered with the occasional people walking, or stumbling, along the sidewalk. As they crossed the road a camp of bats flew overhead. They walked to the shop and began the ascent up the staircase which led them to the front door.

Even though the path was well lit by all types of lighting, the windows of the store were blackened. "Ah, love it. Looks creepy as hell", joked Gary.

As they walked up to the front door a young man in his early twenties walked out with a large grin. "Howdy", he said, without making eye contact.

"Hey", they both replied simultaneously.

Catching the door just before it closed, Gary swung it open again and walked inside, holding it to let Elle follow. "Cool", they again said simultaneously, as they began to take in all the lights, screens and gadgets.

As they let the door close behind them, the room went slightly darker as the veranda lights were sealed off from the wooden door. It was an ambient shade of lighting, but with pockets of light let off by lava lamps, computer screens and other devices. There was a sweet smell that came from an oil diffuser on the back wall, which caught Elle's attention immediately.

"Hello", came a voice from the back left corner of the room, slightly startling them both.

"Oh shit man, I didn't see you there", said Gary. "How's it going mate?"

"Good, good. I'm Apollo", he replied, whilst standing up from his chair.

"Elle", she interjected, whilst tapping on her chest. "And this is Gaz".

"How can I help you guys?", asked Apollo.

"Mate, I've never played the virtual games before. Figured I'd come in and check it out", answered Gary. "Is that what 'Meet Your Master' is?"

"Sure is", answered Apollo. "It's the latest biotech program, actually. Vibrate VR".

"Vibrate VR?", questioned Elle.

Apollo explained that the new technology in virtual reality is hopping into a 'frequency resonator' which aligns the user's consciousness and the electromagnetic fields of the brain and heart to the software program, instead of having a visual experience with goggles.

"It's totally different to how virtual reality was originally developed", he continued. "It uses a collection of magnetic fields and high frequency sound that you cannot hear to shift the awareness of the player. One day I imagine this sort of technology will help heal disease too, as mainstream science is finally acknowledging that the cells of the body don't just communicate through chemical and electrical signals, but also via vibration and nonlocal communication in the quantum field".

"Is it safe now though?", asked Gary, ignoring Apollo's academic rant.

"Of course it is you pussy", joked Elle. "Sounds like fun. How much is it?"

"It's not cheap yet", replied Apollo. "One hundred bucks for an hour, but for the two of you I'll do it for one eighty. You'll have an hour to explore a virtual world that looks and feels as real as now, except there are no consequences for your actions".

"Huh?", Elle responded shyly.

"In other words, you can do whatever you want", Apollo continued. "You can fuck, steal, blow shit up – all without a karmic debt. If you don't like what's happening, you can hit the reset button and start again. It really is unlimited in its potential too, because you bring your own memories and knowledge to the equation. So as you enter this pseudo-reality, you can summon the experience based on your own life, as you see fit".

"Whoa, sounds sort of messed up", reflected Elle.

"Yeah it can be used for some crazy ass things, but it was primarily designed for healing and learning", reassured Apollo. "The inventor, Will Beal, created it so that we can more easily explore our subconscious to understand ourselves better, rather than rely on becoming good at meditation".

"I'm not sure I follow?", reached out Elle in a vulnerable tone.

"Well, our conscious experience is mostly made up of information that we're not aware of", explained Apollo. "From our memories to our traumas, or just all of the programming that lies in the depths of our subconscious mind, it drives our experience of reality even though we don't usually acknowledge it. So if there's things about ourselves that we don't like, such as bad habits for example, we can explore our subconscious to find out what is driving those behaviours so we can heal and develop those neural and conceptual pathways".

"Lost me too", shrugged off Gary.

"Okay, there's definitely a time and place for that, but

right now I want to have some fun!", exclaimed Elle. "Let's do it babe".

Gary looked at Elle, who had a devilish look in her eyes. "Sure", he agreed. "Can we enter the same world together?", he asked Apollo.

"Yep, sure can", he replied. "You can choose to enter the same game, or do it separately. If you're in the same construct, then you'll have to agree on what you want to experience, otherwise you'll split off on different timelines, so to speak. If that happens, just set a meeting point to reengage".

"How do you do that?", asked Elle.

"You speak to each other, which is sort of like telepathy", Apollo clarified. "You say, 'I'll meet you at your favourite beach' or wherever. Then if you agree, you'll automatically be there. It's just like magic; you're manifesting reality with your mind. That's how the game starts. Before you enter the resonator, which is really just a float tank with some magnets and high frequency speakers, I'll hook you up to the monitor. Then you hop in and I'll give you the body sedative, which will make your mind go dark in isolation for a few seconds. Maybe ten. Then you'll be able to talk to each other. It's from that point that you either mutually decide what to manifest, or create your own experience. Make sure you have a chat beforehand to not waste time".

"So if we want to go to the Amazon Rainforest, all we have to do is agree to it and we'll be there?", Gary asked for clarification.

"Yes. Now don't forget, it's not really real. It's not a true reflection of reality. So if you decide to manifest the Amazon, with the information contained in the software as well as both of your minds, it'll come up with a version that fits in with all of that. So if it's a little uncomfortable or scary or whatever, just set your intention to 'reset'. When you do, you'll be back in the blackness. If you want to leave the game entirely, set your intention to 'exit' and you'll find yourself back in the float tank".

"What happens if I want to leave earlier than an hour, will the sedative still be affecting me?", asked Elle.

"No", replied Apollo. "It wears off pretty quickly, it's just a quick way of interfacing with the software. If you exit too quickly and want to go back, I can give you another dose. There's no side effects either; it's just a natural relaxant extracted from a plant.. from the Amazon actually".

"Awesome", Elle and Gary replied at the same time. They both looked at each other and started laughing due to being so synchronised that night, which had been a theme of the whole trip.

"We're gonna have to start playing 'jinx' I reckon", chuckled Gary. "We've got to stop this pretty quickly before we end in a co-dependent relationship!"

"You'll never have enough of me", Elle responded sexually.

"Okay then", Apollo interrupted in a jokingly awkward manner. "Are you guys ready?"

"Fuck yeah", they both responded, which resulted in all three of them bursting out with laughter.

After he recovered from a good belly laugh, Apollo walked over to the door-less doorway in the front left corner of the room and parted the red curtain that covered it. He walked in and then a few seconds later popped his head back through: "I'll set up which will take me about five minutes.

How about you have a seat over there and have a chat about what you want to do. And remember, you can do anything that you can conceive of".

Elle led Gary over to the waiting chairs, which gave him the chance to grab her on her bum again. "Anything hey", he repeated sassily.

"Mmmm, god Gary, I want you so bad", she whispered. "Do you want to fulfil some fantasies in there?"

"So you could fly to another galaxy, or even hang out with your idol, but all you want to do is fuck me", Gary remarked cockily.

"Who says I don't want to fly to another galaxy and fuck both you and Jim Carey?", Elle replied, with a wink.

"Touché", giggled Gary. "Alright, so what do you have in mind?"

"Good question", Elle said in a confused tone. "Everything, really", she continued with more confidence, realising half way through that there was a good pun in her sentence. "How about we start off on a deserted island paradise, naked of course, and then play it out naturally?"

"You're speaking my language", agreed Gary. "So to be clear though, anything goes?"

"Yes baby, anything. Let's have some dirty fun, yeah. Show me how you satisfy your woman, and yourself!"

"Alright you two, keep it in your pants", sniggered Apollo. "Everything is ready to go. Inside the float room there's a dressing area. Strip off your clothes and put these on", he continued, handing them some green and black swimmers. "After you're ready get in your assigned float tank, put on your eye mask and I'll hook you up. Don't worry, the water is exactly body temperature, so it feels perfect. It's also perfectly salted so that you float without touching the bottom. It helps to remove any unwanted sensory noise".

They both nodded, took their gear and headed into the float room. Whilst they were getting changed behind the dressing curtain, Gary ran his finger up Elle's arm, along her neck and across her face, leaning in to kiss her with passion. She reciprocated by kissing him even stronger, and then gently biting his lip. Then with the tiniest amount of saliva she spat it onto his face, and whispered, "see you on the inside".

Gary smirked at the pun.

"Alright Apollo-man; we're ready", rushed Gary. They walked over to the float tanks as Apollo entered the room. It was at that point that Gary saw the monitors with flat lines on them. "What are they for?", he asked, suspiciously.

"We monitor breathing and heart rate at all times", responded Apollo.

"Yeah, I get that, but why? I thought it was safe?"

"It is, it is", Apollo comforted. "It's just to be absolutely sure, given we can't see you inside the tank. If in the unlikely event something does go wrong, the machine will send a notification to the hospital and they'll dispatch an ambulance immediately. It's just part of the deal with the insurance companies".

"Ah, okay", Gary said, sounding more content. "So what do you need to hook up?"

"Before you hop in, I'll place this transmitter on your chest. Then after you're in I'll inject the sedative into your left arm. It'll only be the slightest of stings, and there is no ongoing pain. Like pressing your finger onto the end of a knife or scissors. Any more questions?"

"Nope, I'm good", finalised Gary. "Elle?"

"I'm good too babe, see you on the island", she responded, in a scantily clad voice.

"Alright, arms down by your side", Apollo directed. He then removed the film from the back of the transmitter and stuck it to both their chests, right above their hearts. "The time is 1-54am on the eleventh of September, Twenty Twenty. I'll start the hour at 2am, giving you till 3am. Oh and one more thing. Time is a little distorted in the game, so most people feel like it was a little longer or a little shorter than an hour. If you're one of the lucky ones, you'll feel like it was a lot longer than it actually was".

"No worries", they both replied at once, causing all of them to once again detonate with laughter.

"Now hop in", Apollo said, whilst still giggling.

Gary was already fully submerged by the time Elle was getting her feet wet. Once he was settled Apollo reached in and pricked his arm with the sedative, which Gary only barely felt. He closed the door and turned off the light, and then proceeded to do the same with Elle, completing about ten seconds after Gary.

"Have fun", only Elle heard, ever so slightly.

Gary immediately woke up in a very dark place. He couldn't feel much, even though he felt basically normal, which he found very interesting. "Elle?", he investigated. With no response, he figured it was a little too early as he had been put under first. "So, a deserted island all to ourselves and our desires", Gary thought to himself.

"That's right baby", responded Elle. "I'm here. You ready?"

"Created ready baby", Gary said with confidence, trying to mask the shock of Elle being able to hear his thoughts.

The very next moment they were staring at each other, naked, on a stunning white-sanded beach. The sun was shining without a cloud in the sky. Deep green rainforest carpeted the landscape with eclectic bird sounds filling the airwaves. It looked exactly like reality itself.

"Holy fuck", asserted Elle. "I feel like I just had a massive toke on a joint".

"Yeah I feel ya", Gary laughed. He was already thinking about how disorienting it was, adjusting to the game. "It's like waking up from a really deep sleep".

"Okay, now we're awake, what do you want to do?", Elle said slyly, as she watched a blue and red butterfly dance around them both. She turned to look at Gary, who was swinging his penis in circles whilst yelling, "Get to the chopper!"

Elle almost fell over laughing. "Alright, alright, I'll take the lead on this one. I want to manifest a gorgeous beach house with a view of the ocean and the neighbouring islands".

"Done", agreed Gary, which immediately created her wish.

"Oh my god baby, it's like we're genies! Let's go in and take a look", Elle said enthusiastically.

They entered the large cabin and walked upstairs to a master bedroom with a view to die for. Dolphins played magically about one hundred metres to the front left. Birds were flying past the window, almost like they were trying to get a sneak peek at these human sex symbols.

"Jeez, she looks so bloody hot", Gary thought. "Hmm, could you hear that?" Gary asked in thought, remembering that telepathy was a thing in this world.

"Hear what?", Elle replied in thought.

Speaking normally, Gary said "Okay, well I had a private thought about you and then remembered that we can hear each other's thoughts, so I asked if you heard it. But you didn't, which means that you can only hear what I think, if I want you to hear it".

"What was your thought?", Elle asked in her mind.

"That you're deliciously sexy", answered Gary, telepathically.

With that they embraced each other and kissed passionately. They began to explore each other's bodies with their hands, which stoked their sexual appetite. Their genitals started to juice for each other, reflecting that they were ready to have their fun.

"I wonder if you can get drunk in this game", Elle excitedly shouted. "I want a sexy naked butler to bring me some Pina Coladas!"

There was no change.

Elle continued: "Gary, I want a sexy naked but…"

"Oops, my bad", Gary interjected, whilst sanctioning her request in thought.

Instantaneously a man walks in with a tray of Pina Coladas. "Bring them here and then sit down in that chair", ordered Elle. "I want you to watch me make love to my man".

Gary and Elle grabbed a drink each. Gary raised his glass and said, "Cheers baby. Cheers to our love, and cheers to our lust. I couldn't have a more beautiful, amazing relationship and friendship, even if I were to try in this outrageously crazy game".

And suddenly, Gary was gone.

CHAPTER 2

Absorber

"Elle? Elle … are you there?"

Gary was wandering through an empty street in a city. "It is eerily beautiful", Gary thought. It looked brand spanking new, like it had never been lived in. There were no cars, no people, and no signs of life.

"What the fuck happened?", he then contemplated verbally. "So I was in bed with Elle, and suddenly I'm here. I'm obviously still in the game, so I guess I should manifest back to the island".

And with that intention, Gary was back where he originally started. There was no mansion, no butler, and no Elle. "Can you hear me, Elle?", he yelled. Feeling a little amused now, he said it again telepathically. "Can you hear me, Elle?"

Nothing.

Gary began reflecting on what Apollo had told them. "I can go back to the reset maybe, but obviously our intentions were split so we must be on separate timelines. Although he did say that we would be able to communicate".

He looked around and was involuntarily taken aback in awe at how pristine and pure everything looked. "Yes its amazing mate", he said to himself, "but get back to the issue at hand. Clearly I should be able to talk to her, unless she's out of the game. So maybe I should exit to make sure she's okay".

Gary thought about this for only a split second, and then said, "Exit game".

Nothing.

"I want to exit the game", he continued.

Nothing again.

"Reset game. RESET GAME. EXIT THE FUCKING GAME GOD DAMNIT".

Still nothing, although this time he felt a little woozy. "What the hell is going on", he thought. "I'm starting to feel sick. Why can't I exit the gam…"

Gary felt himself falling, although he didn't hit the soft sand. He kept falling until his consciousness had almost completely faded. But then there was a light. A faint glitter of sunshine sparkled through his heart. "I must be exiting", he celebrated.

When Gary opened his eyes he was disappointed at what he saw. He was standing in the street of the empty city, exactly where he found himself before he went back to the island. "This feels insane", he thought. "It must be a dream. I cannot be lost in a damn video game for fuck sake!"

Considering the idea of being in a lucid dream, Gary thought about all his memories. "They're too consistent, they're too linear", he remembered. He backtracked through his experience, whilst walking down the middle of the road. "I succinctly remember my day", he continued. "Lunch, drinks, clubbing, walking home past the video game store. The whole conversation with Apollo. It just feels too real", he concluded.

"Okay, for now, I need to take this seriously. I need to have my wits. I could be in serious trouble", he said to himself. At that moment, a loud bang filled the air, startling Gary back into the experience. "It came from down this alley", he acknowledged.

Gary was feeling determined to get to the bottom of what was happening. He took a right turn into the small empty street and moved his way through the cleanest alley he had ever seen. There was no graffiti, no rubbish, and no signs of wear and tear. "This definitely isn't a normal city".

Moving towards a large metal door, he heard some more sounds. They were coming from machinery of some type. "A factory?", he pondered.

He opened the door as quietly as he could and peered into what turned out to be a very large room filled with production lines and people. "Oh my god, yes!", he said with great satisfaction, noticing they were all naked at the same time. He scanned the room and saw that they were all middle aged and looked really healthy. There was not one old or overweight person that he could see. They all had long hair too, including the men, which were tied back in a ponytail.

Gary slowly walked towards them but then rushed his pace towards the closest person he could see, who was around 25 metres away. Most of them were working on conveyer lines, although Gary found it odd that none of them were talking, or even interacting.

"Excuse me mate, I need your help", Gary stated, whilst

still walking up behind one particular man. "Excuse me", he restated, after he was ignored. Yet, he received no response. Not one of these people had looked at him, or even looked up. He walked right up next to one of them and said, "Mate, I really need your help".

He received no response.

"Fuck, can you hear me or what?", he said with a hint of anger. Gary tapped him on the shoulder, to which the guy waved his hand like he was shooing away a fly. He then turned to several other workers across from him who were busy shuffling through metal pieces on the moving belt, and started waving his hand towards their faces as if he was trying to determine if someone was awake or asleep.

Nothing. No response at all. Gary picked up a piece of metal and threw it across the belt, trying to gain their attention. It landed on another piece and ricocheted onto the left forearm of a female. Immediately it made a small cut and started to slowly bleed. The worker looked at it, put down what she was holding and proceeded to walk to her right.

"Shit, I'm so sorry", yelled Gary. "I didn't mean to hurt anyone, I was just trying to get your attention". It didn't matter what Gary had said anyway because given the loud noises in the place, she was almost out of earshot by the time he had finished. "I need to follow her", he thought.

Gary navigated under and around a few machines, trying not to lose sight of her. He raced up behind her, where he noticed on the back of her neck a tattoo that looked like a code. After acknowledging the strangeness of it, he moved in front of her and tried again to gain her attention, but she didn't respond. He looked directly into her eyes whilst walking backwards in front of her, but it was like she was looking straight through him.

"She looks completely dead inside, like a robot", he thought with deep concern. "Jeez her tits look good, though", he then joked, as an attempt to bring some light to the moment.

The woman maintained the same pace, which made Gary stumble a little. He moved out of the way and followed her down a corridor and into a small room. In it was a large table holding a machine that had a pointy end to it, which looked like a pen attached to an arm. The woman stood on a glass panel on the floor that encircled the entire table. There were glass pads on the table too, one of which she waved her right forearm over. The machine's lights lit up, moved along a rail attached to the table and proceeded to scan her with a fluoro yellow light. A green coloured one did the same from underneath her feet.

Gary walked to the table and waved his right forearm over it too, thinking it might be what he was meant to do. A monitor in the table immediately lit up with the words 'ERROR: INVALID CODE 7G-3311429V'.

This escalated the fear in Gary so he slowly backed away. "What the hell is this place?", he quivered.

He was starting to lose focus, like he was so drunk he couldn't see straight. The fear really started to grip him. His vision began to blur in and out. The last thing he could remember was the machine moving to the right forearm of the woman and the light switching back on, but this time it was a deep fluoro blue. It advanced a laser-like beam onto the wound, as Gary blacked out.

"Wake up mate!", were the first words he heard. "Come on, you can do this", the person continued.

Gary opened his eyes to see an older man of at least sixty, leaning over him. He was lying in a dark place and couldn't really make out much except for the combat attire the man was wearing because of a few flashing lights on his equipment and a small fire which was petering out in the distance.

"What happened?", Gary asked.

"You got hit by a sensor shell", he replied. "It tore your right arm off. I've rebuilt it already, so you'll be good to go in about five minutes. You just need to relax. While you recover, I'll go through the next phase of the plan. Corebase uploaded it just a few minutes ago".

"What plan?", enquired Gary. The man instantly laughed in response. "What plan", he said sarcastically. "You're a classic Feddy".

"No seriously, I don't know what you're talking about or who you are", Gary reinforced.

"Oh shit, really", the man acknowledged. "I did a head scan but it reported no damage. No major issue though, you've probably just got a touch of shock residue blackening your memory. You'll be fine in a few minutes, so don't stress. For the time being, my name is Lez. I'm your superior in the Nitro unit".

"Nitro unit?", Gary quizzed softly.

"Yes, our unit is in charge of dropping the Corrosion Cluster – CC for short. Fuck brother, don't tell me you can't remember any of this?"

Before Gary could answer, Lez continued explaining. "Listen, Corebase is one of only a dozen or so impenetrable safezones for the Peeps. Do you at least remember the Peeps?"

"No", Gary murmured.

"Fuck! Alright, twenty two years ago there was a breakaway civilisation where humanity was split between the upper and lower classes. Those with the money and power – which we call the Creeps – decided to go underground and undersea to weather the flipping of the earth's magnetic poles, but it didn't happen as destructively as their models predicted. The poles did reverse and there was massive carnage, but around ten per cent of us on the surface still originally survived".

"What?", Gary said with utter confusion.

"Listen Feddy, just listen", Lez interrupted abruptly. "We're running short on time and it will help you regain your memory. There were nearly ten billion people on the planet when this occurred leaving around one billion of us after the flip. The Creeps only sent around half a million of their own to their safezones, but since our war began there's only twenty five thousand of them left. We've got only ten per cent after all the starvation and disease, meaning there's around one hundred million still remaining. But we're stronger than them now. Our numbers are increasing again, too. We're recovering just like the earth's natural systems are, which initially fell apart. Try to remember. Animal and plant life died out on masse, with raging fires all across the planet. Those fires, hey, hard to forget them. Anyway, remember how it took nearly two years for them to subside? Remember when we started to see the sun properly again?"

Gary watched as Lez got lost in thought for a split

second, like he was experiencing nostalgia. "No, I don't. And my name is Gary", he enforced anyway, almost rudely.

"No it's not, it's Feddy", he responded, with a fierce tone in his voice. "Look at me, we've known each other for a long time. I've been with you since nearly the beginning of this mess".

Gary felt like it was the first time he'd ever seen his face.

"Just hold on, you'll be back shortly. Anyway, the rest of the population, which we call the Peeps, started to organise against those who condemned us to death. After many years we found most of their secret bases on land, but without the proper technology the only way we could access the sea was through Tripping. That's where most of them still reside today, but we can get there now in the flesh. That's where we are right now".

"Wait, we're under the ocean? Which one?", asked Gary.

"Off the coast of what used to be known as Hawaii. Is any of this coming back to you yet?"

It was too much for Gary to handle, so he was starting to become unsure of himself. "No, not yet", he answered.

"Okay okay, let me finish the summary. Before the split there were two dominating sciences. One was the mind travelling programs and the other was the intelligence programs. The Creeps had secret AI technology they were working on which went rebel not long after the flip. This desecrated them. They managed to reign them back in under their control again, but not before they had destroyed a huge amount of them. We only had a few casualties, mostly because we were still highly fragmented at that stage. Because of the inherent dangers associated with AI, there are now dependable failsafe's built into both their hardware and software. It's one of these that we'll be activating as part of this mission".

Gary couldn't believe what he was hearing.

"The mind sciences on the other hand began their surge about two decades before the flip", continued Lez, without missing a beat. "The latest teleportation technology isn't fundamentally of a physical nature, it was achieved via consciousness manoeuvring through the quantum realm. It began with the development of telepathic skills, as well as the remote projection of information intentionally emitted by a mind, but then the mind began to follow the information. There were only a few, select individuals who had the capability at first, but with our collective consciousness slowly evolving to accept quantum travel and the non-physical realm, certain people got stronger in their capacity to navigate the material realm with their minds".

"Fuck off", Gary pronounced, amazed with the information Lez was providing.

"We call it Mind Tripping, or Tripping for short. Eventually the Trippers started to have measurable physical effects on the environment they occupied, even though their physical body was still in the original location. That included possessing and controlling a human receiver, at least to an extent. It was only a matter of time too before the transmitter body began to show effects, such as wounds if the mind was subject to dangerous conditions. This happened not long before the Creeps went off grid".

"You're kidding me, right? Don't fuck around with me Lez", Gary barked. He was starting to forget his own story, by this point.

"It goes much deeper bro. Listen, I need to speed this

up, it's been close to five minutes already". As Lez finished the sentence, he pulled out a circle-shaped metal device from his pocket and a green fluorescent light scanned over Gary. "Yep, your vitals are fine. Your arm is very close to 100 per cent health. There's no reason why your memory shouldn't start to return very soon".

Gary felt a wave of relief wash over him, which ended in anxiety. "Wait a minute", he thought. "I'm Gary, not this Feddy person".

Before Gary could continue on his line of thinking, Lez interrupted again. "So the Creeps disappeared to their safezones, leaving us to fend for ourselves. They mistakenly assumed we'd all end up dead, so they had little plan to deal with us after the flip. They kept it quiet from us the whole time, justifying the changing conditions as sourced from both natural and man-made changes the climate. We were unprepared; well, most of us were. Some of us had been trying to warn the rest of the population for decades of the vulnerability of being so dependent on a highly fragile economic and social system, but it fell on deaf ears. The Creeps controlled all the official narratives by this stage".

"Then what happened", said Gary, feeling like he didn't say it at all.

"The Peeps began to understand that something had changed. Whilst the Creeps still controlled the official information from their bunkers, many people started to realise that so many of the financial and corporate elite had not been physically seen in months. Some celebrities had disappeared as well, even though they were still communicating on their social media accounts. It was starting to become obvious that something peculiar was happening, so more and more people started to explore the unfiltered media. That's when the rumours of a coming cataclysm took hold on the masses. They began to panic. Some of them sought out their own safezones, whilst others just continued on with their lives. As supplies began to slowly diminish over the following months, the earth changes increased. It was almost in perfect unison".

At that moment a large explosion occurred in the far distance. "Fucking hell, they're coming to investigate. They'll be here in around ten minutes. Fortunately they've still got two doors to penetrate. Listen Fed, you need to remember. You need to remember who you are. I need you to help me complete this mission, mate. You're the only one who has the code".

"I'll try Lez", Gary said, this time knowing he didn't say anything at all.

"Okay Fed, we're gonna get through this. Try to remember. Try to remember the flip. It sent tsunamis all over the planet, it set off megaquakes and supervolcanoes, and it pretty much instantly destroyed about half of the habitable land. So much death and destruction. Ninety per cent of our critical infrastructure was gone too. But the WhiteRavens, Fed, if it wasn't for them none of us would probably be here. We wouldn't be here; they saved us. Surely you remember?"

"Yes, I'm starting to", Gary heard his body say. It wasn't him who had answered though. It was at this point that Gary looked into a badge on Lez's jacket, which slightly mirrored his reflection. But who he saw wasn't him.

"Good, good. What happened from there?", encouraged Lez.

"Um, well, I'm not sure", Gary's body replied.

"Feddy, please try. Remember when we were with our families in the hills of The Web. The WhiteRavens found us and took us to Corebase One. This was about four years after the flip. They explained to us that they'd developed their Trip capacity to the point they were sending in their best Trippers to destroy the Creeps from the inside. That's when we started to work on our own mind travelling, remember? I know you can't possibly forget that you beat me first to possessing a Creep, right?"

Feddy laughed out loud at this stage, forcing himself to speak. "Of course I remember that, the competition went for nearly a decade!"

"Excellent, welcome back soldier", smiled Lez.

Gary was feeling so dazed by this point the voices begun to merge into one another, however that was quickly overcome by the sound of another large explosion.

"Damn, only one door to go!", yelled Lez. "We need to get to point C. It's only fifty metres to our northwest, through two uncoded doors. The power has been suppressed for us. We have about ten minutes till it comes back online. We should have plenty of time to inject the CC, but let's not waste any more time".

"I want to go home!", Gary screamed.

Lez looked at Feddy again with a puzzled facial expression. "Huh?", he said.

"I don't know why I said that", said Feddy, looking just as puzzled. Gary's sudden outburst had made him feel even weaker, which led him to fall deeper into an observer role.

"Are you okay? Are you ready to go?", asked Lez.

"Help me up!", Feddy replied, confidently.

Lez grabbed Feddy's left arm and dragged him to his feet. He stumbled a little but quickly regained his footing. Stretching his back and arms, Feddy squatted a couple of times to rebuild his self-control. "I'm good to go".

They both hit a button on a flashlight attached to their vest which lit up a door to their right. The room was filled with laboratory equipment, including fridges filled with various substances. There were also benches with chemistry paraphernalia spread throughout the room.

"Okay, the CC needs to infect a security update. It's for AI7 - the latest wave of AI. If this works, it should send them back to pre-flip progress. This will be the beginning of the end for them!", Lez shouted with confidence.

He pulled out another small metal device, pointed it towards the side of the door and pressed a red flashing button. A series of numbers flickered on a panel near the door which resulted in a green light. The door opened swiftly and quietly.

The two men ran up a corridor which was only lit by their flashlights. Gary could see doors to both the left and right every ten metres or so. When they had ran for about fifty metres, Lez pulled out the same device and proceeded to open the door at the end.

It opened exactly as the previous one did. Lez headed straight for a large desk which Gary thought looked like a massive computer because it had monitors and buttons built into a top panel which was slanted on a forty five degree angle. "Okay, this is it Feddy. Let's power this sucker up!"

Lez took off his backpack and opened it up. From the large compartment he pulled out another gadget, which reminded Gary of a multimeter. There were two wires that

Lez unwrapped from it; one he plugged into the side of the computer panel and then he pushed a button on the device.

As the monitors and lights powered up on the computer, Lez turned to Feddy. "Alright mate, what's the code?"

"It's seven, G, dash, three, three, one, one, four, two, nine, V", replied Feddy.

Lez typed it into his gadget and plugged the other wire into another port on the computer. Then he lined up his pointer finger and pressed a large button. "Alright, CC is in flow. We've got about a minute for upload".

"So how does it work, Lez?", asked Feddy.

"Mate, you know how it works. It sends nanodust into the core of AI7 which distributes the corrosive chemical into the network", explained Lez anyway.

It was like an action movie, Gary thought, feeling more entertained and less scared by this stage. "I know I need to understand what this is all about. I need to understand its purpose".

Lez continued: "Once it gets past security update 211, it cannot be stopped. The virus will infect all of the AI's physical infrastructure and literally dissolve the material it's hiding in. Instead of attacking the software or its intelligence, it forces it into a corner and then eats it alive. It's never been tried before".

"Update 211, hey", Feddy repeated. He reached behind his back and under his shirt, but was stopped by Lez's fierce voice.

"Not so fast Fed, I know you've been compromised".

Lez already had a gun pointing directly at Feddy's face. "How could you do this Fed? You were meant to be on our side. You were meant to protect us. That was your role. After everything we've done for you".

This was sending Gary's mind into hyperdrive. "This is unbelievable", he thought. "This cannot be real!"

"What the fuck you say?", replied Lez. Once again, Gary had spoken for Feddy.

"That ... that, wasn't me", said Feddy, his voice laced with fear. "Someone is trying to Trip me".

Another explosion rocked the airwaves, which made Lez take a step back. He looked at his device plugged into the computer and noticed it was flashing blue. "It's done, Fed. You're done. We're both done. I sacrificed my life for the Peeps and you tried to take that away from them. You tried to take it away from me. After everything I did for you, you were prepared to let me die for nothing".

The voices and footsteps were getting closer to their position. "I did it because I belong to the breakaways", replied Feddy. "They're my real family".

"Not anymore", Lez interrupted. "Say hello to your death".

Lez raised the gun to align the barrel with the middle of Feddy's forehead. The experience went into slow motion for Gary, as he watched Lez squeeze the trigger and the bullet exit the chamber. In rich graphics, he could see each individual spark in the wake of the bullet hurling towards him. He even knew when it entered the head of Fed, even though he felt no pain.

And suddenly, Gary was gone.

CHAPTER 3

Motivator

Gary slowly began to regain consciousness. It was all black, with faint sparkles of light becoming increasingly observable. He was scared to try and see more, but never got a chance to make a choice. His vision rapidly filled with light, until it had readjusted into an image of his surroundings.

But it was all dark again.

"Gary baby, are you there?"

He was so relieved to hear Elle's voice. "Yes, I'm here Elle, where are you? All I can see is black".

"I'm back on the island. You must be in the entry point. See if you can exit baby".

"Exit game", requested Gary, to no avail. "I tried this before, but nothing happened. I couldn't get to the reset point either".

"Try again", pleaded Elle.

After several failed attempts Gary began to panic. "It's not fucking working. IT'S NOT FUCKING WORKING", he shouted in an alarmed state.

"Set your intention to come here", stated Elle, much more calmly.

And with that request, Gary was standing back on the beach, next to Elle. "It's SO good to see you. What the fuck is happening?", he asked fearfully, whilst wrapping his arms around her.

Elle grabbed him by the shoulders and pushed him back to look into his eyes. "Baby, you need to listen carefully. I woke up back in the store after you disappeared. Apollo was freaking out, because something happened to you. Your vitals are showing signs of distress. You're okay, but you're lost in the game baby. You need to figure out how to exit otherwise you're going to get worse".

"How long has it been?", he asked Elle.

"Around fifteen minutes", she replied.

"And what did Apollo say I should do?", questioned Gary.

"He said he's never seen or heard of this before. He doesn't know exactly what to do. He did say to try and navigate through your experience with the sole intention to exit. He said it's like a maze. A puzzle. It's your own puzzle. He thinks you're creating this. He thinks that somewhere in your mind you've set an intention that you're not conscious of. You need to figure out why you won't let yourself exit baby. You need to come home".

Elle began weeping, which triggered deep beats in Gary's chest. "I'll fix this babe, everything will be okay. Everything will be back to normal soon".

Gary's consciousness faded very quickly into darkness, but then just as quickly re-emerged into a light. This time it was easy for Gary to adjust because he could smell pizza, which is his favourite fast food.

He looked around and immediately recognised that he was in a shopping mall, although he had never been in this particular one. There were dozens of people walking in every direction, some with kids or friends, and some alone. One mother walked passed him with her daughter, who was asking to buy some lollies. "I said NO, how many times do I have to tell you!", she screamed disproportionately. She then violently grabbed her daughter by the arm and pulled her in the direction she wanted to go.

"That's near child abuse", Gary thought.

Gary noticed that the woman he had embodied was blonde, because he watched her brush it out of her face. When they walked past a shopfront, he glimpsed her reflection. She was in her early-twenties, slightly overweight and had thick makeup on her face. She was wearing very skimpy clothing, with a short skirt and low cut top. When she looked down to reshuffle her bags, Gary noticed her breasts almost falling out of her singlet. "This could be a bit of fun", Gary salivated, before he thought of his gorgeous girl. Then he just missed her.

The woman was with a female companion of about the same age. "Let's go have a smoke Brittney", the friend suggested to Gary's temporary home.

As they turned down an isle on the right and proceeded towards a side door that led outside to a Chinese styled garden, Brittney sparked a conversation. "Remember that bitch from high school, Harriot? I saw her yesterday. She looked so fat, like she'd put on at least ten kilos. She said hi to me and I just ignored her. She was always a dork. Never knew what she was thinking. Thinks she's so fucking smart. So above us. Doesn't surprise me though, when her oldies were so fucking retarded. Remember when they turned up at my party and dragged her out?"

"Yeah, that was hilarious!", remarked her sidekick.

"Apparently she's at Uni now, pretending like she's all that", perpetuated Brittney. "She might know education better than me, but she don't have my sass. She'll never be as good as me".

The girls walked over to the seating area and chose a table with bench seats. They sat down next to each other whilst Brittney pulled out two smokes. Before they lit them, a couple of males in their late teens walked by, one of which wolf-whistled at them.

"Show us your tits baby", said another one.

"Fuck off losers", replied Brittney, lighting her cigarette.

"Whatever slut, we know you want it", responded the one who whistled.

"Just because you have little penises and can only fuck your little slut friends doesn't mean I'm one of them", she reacted, aggressively.

"I'll make you suck it", the whistler continued, as they walked through the mall doors.

"Wankers", she elaborated, loud enough for them to hear.

"Yeah, who do they think they are?", her friend agreed rhetorically. "Why do they think they can treat us that way?", she continued sincerely.

"They're just children Mel. They're immature", she replied, after taking a deep draw on her smoke.

Mel looked down, took a long puff on her smoke too, and said, "Yeah, that must be it".

Gary didn't know what to believe after witnessing this whole scene, however there was one prominent question which raced through his mind: "Does the younger generation regularly act like this?"

At that moment one of their friends, David, walked up behind them. "Hey you crazy bitches", he stated, startling them both.

"Fucking hell David!", they both said simultaneously.

"What?", he replied, sitting down next to them. "I didn't mean to scare you".

"Nah, all good, we just had a couple of knobs give us some shit. Sorry, didn't mean to take it out on you", Brittney reassured him.

"What happened?", he asked genuinely.

"They just walked past us and abused us", Brittney continued.

"They told us to show them our tits, and then called us sluts", elaborated Mel. "It always happens to us. I'm so sick of it!"

"Why do you think it always happens to you?", David examined.

"I'm sure it happens to all women", Mel assumed.

"I don't doubt that it has happened to most women at some point, but why does it keep happening to you?", he asked politely.

"Probably cos' I'm hot", Brittney answered, in both a sarcastic and seductive tone.

This gave David a troubling look. Both Mel and Brittney

picked up on it. Mel stepped in to defend Brittney: "What, don't ya think she's sexy?"

David thought for a moment and then replied. "Yeah, you're pretty Brittney, but that's not the point".

"What's the point then?", continued Mel.

"Well, don't you think you both dress overly provocative?", he reflected.

"Uh oh", Gary thought with a sense of impending entertainment.

"I should be able to walk around naked without being objectified like that", defended Brittney. "I'm a proud woman. I'm self-made. I have self-respect. I might show my body off, but that doesn't mean I should be treated disrespectfully", she roared.

"No of course not", David countered. "I'm not saying that you deserve it, but what I am saying is that with the way the world is, you clearly should be expecting it by now if that's the way you choose to dress. It keeps on happening, right? Most guys haven't matured properly. In fact, most girls haven't either. The entire world has image and respect issues. Actually, the world has many more issues than that. Our society is degrading on so many levels, and this is just one of them".

David breathed in deep and thought about his next words. "If you want to dress like you do, that's absolutely fine, but don't expect there aren't going to be negative experiences because of it", he said with utter compassion.

"Nice save", Gary joked to himself, as he watched a bee buzz past Brittney's face.

This made the girls think for a little while. Before one of them spoke, David continued. "Listen, I'm studying a sociology class right now on feminism and the patriarchy. It's made me think about a few things. I've been doing my own research on it because I didn't think that the lecturer really gets the bigger picture. There were too many gaps in the information he was providing".

"Alright David, you know we always love your opinion. What have you got to say? Just don't pick on feminism!", Mel requested, before drawing on her last puff and putting it out under her right foot.

Gary thought about the hypocrisy of their attack on Harriot.

"Well, there are some issues with it", David said timidly.

"Like what?", she asked sincerely.

"I'll get to a major one later, but one that really bugs me is how most feminists solely focus on the porn industry fucking up women", he replied, with a bit more confidence.

"Well, that's true!", Mel said suspiciously.

"Yes, of course, a few women feel empowered with that career choice but many are being objectified, sexualised and just outright disrespected", elaborated David. "I'm not denying that, but how severe the authentic male has been damaged from the porn industry is missed a lot. Men get addicted to it, it fucks up their relationships, it changes their perception on what love and sex is and it has literally created a culture of men who only want a girl who is a porn star in the bedroom. The whole thing is a mess, not just for women, but men too!"

"Yeah, you're right. I once had this young, inexperienced guy who wanted me to do anal on the first date. I couldn't fucking believe it", laughed Mel.

"You would have done it, you skank", teased Brittney.

Laughing, Mel replied. "Yes, well, I like anal. That's not the point. The point is that this guy had hardly had sex before and wanted to fuck my ass straight up. Clearly he had been watching some porn in his time".

Gary found himself enjoying the conversation a little too much.

"That's what I mean. The porn industry has desensitised so many people and sometimes even destroyed their concept of love, and it should be recognised as such. Now don't get me wrong, there's nothing wrong with sex in and of itself, or lust for that matter. But when it becomes an addiction, when it becomes an imbalance at the sacrifice of other values and experiences, then it becomes a problem".

The girls looked at Gary with curious looks on their faces.

"This issue is directly connected with a myriad of other issues. Materialism, consumerism, a lack of real education, the collapse of social values – a whole bunch of complicated stuff!", David continued. "Anyway, I'll get back to the original point. I'll try to make this as clear as possible, but it's a complex subject and I've still got so much to learn. If I don't make sense, you better not give me a hard time for it!"

"We won't let you live it down", clowned Mel.

"Okay, let me start with sex and gender. Actually, I might record this to reflect over later". David pulled out his phone from his pocket, hit a few buttons and placed it on the table.

"Alright, sex is typically defined as either male or female, or more specifically, a person who has male or female reproductive organs. Now it gets a little tricky when it comes to hermaphrodites because in most cases they are completely infertile, meaning they cannot reproduce. But most people, they are either male or female, in the strict sense of the definition. This is where gender comes into the equation".

"I thought they were the same thing?", asked Brittney.

"No, they're not. Gender more refers to the masculine and feminine roles and behaviours which are influenced by culture. So a classic example in our so-called modern society is that men are more thought of as the provider and women as the nurturer. Another one is that men are more logic-based and women more emotion-based".

"Yeah, nah, that's the point of feminism David", barked Brittney. "Women are equal to men meaning they can be logical too!"

"Yes, of course they can", agreed David. "I completely agree. But in general there are differences between men and women, like it or not. So taking the two examples above, clearly the provider and nurturer expectations are based on not just the fact that women have the babies, but also the way civilisation and our economies have evolved. We have certainly been more likely to fulfil these roles in the past, but obviously that's changing. So this difference is more fluid and ambiguous".

"You're not going to say that women are more emotional now, are you?", Mel remarked cheekily.

"Well, sort of. It's based in science. There are multiple differences between male and female biology, including in their brains, at least generally speaking. One example is that males have a much larger lobe associated with mathematical calculations, and females have a larger hippocampus and a deeper limbic system, which facilitates a greater experience on the emotional spectrum".

"Are you shitting me? Our brains are different? I betcha women's brains are larger than men's!", laughed Mel.

David laughed out loud, but then responded swiftly. "Well actually, men's brains are typically ten per cent bigger than females". David finished his sentence by winking at them with a cheeky smile.

"Bullshit!", laughed Brittney.

"It's actually true, but only because men are also generally ten per cent larger than females. We need that extra brain space to carry around our strong bodies", he said, whilst flexing his right bicep.

"Shut up you dick", giggled Brittney.

This conversation was really giving Gary a good laugh.

"Anyway, in general there ARE physiological differences between males and females", persisted David, "which no doubt leads to psychological and behavioural differences too. There's no arguing that; scientific research has been super clear".

"Is that why men have deeper voices?", asked Mel.

"Yes, the deeper a male's voice, the more testosterone he likely creates", he replied, without a missing beat.

"Is that why gay guys talk more like women?", Brittney questioned inquisitively.

"Yeah, sometimes. Many gay men talk like a typical guy though. It no doubt has an impact, but some of the time the guy might be enacting a female stereotype, regardless if he's aware of it or not. Another reason is that homosexuals have been so suppressed, they've felt so isolated, sometimes they haven't had much focus on developing themselves because they're still trying to figure out who they are in the context of society. Take one of my best gay mates, Rob, for example.

He's more like an adolescent in an adult's body. He's still very immature and talks like a child, which was most likely influenced by a fear to be himself in a society that regularly condemns people outside of the norm".

"So you're saying that gays are immature?", Brittney asked seriously.

"Of course not!", David laughed. "I'm saying that some of them might be because they didn't express themselves when they were young adults, so they didn't get to know themselves as much as others might have. They might have even condemned themselves too, stifling their own development. They may have been unsure of who they are and who they want to be. But it's not just gay people though. I mean, c'mon, so many people are stunted in their self-development for so many reasons".

"So what the fuck has this got to do with wanting to show my puppies to the world!", hooted Brittney.

"Hang on, let me finish this first. So just like there are differences in races, in cultures and in people in general, there are traits that are more likely prevalent in women than men, and vice versa. This isn't just the result of social and cultural conditioning, but their physiology too. If you disagree, try telling a gay man or woman that they're only gay because of their environmental influences. They will crucify you, because they strongly believe that they are that way because of their genetic makeup. Their argument is that it's nature, not nurture".

Both the girls started nodding their heads.

"The thing is though, and this is a necessary tangent, I believe in some cases it's both. It's not just nature, but nurture too. We're all on a spectrum. We all have testosterone and we all have oestrogen, both of which are mostly made in the balls of men and the ovaries of women. It's just that we have different mixes of the two. Some men naturally produce higher levels of oestrogen, which makes them express more feminine characteristics in certain ways. Just the same for women. Some have heaps of testosterone, making them feel more masculine. Then there are both men and women who are more in the middle. They are more balanced in their hormonal production, which means the way they're conditioned is going to have more of an impact on their sexual choices and tendencies. Not only that, it will circle back into their physiology, reinforcing a greater production of the relevant chemical. It's called epigenetics".

"Epi-genetics?", Mel retorted.

"Epigenetics. You've never heard of it?", David said, with little surprise.

After Mel shook her head, David continued. "It's a relatively new science that has been more accepted in mainstream thinking over the last several decades. It illustrates that environmental conditions impact the activity of particular genes. That's not just referring to culture and stuff, it's also referring to what's happening in our minds. Our beliefs and thoughts and perceptions. So if you have a genetic history of heart disease, for example, epigenetics says in theory that if you really take care of yourself physically and emotionally or whatever, then the genetic weakness is less likely to be activated in your body. That's a very simple way of explaining it, but ultimately the way we live can change the way our genes operate. Crazy, right?"

"I really have no fucking idea what you're talking about", Brittney joked. Both of the girls erupted in laughter.

"Wait, so what I'm saying is that some men and women are naturally gay, because of their physical makeup. But some people are more in the middle, some of which are bisexuals. Some people are literally attracted to both sexes. Then there are others who have had certain experiences which either subconsciously or consciously led them to become either gay or straight. I'll give you a perfect example. There are no doubt tens of thousands of men who are not just attracted to women, but also men, but because society hasn't been as accepting of homosexuality compared to heterosexuality in the past, they have suppressed it in themselves so they aren't rejected by their family and friends. The crazy part is that many of them might not even be aware of it".

"You coming out of the closet David?", Mel joked.

"Then there's the people who flip-flop between being gay or straight because of the social circles they interact with", he continued unabated, with a slight grin. "They might jump the fence for a while because they feel an attraction, but then they realise it's not for them".

David intuitively looked up to his right and watched a bird fly past him, missing his head by only a few feet.

"Now let's take a look at the transgender movement", he continued. "There are many people who identify with the opposite sex they've been born as. Some people don't identify with either of them, as strange as that may sound. Now, those who feel they're a boy living in a girl's body, or vice versa, probably feel that way for a couple of reasons. The first is obviously biologically related; the chemical cocktail they make internally, as well as their genetic expression, no doubt influences that feeling. But then so do social and cultural expectations of gender. If someone feels like they're

41

not fulfilling the gender role that society expects of them, then they might disassociate themselves with that particular sex. Another basic example is that if society says that to be a girl you need to have children and be a stay-at-home mum, then those women who don't want to do that will feel conflicted. If they believe the cultural perception, then they won't feel female".

"So are you saying that they're really female, just not society's version of it?", Mel asked sincerely.

"Well, sort of. If you have female sexual organs, then you're female. That's the definition of the word. The same goes for males. But gender is different. Because so many people don't feel they fit the gender stereotype, they feel they're not the sex they are. But they are; they have those organs so they're either male or female".

The girls and Gary watched David carefully navigate through his thoughts.

"Listen, this whole transgender thing is causing a lot of confusion. Unless you're a hermaphrodite, you're either male or female. It's that simple. Now, how you express your individuality, your sexuality, that's a different story. For example, I feel very feminine at times. There's different feelings I have, which makes me feel more analytical at times and more intuitive at others".

"David has titties", Brittney laughed in interruption.

"Very funny, dickhead", David joked. "But seriously, there's so many vulnerable people who want to be accepted as who they feel they are naturally, but then they're injecting themselves with synthetic hormones and sometimes even undertaking physical sex changes. These unnatural hormonal states amplify the mental health issues that many of them have, which leads to suicide in many cases too. It's just so sad".

"But some people want to look how they feel", responded Mel.

"Yes I understand that, and we're all free to do as we choose. If that's what you want, go for it. But if it's hurting yourself, then I wouldn't say it's a wise move. Look, I believe that we have everything inside of us, we have both of what some people would call masculine and feminine traits. That's why I think it's silly to believe that our gender is either masculine or feminine, because we all think and behave according to both stereotypes. Sure, we might predominately feel one more than the other, but it's a wide spectrum of experience which is difficult to label as this or that".

David scratched his right cheek and then continued. "Now, are we more likely to behave in certain ways than others? Yes, of course. That's what makes us different. Some traits are more naturally prominent and others are more prominent because of our training. For example, I might be naturally better at maths than you, and you might be more empathetic than me. And that's perfectly fine. But if we both focus on improving our weaknesses, then one day we might be just as good as each other in both areas".

"Yeah, sure", yawned Mel. Gary on the other hand, was completely fascinated.

"Okay, I'll take that as a hint", David mocked. "Look, a major point I wanted to make is that feminism only focuses on the rights of one group, when it's super clear that everyone's being fucked by the system. Of course women should be treated equally, as should everyone! When it comes to transgenderism, the same applies. The fact remains that most people are just as dazed and fucking confused as everyone else, regardless if they have sexuality issues or not. Most people are either sick, sad, stressed, or all of the above. What type of world is that to live in?!"

"Yeah, I'm hearing you", Gary thought to himself.

"I'm just over all the hatred and bigotry and fighting against each other", continued David. "The 'isms', the sex and gender wars, they're all distractions to a degree. They're just more divide and conquer strategies, not by the patriarchy, but by the ruling class. All this has led to so many people being less connected from each other and their true self for that matter, including being seriously unhealthy in their thinking and behaviours. Like seriously, appreciate your unique energy, but honour that in everyone else too. And if you're going to stand up for the rights of one group, it's important that you be counted for representing our collective needs too".

"Makes sense", Gary acknowledged.

David took a deep breath like he needed to calm himself a little. "But let's get back to the idea of the 'patriarchy versus the ruling class', to wrap it up. The feminist thinking is that men rule the world, or the system is designed to foster the success of men over women, and women have been subjugated or treated unequally because of it. Just a quick look at modern history shows that women, as well as specific races and cultures, have been treated highly unfairly. It's a disgrace".

"Now you're talking", snorted Brittney.

"Some feminists certainly made great headway for women, that's for sure", he endured. "However, the reality is that it's not men per se who rule the world, it's the corporate, financial and political elite who do. I like to call them the 'ruling ass'. They've got their secret societies and shit, and sure, men are more likely to play a more dominant role in many areas of our society, but there are many women involved in this process too. For example, there always has been queens and princesses and any other women who are part of the aristocracy. So there might be more men than women in these hierarchies, but all the effects we see on society, including the oppression of women, stem from this systemic design, including the left-brained cultural dominance. So women and other particular demographics still to this day have issues of prejudice and discrimination, but it's obvious that we're all being cheated and degraded, whether we're white or black, male or female".

"Aww, you had a tough life princess", Brittney joked, leading David to burst out laughing.

"Yeah, putting up with you has been tough", he replied wittily. "Listen, it's important. Yes, as a white male there are no doubt certain advantages that I get over others, and I'm not denying that. That might even include a higher-paying job in our crony capitalistic world, not that it's much of a benefit when most people either hate their work or are filled with stress and a stupid addiction to more fake power. Who really wants that anyway? Regardless, just like pretty much everyone else I know, I've really struggled to understand who I am and who I could be. We're put through schooling that is clearly an indoctrination process into the status quo, which designs us to be robotic cogs in this sick system. I learned very few life skills at school. I never learned how to think for myself. I was so lost and confused when I left that I had no fucking idea what was going on".

"Well, that's your parents job, not your school's", Mel interjected.

"Agreed", Gary thought.

"So what happens if your parents don't have the knowledge and skills to do that?", David asked rhetorically.

Before anyone could answer, he continued. "Most don't. That's why we have so many issues in our society, because the older generations weren't educated properly, they didn't educate themselves properly, so a toxic cycle continues. We need to think about how we educate the younger generations so much more. The reality is school is for learning. Kids spend so much of their early lives there, so they need a holistic education. Emotional development, social development, creative development; that sort of thing. While English and maths have their place, so does learning about how to be a successful human, not just a human with a successful job".

"Absolutely", agreed Gary.

"So most kids leave school totally disconnected from their own nature. They're not empowered, they've primarily been conditioned to think that they need to get a good job to be successful in the world. So that's what they do, generally speaking. They chase money and stuff and hurt themselves and others along the way. It's the opposite of being authentic to our real needs. We're taught to want things, not to understand what we need".

"What's the difference?", Brittney questioned.

"Well if we're too busy chasing stuff, like a successful career, a big home, the latest phone, that sort of thing, then we forget to focus on what we need. Health is a great example. A healthy body, a healthy mind, healthy relationships. They're needs. I mean, who wants to have all the money in the world if they're unhappy or don't have great relationships with their friends and family so they can share it? So to be a successful human, we need to honour our needs. It's living the authentic self. The beautiful aspect is that we can WANT that, which means our needs and wants are aligned. The problem is most people haven't done this. They've been trained like a dog to chase their wants without reflecting on what they truly need".

David took another deep breath. "That's why we're all in the same boat. We've all been distracted from being genuine to ourselves and genuine to each other. I do admire that many people stand up for this cause or that cause, you know, the challenges faced in this day and age, yet most don't recognise that the strong majority of us are suffering because of everything I just talked about".

This hit Gary in the chest like a sledge hammer, as he felt it was directly applicable to his own life.

"Plus, getting back to the gender clusterfuck, each individual is made of both masculine and feminine energy. In this sense, we're all the same too. We express those energies differently to each other, and that's what makes us unique. But I see it as a serious issue if people are only fighting for the rights of a specific group, without also acknowledging that we're all being suppressed on a grander scale. Why else would there be so much pain and hatred and anger in this world?"

"Suppressed by who?", Mel queried with great interest.

"The ruling ass, of course", David resolved. "Once

people realise they don't need to fight each other, and instead should look at how the entire social system has been hijacked by these parasites, then they're in trouble. They don't want an empowered populace. They want us to fight. They want males and females to fight. They want to divide us, to conquer us".

"Hijacked how?", said Brittney.

"Yeah, hijacked how?", deliberated Gary.

"Well, how money is created in our society should be a public utility, but it's not. Private banking organisations create new money out of thin air and then reap the profits from it. All those profits should be reinvested into community programs and infrastructure, but instead it lines the pockets of the super-rich. That's the single biggest issue, but there's others too. For example, the major media platforms have been monopolised, meaning they control the official views for society. Another is medicine, which has been corporatized too, and has resulted in the suppression of cheap and effective cures, especially natural ones they can't patent or actually cure certain illness. And then of course there's governments. Because they're in debt to the money makers, they're under their control. The system we have today is called a corporatocracy, where big money controls the political show. The people at the top of the power pyramid design macro policy through lobbyists, bribes and political puppets, ensuring that we don't evolve the system so it actually benefits the people".

"Wow", Brittney, Mel and Gary gasped simultaneously.

"So that's why they want us fighting each other. They want feminists to be angry at men. The patriarchy is the scapegoat, because it means their focus is on men, not on how the system is designed itself. They want us to be so distracted with our individual plights so that we don't collectively put an end to our debt-enslaved society. Now of course I'm not saying that many of these issues aren't important, but if we want to have any chance at resolving poverty, homelessness, community breakdown, psychopathological pandemics and our sick society in general, then we need to put our differences to the side and together focus on the bigger picture".

Mel was staring deep into David's eyes. "How do we do that?", she mumbled. Gary was thinking the same thing.

"I don't exactly know. But what I do know is that we need to realise we're on the same team and start acting like it, no matter our differences. We need to focus on becoming as authentic as we possibly can, which means we're gonna treat ourselves and other people much better. We really need to bridge the gap with each other. We also need to demand an honest public debate on the entire system with a view to bringing true justice to it. Politicians, journalists and the ruling ass need to be held accountable for letting all this happen. It's absolute insanity".

"Alright, titty talking time", Brittney disrupted. "So why can't I show my breasts in public?"

Shaking his head with an awkward laugh, David continued. "Well, surely you don't want to attract that energy into your life. Surely you want to have a bit more class then waving your bits in people's faces. There's a time and a place Brit, and maybe a mall isn't really one of them", David said in a mechanical fashion.

"Plus, it's just another division", he continued. "The division of love and sex. I'm not suggesting that you should only have sex with those you're in love with, but you should at least hold some respect for the person. Love and sex needn't be separated; it doesn't mean you need to be head over heels for them, it just means you should honour anyone you fuck. That includes a one night stand. It's just another aspect of the authentic self crushed in our society. People are having sex for so many reasons other than experiencing a sexual connection with that person. It's like two robots fucking".

This made everyone chuckle to themselves.

"Hmm, okay. Shit. I'm just trying to get attention from boys, but you're right, it's usually attention I don't really like. I think I need a wardrobe change", Brittney admitted, almost in embarrassment.

"Excellent", David agreed, quietly.

Gary really struggled to get his head round it all. "Why am I listening to all this?", he pondered. He was lost in thought when he heard someone unexpectedly yell at Brittney.

"Hey bitch, who you think you are bitch?", said the voice of a female teenager. Brittney turned around to see five girls in their late teens walking from the side doors. With them were the boys from earlier, laughing at them. They increased their pace as Brittney, Mel and David rose to their feet.

"They don't want any trouble", David interjected.

"Well, she's got it", the girl responded in pure rage. As she finished screaming her words, which saw saliva spraying from her mouth at the same time, she threw a straight punch directly at the side of Brittney's head. As Brittney fell to the ground, Gary saw the bench they were sitting at fly past his vision, with the last image being her head buried in her cleavage.

And suddenly, Gary was gone.

CHAPTER 4

Balancer

Gary woke up instantly in a boardroom. There was a long table with about twelve chairs, with only one chair empty at the very front. The windows were floor to ceiling, letting a lot of natural light into the room. Outside were buildings and skyscrapers, signifying he was in a city. He couldn't see the ground, which illustrated he was quite high up.

Once again, he couldn't move. He could only observe what was happening, with the only control limited to his thoughts. "This is insane", was one of the first assessments he made in this scene. "I had some control in Feddy, but completely lost it in Brittney. I need to get motivated. Let's see if I can get back in the driver's seat".

The body that Gary was visiting walked over to the spare chair and stood behind it. He was in a male this time, as he could see his hairy hands resting on the back of the chair.

"This is an absolute joke", said the man, angrily. "If we don't fix this, the company is going under real fast".

"Sir, there's one option we haven't considered yet", said the young man sitting directly to his left.

"And what's that, John?", he responded with almost disdain.

"We could diversify our portfolio by investing whatever liquidity we have left in precious metals", John suggested. "Given the collapsing stocks don't look like reversing anytime soon, the gold and silver markets still have a lot of room to manoeuvre. They've risen 45% in the last week, but some projections I've been following are estimating up to a 500% increase, maybe more. It's a big risk, but there is an opportunity to easily recuperate our losses, and maybe even double our original net worth".

"You want to take what capital we have left and put it into gold and silver, you moron?", shouted the man. "Do I look like a fucking idiot to you?"

"No of course not James, I mean Sir", he nervously replied. "I was just thin…"

"Enough thinking from you, for fuck's sake", interfered James. "Right, I'm out of here for the day. There's no way I can handle your poor excuses any longer. I want you all to brainstorm ideas. As long as it takes. Tomorrow morning I want you all here at 8am, and we'll reassess. I want practical ideas with maps to achieve them. Do I make myself clear?"

"Yes sir", they all bowed in almost exact unison.

Gary just tried to relax and endure the entire experience. It was unpleasant, but interesting to him. James stormed out of the room, slamming the door behind him. He marched up a hallway towards a fancy door at the end. He opened it and walked into a room twice the size of the boardroom, with a massive desk, other furniture and ornaments filling the rest of the space.

James moved around the back of the desk, in which Gary noticed a large Elephant's head mounted on the wall. He sat down and opened a draw to his right. He reached in and pulled out a large plate with a handful of white powder on it. He grabbed a metal straw, moving some of the powder away from the pile. Then he leant over and took two very large sniffs through the straw, sending powder up his nose.

"Ahh, needed that", James said to himself.

Gary could feel a slight change in his own consciousness. In fact, it was like he could feel just a touch more than when he was in Feddy's body. It made him think how lucky he was not to feel the gunshot he sustained.

James leaned over and pressed a button on the phone. "Goldie, get the chopper on standby. I'll be up shortly. And tell Johnny I want him up there now. He's coming with me".

"Yes sir", she responded quickly.

By this stage, Gary was still giggling at the chopper comment. "Ah sweet memories", he said to himself, whilst thinking about his silly behaviour back on the deserted island. This made him lose attention for a moment, so by the time he was watching James again he was just finishing another couple of lines.

"Great coke", he spluttered to himself, almost out of breath.

He grabbed a bag from under the desk, stood up and walked towards the door. He exited the room with the briefcase in hand and pressed the button on what looked like a private elevator. The doors opened immediately and he entered. After pressing the highest button, a swift upwards rush occurred. Gary wasn't sure if it was the elevator, the cocaine, or a combination of both.

The doors opened to a bright sunny day. Once Gary had adjusted to the light, he realised he was on the roof of the building. Over to the right, about twenty metres away, sat a black and blue helicopter. The rotors were just starting to wind up.

John rushed from around to the left, indicating that he had come from a different doorway. "I'm here sir", he yelled, trying to be heard over the increasing sound of the chopper.

"Alright, get in", directed James.

They both entered through the right door and strapped in. The pilot checked to see if his passengers were ready, to which they both gave thumbs up. The chopper began to slowly rise and then made a sharp left, whilst still escalating in height. Within a minute it was soaring at the desired height and heading away from the city.

"Oh my god, it's beautiful", thought Gary. He was absorbing the sights that filled the landscape, which included high-rises, a large winding river, and the ocean. Suburbia was littered in all directions, although there was so much greenery that it felt like this city was built amongst a forest. It was a nice balance between urban and natural living.

"Okay John, I don't want you to pull any punches. That was brave what you did in there. It was out of the box, and right now that's what we need. I still don't like your idea but only because there isn't enough cash flow to facilitate it. I couldn't let you be acknowledged for it in front of everyone either because I couldn't have their heads in the wrong mind frame. But my personal affairs, that's another story. I know you've been reading and watching alternative views on what's going on. I've known for a while, because we monitor our employees' internet activity. I know you were preparing for something like this, and I should have come to you sooner. I just didn't think it was going to happen. So for the love of God, tell me what's going on John".

"I'll try sir", John said anxiously.

"Please, call me James. This is personal now".

"Okay James", he reacted compliantly. "Look, it's going to be hard to explain. Essentially we operate under a fiat monetary system, meaning that there is nothing to back the paper currency. For thousands of years we have used metals like gold and silver to underpin the money, but for the last several decades that was removed in its entirety. There has been fiat systems before mind you, but they all failed eventually. That's what might be happening here".

"Go on", encouraged James.

"So many people are pissed. The libertarians. The anarcho-capitalists. Sovereignty advocates. They've been warning us for so long that this was going to eventuate.".

"Anarch-what?", James interrupted.

"It's a combination between anarchy and capitalism. Anarchy fundamentally means 'no rulers', not 'chaos', as is widely believed. So anarcho-capitalists want a free market with little or even no government intervention. Some even want to remove governments completely and operate independent of any hierarchy, however others believe that would result with other non-governmental monopolies and conglomerates taking control, both domestic and foreign. The idea of anarchy is a little romanticised, but that's just because it's such a complex issue. It's hard to know the right way to move forward, what the right social system will be for our future, especially now that we're operating on the world stage with so many cultures and ideological positions. And that's not even considering the risks and dangers that come from all the crazy technology and weaponry that exists in this day and age".

James had a puzzled look on his face, but that didn't stop John's rant. "Back to the financial issue though, there are many people who have been advocating for a return to some sort of backed monetary system, which would most likely be precious metals. As I said, they've been expecting the economic chaos that is happening right now. There are several allegations about what's causing it too. One is that it is a controlled demolition to bring in a global reserve currency. Another is that it's spiralled out of control and the aim might be to move back to a precious metal standard. The final one is the oligarchy want to crash the economy to depopulate the earth, because our population is increasing at an unsustainable rate".

"You're talking about mass murder now, John", James replied, with deep cynicism.

"Look, it's difficult to ascertain what is true, it could actually be a mixture of them. But ultimately the house of cards is crashing due to its unstable foundation. This might be intentional, it might not. It's hard to say if the shadow government and the ruling class have this under control or not".

"Shadow government? Ruling class? What are you talking about?", questioned James.

"Sir, I mean James, the world doesn't work as we've been told", John said confidently. "The governments of the world have long been infiltrated by the aristocrats. They control the banks and the media too. That's why I research through independent media, because it's the only way you'll get the big pictures".

"That's just conspiracy", James stated weakly. Gary wasn't so sure, as he thought back to David's spiel.

"No, it's not. Don't be so naive", replied John, with increasing confidence. "There's always been people behind the scenes running the show, it's cemented throughout our history. The same applies now too. Simply, when you control the money especially, you control everything else. That's what the transnational banking institutions are designed to do for them. They control the creation of new money, or should I say currency. Money in its strict definition doesn't equate to what we have today. Currency is more accurate. So currency creation has been such a powerful tool that they've been able to grow shadow power structures, such as a secret government. Some people call it the deep state. What it essentially means is that politicians, and even the President, are subject to the shadow players. The whole system is totally rigged to funnel the wealth and the power to this ruling class".

"Are you sure?", James asked inquisitively.

"Yes James. I'm sure. There's a whole network of people, called civilian investigators, who have long exposed how the world is really run. The evidence is unquestionable".

"Okay, okay, but what does that mean for me", James shifted. "Most of my wealth is tied up in stock portfolios and real estate. If the stocks continue to fall, I'm not going to have much left. Do you think I should invest in precious metals?"

John contemplated for a few seconds, indicating

he was deep in thought. "Yes", he resumed. "That and cryptocurrencies".

"Crypto-what?", James quizzed.

"Cryptocurrencies. You've never heard of them?", asked John.

"No, I haven't", he responded.

"They're digital currencies and services that operate through the blockchain technology, which is essentially a decentralised, digital ledger. Crypto means hidden or secret, meaning people who have cryptoassets apparently cannot be traced if they don't want to be. However, the blockchain has total transparency with transactions and other records, meaning even though you can't identify who each person is, anyone can still access all of its activity. This technology has the potential to decentralise the entire monetary and trade systems, as well as other operations. This is why cryptoservices, which are transparent operations coupled with anonymous parties, are so attractive to so many people, especially because they allegedly can't be controlled by the corporatocracy. Well, that's one perspective anyway. Others believe they were secretly founded by the financial elite to transition the world onto a solely digital platform which they will ultimately control, whilst others believe it was an authentic invention but it's being hijacked or co-opted. I'll explain in more detail later, it's too hard to do with this noise".

"I definitely want to hear more", James replied.

"The other thing that's important is whatever you need to survive. If the entire fiat system implodes then all that paper wealth will be wiped out. Companies will collapse, the boats will stop turning up, the trucks will stop delivering.

There will be no food in only a matter of days. There might not even be electricity".

"Fuck, really?", responded James in a fearful manner.

"It's not a certainty, but it's certainly a possibility", John continued. "Listen, that's why gold and silver are so sought after. I'm not talking about the paper markets, I'm talking about real physical metal that you can hold in your hand. If you can hold it, it has much more value in times like these. That's why food, water and other necessities are a wise investment too. If this blows big, you'll be thanking your lucky stars you were prepared".

At that moment the pilot starting speaking through their headphones. "Okay, we've arrived at the residence. Ready for landing", he stated, rhetorically.

"We'll finish this later", said James. "My accountant is in my second office. Meet up with him and tell him what you told me. Get him to show you the books. Come up with a couple of plans and we'll talk in about an hour".

"Okay, will do", said John.

Gary was enthralled by the conversation, especially because it reinforced the perspective David had. He's heard of conspiracy theories before but never gave many of them too much attention. Whilst he was aware of the many problems with the world, he simply blamed humanity in general. It had never occurred to him that the system might be so deeply corrupted by a small group of people.

"I wonder if that's why I'm stuck here?", he thought. "To learn? Maybe. I can't wait to hear the rest of the conversation either way, though".

He began to contemplate his own life. He thought about how he had wasted so much of it. His aspirations were nearly non-existent; all he wanted to do was have fun. "Not a bad outlook really", he philosophised, "but when my job is mundane, my intelligence has never been properly utilised, and my engagement with the world was mostly limited to mindless TV and media, I feel a little stupid. The best thing going for me is Elle".

A surge of inspirational energy spiralled up through Gary's awareness. "There's so much that I don't know", he acknowledged. "That is something I definitely need to change".

A forgiving thud stirred him from his deep thought. He had never been in a chopper before, so it was a surprise when it landed so softly. It almost felt like a dandelion floaty having the wind taken from underneath it.

James hopped out first and ran to his back door. Waiting there was a well-manicured woman. "Inside", barked James, very rudely.

The two of them walked briskly through the door, leaving John well behind them. "We need to talk now", he growled.

"What about this time?", defended the woman.

"Just follow me Carol".

He led her up a flight of stairs and into a large bedroom. Gary assumed it was the master bedroom. "Carol, we're fucked", he stated, whilst pulling out another bowl filled with cocaine from a desk draw.

"What do you mean, we're fucked?", Carol screeched.

James finished snorting some coke and then coughed briefly. Clearing his throat, he said, "the company is going under. The entire system has fucked us. I need to move as much money as I can out of the stock markets. We've already lost a third of our worth in the last week. If this continues we'll have nothing left".

"We already have nothing left", Carol interjected, insultingly. "Look at us. Look at you. Snorting coke before lunch you feral".

"Shut up you hypocrite", yelled James. "Why don't you go pop some more pills you junkie!"

"Fuck you James, you know I'm not well. You know I've got anxiety issues", she squealed.

"And you've done nothing about it but pop those damn pills and see that hopeless psych of yours. Newsflash: whatever the pills do, whatever he does, it hasn't been working. You've been getting worse every day for the last few years. You look like an empty shell. You're an emotional wreck. You're a poor excuse for a wife and mother", James blasted.

"I've been having an affair James", Carol reacted spitefully.

"No shit, we've both been having affairs for years", James said, shrugging it off.

Gary was surprised by this quick turn of events. It felt horrible watching these two people verbally and emotionally abuse each other.

"I don't love you anymore. I don't know if I ever loved you. I can't do this anymore. This has been a nightmare. I might have all the things that I could ask for in this world, but I'm not happy. I don't feel real. None of it feels real. I've been hating this life more and more since the company expanded internationally. We've been flying around the world attending all these events, but we hardly see the kids.

They don't even know who we are. We don't know who they are!", Carol exclaimed.

"Well, perfect timing, as always", James said condescendingly. "The world is falling apart and now you want to break up. Perfect. This just keeps getting better".

James began to tear up.

"Sit down James", said Carol, guiding him to the bed. James sat down at the same time with her on the end of the bed. Carol took his hands into hers. "Baby, remember when we were in love?"

James nodded in acknowledgement.

"I'm sorry I said that I'm not sure if I loved you, because you know I did", Carol continued. "We were deeply in love before we had all this money. We used to dance and play and have so much fun with each other, all those years ago. But then our relationship took a backseat to your job".

"And your desire for stuff", James interrupted.

"Yes, you're right. I got lost in the material world", Carol agreed. "I wanted the perfect life, with the perfect house, with the perfect family. Somewhere along the way I got lost. I was confused. I was broken. I was told by society that all I needed to do was have money and I could have the perfect life. But it hasn't worked out that way James. I'm miserable. We have millions of dollars at our disposal and we're not even happy!"

"We might not have it for much longer", James remarked.

"That might be the best thing for us", whispered Carol, with a gentle smile.

Gary was feeling better now that they had relaxed a little. He'd never been in a mansion before, let alone listened to a rich couple having a fight. He'd seen many celebrities over the years break down and end up in a sick cycle of addiction and self-abuse, so it didn't surprise him the same occurred to those who were less in the limelight.

He felt sorry for James and Carol too, because he knew what he had with Elle. "We might not have grown up that much and actually took the time to look around and see what was truly happening in the world, but at least our love kept growing for each other", Gary reflected.

He had never felt so in love with Elle.

What felt like a minute or so later, Gary began to feel sleepy. His consciousness started to fade. He refocused on James and Carol, realizing they were cuddling each other, laying down, and James was drifting off to sleep. "Wait, no!", Gary exclaimed. "I want to hear the rest of the conversation with John!"

James suddenly sat up, like he was startled. "What's wrong baby?", asked Carol.

"Nothing babe, nothing". He put his head back down into Carol's chest and closed his eyes.

And suddenly, Gary was gone.

CHAPTER 5

Explorer

A s soon as he became aware that he was becoming conscious again, Gary was excited to find out his next location. He was starting to feel positive about the experience, particularly because he could feel there was a purpose to it so he wanted to connect with it. Once he concentrated on his new surroundings, he noticed he was standing in a cemetery full of hundreds of mourning people with a black, lacy veil covering his face. He couldn't move how he wanted, or say anything. Once again, he was bound.

He watched hands being put over his face. But it wasn't him that was doing it, it was his body. He was just able to see an old woman of about 90 years of age touching him on the shoulder, as his body seemed to weep into its hands. His body then turned to face the woman.

"Annie, Annie, I'm so sorry honey. I'm sorry for your loss", said the elderly lady.

Gary had a momentary relapse and begun to get really anxious. He started to consider that something had gone seriously wrong and that he was in the consciousness of another person in the game. "Please, please, make this go away", he pleaded, without thinking about who he was pleading to.

"It's okay Freda, it really is. It was her time. I was ready, I had been ready for a while", responded Gary's body.

This confirmed to Gary that he was definitely seeing through another woman's perception, regardless if it was real or not.

"Yes, but it's still hard honey", Freda replied. "You have all the love I can give you".

Gary reflected again on the fact that he couldn't feel much of anything, just like it ended when he was in Feddy's body. The difference was he sort of felt the anxiety of Annie, but only vaguely. He could sort of feel the clothes and the veil too, but even less slightly.

"Thank you, you've always been there for me. Are you coming to the wake?", Annie continued.

"Yes, yes, I'll be there. But not too long. I've got to get back to Apollo tonight, he relies on me".

"Apollo hey, that'd be right", Gary snickered. This helped him relax a little more into the experience.

"I'll see you there", replied Annie. "I'm heading over to the hotel now to freshen up. Love you".

Annie turned around and proceeded to a man standing by a large willow tree. "Majestic", thought Gary, as he scoured it. He had re-centred himself again, by this stage.

She walked up to the man and Gary felt her smile, only a touch. "Let's get out of here", said Annie. She and her mysterious looking man headed towards a large car park about 50 metres away.

"Well that was fun", she chuckled. "About time that bitch was laid to rest Mike".

Gary was beside himself at this point. Well, even more so, given the context. He couldn't believe not only what he was experiencing, but what he was hearing too. "She fucking killed her", he thought. "That psycho!"

They walked over to a black sports ute and hopped in. "Now I want you to get onto Gazza over at the shop. Tell him that I'm ready to speak now", demanded Annie.

"Sure thing Ann", replied Mike.

Mike got onto the phone and started talking to Gazza. Gary found this even funnier than the Apollo connection, making this feel more in a game than ever before. "I don't know what my mind is capable of anymore", he giggled in thought. "It feels like it's all connected, somehow".

They raced through a mix of suburbia and farmland. At one point he noticed a Ram standing still on the side of the road, which seemed to stare directly at him with its piercing eyes. Gary absorbed as much of the surroundings as he could, whilst also thinking about Elle and what was happening to him.

In what felt like a flash, they arrived at a large warehouse that was made of steel and aluminium. Looking around, he concluded he was in an industrial estate. There were a few cars parked on the street and in the car park. They pulled up in what looked like a designated spot and hopped out.

"She's here", Gary heard someone say from the entrance.

"Alright, I have to be quick. Get me inside and on stage", ordered Annie, impatiently.

"Follow me", said the host. "We're so glad you're here".

They were led through a shed of about three hundred

people. "Not what I expected", thought Gary. There were cheers and wolf whistles from the crowd. Mike and the host moved off to the left before Annie walked up onto the stage. It was just her, and Gary, in front of a large audience.

"She's dead", Annie began, to the sound of more cheers. "My mother was everything that we despise. She had no respect for her community, let alone her family, or herself. She was a parasite to all of us, which is no doubt why the heavens made sure she contracted the virus and left us to resolve this mess".

The crowd erupted in laughter and applause. "Off with her head", someone yelled over everyone else.

"As you all know, I had been spying on my mother for over three years because it became clear she wanted to rid society of free thought. With the power of her bloodline and her money, she created a thinktank which forged an alliance with the government. She really believed that humanity is a cancer on planet earth. Her whole purpose in her later life was to subject us all to their whims".

"Booooo", the crowd vented.

"She was a major part of the widespread campaign to indoctrinate the masses into their official narratives. Their propaganda is still accepted by so many, especially here. A huge portion of the population still don't understand that her organisation wanted to not just tell us how to think and how to act, but purge us too. They don't know she sanctioned the depopulation program of 'Humrid'. They don't even know the program exists. So far we have lost over 100 million people around the world, to their virus. And this number continues to grow every minute. We estimate that by the end of the cycle, that number will have reached

500 million. They will be the last of these souls before we build collective immunity".

"Why God, why?", a woman screamed in obvious pain.

"Why?", acknowledged Annie. "Because they think they rule the world. They think they are the gods that you pray to. But they're not. We know they're not. Without all of you, our network, our rebellion of over 10 million people, they would have already shed us. But they won't. Do you know why?"

"Why?", the crowd shouted unanimously.

"Because we're humane. We care. I know you care, that's why you're here. You care about your own sovereignty, as well as the sovereignty of your family, your friends and your community. You care about humanity, instead of treating us like a problem to be managed. Now of course we have a problem with the way the system is designed, which caused a lot of severe consequences to not just our species, but planetary life too. But these issues are the direct result of those who hijacked the systemic processes to meet their own greed for power and money".

Annie continued, but with a greater sense of conviction. "My mother is just one head of a snake in a pit full of snakes. They won't stop, until they either achieve their goal, or readjust their perspective. After all, they're human, just like you and I. They're hard on the outside and soft in the inside. Just like us, they need to be nurtured and cared for. They need love".

"They need to die", someone screamed from the crowd.

"Yes, that might be true. They might need to leave this plane of existence if they cannot change their ways. But let's not forget that they, themselves, are sick. They are sick mentally. They are sick in spirit. What we need to do is to continue to build our network so that all their minions realise that they're working for the wrong team. They need to be left stranded, fighting among themselves. For they are few in numbers, and we are many. There are already so many people who used to work for them but now they've converted to the right path, including tens of thousands of genuine people from military, police, intelligence and other governmental agencies".

Annie walked to the edge of the stage. "How many of you used to do the deeds of this madness? Come up here now, and confess to all of us your past choices".

At least a dozen people began walking to the stage.

"Remember, this is stepping into your freedom. This is stepping into your truth".

Around thirty people made their way to the platform. Annie looked at the first person to arrive and said, "You sir, please join me up here". As he climbed up onto the stand Annie asked, "What is the greatest guilt that you hold in your heart?"

Walking up to Annie with his head held low, Annie continued. "Do not look down on yourself, for you are making amends. You are acknowledging your mistakes and taking responsibility for them. Without you doing that, more people would have died".

The man of about 40 lifted his head and stood next to Annie. "I was part of the military. I followed the orders of my command. The worst act I have ever done is took part in the killing of 44 innocent civilians. I knew it was wrong, I knew they were victims. I left the military as soon as I could escape and found my way here. I want to help. I want to make amends".

The crowd applauded, almost quietly. "What is your name?", asked Annie.

"My name is Vikas", he replied.

"Vikas, you've made the right choice. You were once brainwashed, you were once blinded. You were forced to do things against your natural tendencies. You were made to think that power is power over others, but you rejected it. You learned that you deserve your freedom, just like everyone else does. You learned that there are other positions in life more powerful than subjugating others. You became more of you than you've ever been before, only because you made the right choice for yourself, and your family".

"Thank you Annie", he replied graciously.

Annie directed him off stage whilst looking through the other men and women standing right in front of her. "You", she said, whilst pointing at a woman nearing her fifties. "Please join me".

"What is your name?", she asked.

"Bella", she replied.

"Okay Bella, tell us your sin".

"I was the wife of a very powerful man. He gave me everything I wanted, and I gave him three wonderful children. Two girls and a boy. I thought he was the love of my life, until I found out what he was doing. I watched him shape the minds of my children with hate and disdain for their fellow men. He made them out to be monsters, just like him. One day I heard him on the phone, talking about the execution of a group of people. 'They can't be heard by anyone else', I heard him say. He demanded that they kill them now. It sounded like they didn't have any weapons, because he insisted that they kill them with whatever they could find. The last thing I heard was 'strangle them with your shoelaces if you need to!' It was from that moment that everything fell into place. I finally saw him for who he was".

"So what was your sin?", Annie reiterated.

"Deep down I knew it all along", she confided. "I hid it from myself, to stay comfortable in our lives. I supported him when I knew that he was committing monstrous acts against his people. I cooked for him. I bathed him. I should have killed him instead".

"Thank you for your honesty Bella". Annie then turned back to the people who walked up to the stage. "And who else wants to tell their story?"

"I do", said a middle aged man with a fit build. He hopped up on stage and faced the crowd. "I was part of the police force. I worked there for nearly two decades, trying to provide a proper service for my local community. I did provide a good service for the first half, I was protecting my people. But then I noticed big changes. We were slowly being militarised, turning our role into one which protected the political and financial classes at the expense of the people. It was like a slow death of the role to serve our community".

His eyes began to weep.

"What is your name?", Annie asked gently.

"It's Andre", he replied. "It was horrible to watch, even though I was being conditioned to justify actions that I knew were unethical. At first I believed that it was for the greater good, but then it just kept on getting worse. We beat protestors. We arrested good, honourable people. We murdered innocent civilians because we were told to. I murdered innocent people. I'm so sorry. I'm so disgusted in myself".

"But you're proud for leaving and standing up for justice?", Annie enquired.

"I suppose, but it's the least I could do. I just had to do what was right", he answered.

"Now do you see the power of the conscience of humanity?", Annie asked the audience. "Do you see how we must shift the power back to the people?"

The group responded with nods and words of approval.

"The people who support the power structure are just people", continued Annie. "There are some psychopaths, there are some sociopaths, but they're the exception, not the rule. We need to reach out to the good ones and let them know they're our ally, not our enemy. They need to understand they can come join us, no matter how many atrocities they've committed. They need to be nurtured to overcome the deep programming and trauma they've been subject to. They need our love, and we need theirs".

Annie noticed a young woman climbing up onto the stage. "Do you wish to confess?", she asked her.

"Yes, I do", the woman replied quietly. She walked up to Annie and looked her deep in the eyes. "I confess to my saviour. I confess to Lord Archon".

In a swift move the woman pulled out a small pistol and unloaded two shells into Annie's chest. Gary felt like he knew it was going to happen, before it did. He watched the woman being tackled and disarmed by those closest to her. He watched all of this whilst Annie's body fell to the floor.

And suddenly, Gary was gone.

"Where am I now?", was Gary's first thought. As his

awareness crystallised into clarity, he noticed something odd straight away. He was in what appeared to be an underground bunker.

"Adam, we've got to go mate", explained someone from behind Gary's and Adam's view. Gary assumed that Adam must have been the body he was inhabiting. Adam stood up and turned around to look at the man who had spoken to him.

"Alright, let's do it Bobby".

As Adam and Bobby walked up a long, narrow corridor, Gary noticed lots of shelving with plastic boxes. They were marked with various labels, such as 'Grains', 'Seeds', 'Milk', 'Batteries' and an array of other survival goods.

Immediately Gary had an exciting thought: "Did I manifest this because I wanted to learn more about it?"

"What time is it?", asked Adam.

"It's already after four", replied Bobby.

"Oh shit", said Adam. "My talk is meant to start now".

They headed to the end of the corridor and took a left. Gary was expecting to see a ladder leading them out of the bunker, but instead there was a metal door. It was already open so Adam walked through it into what looked like a standard basement. There were a set of stairs leading up to another door, which Adam and Bobby climbed.

They exited through the next door into a hallway. They took another left which led them into a normal-looking dining room. They grabbed a bag each that was sitting on the table and proceeded to walk out the front door. "Ah well, at least the world's population hasn't been decimated in this reality", Gary giggled to himself.

Outside was a forest with several little cottages spread

amongst the trees. To the left was an expansive view, down a valley, to an ocean about ten kilometres away. On the flats before the water was a giant metropolis, with skyscrapers, bridges and harbours. It looked like a light smog was blanketing the entire city.

Walking a little quicker, they crossed through a path in a vegetable garden and across a dirt road, heading towards a neighbour's house. A large, black snake slithered under one of the cars which were scattered throughout, parking in seemingly random areas. A white cat stalked the snake from behind.

Gary could hear talking and laughter coming from the premises, indicating that there was some type of gathering. They walked straight through the front door without bothering to knock. "They're here everybody", someone yelled from an adjacent room.

Adam and Bobby walked into the room where the voice came from. "Hey Nazim. Hey everybody", greeted Adam.

Everybody said their hello. There were around fifteen people in the room, with more in the kitchen and the backyard area. "Alright, where are we doing this Nazim?", asked Adam.

Nazim pointed towards the back. "Out there", he explained. "It's all set up and ready to go".

Adam grabbed a beer from an esky and proceeded outside. He put his bag next to a microphone stand, cracked his beer and had a long skull. "Jeez, he must have been thirsty", thought Gary, noticing that he had drunk half of it. Feeling a slight buzz, he thought, "I can't wait to hear what he's got to say".

By this stage most of the crowd had gathered outside,

finding their own seats. Adam pulled the microphone off the stand and tapped it. "Testing. Testing", he said into it. A soul-curdling screech filled the air. "I don't think I need this", laughed Adam.

He placed the microphone back on the stand and moved it out of his way. "Alright, friends. Stoked to be here. Always good to be around likeminded people".

Adam waited for the remaining few people to be seated. Bobby was sitting to his right, going through his bag and pulling out some paperwork. Nazim was at the back, standing in anticipation.

"So, welcome to Prepping 101", began Adam. "I'm taking you're all here today to learn something new about being a survivalist. Well, I hope I can offer you something new, as I'm sure you've all done your own homework regarding this practice. First, I want to acknowledge the traditional owners of this land. The original people were the Ramarinji tribe and they would still be prospering if it wasn't for the imperialist, corporatised machine. As the original custodians of this land, I honour their wisdom and history. I honour their sacred ways. They're fortunately still with us today, however they're broken and fragmented. But they are rebuilding. We hope to help them on their journey of healing and regrowth".

The listeners nodded and verbally agreed.

"Now, let's start with the basics. Prepping is the practice of building the capacity to survive if something goes seriously wrong in our society. As you all know, we are highly dependent on the system continuing to function. The strong majority of people do not have more than a few days of food in their homes. They don't grow their own, let alone know how to grow their own. If there was a malfunction in the food delivery system, which could happen in a variety of ways, the supermarkets and other convenience stores would be stripped almost immediately, giving us very little time to prepare in the event of an emergency".

Gary was on the edge of his metaphorical seat.

"This is why it's so crucial for us to become more independent from the system. What we really should be doing is decentralising our governmental apparatus, migrating from the cities back into smaller communities and re-empowering our society to be more self-reliant and self-governing, but that's not what's happening so we need to at least do it on an individual level. I mean, who wants to contribute a third of their lives to an economic structure where a small few benefit at the expense of the rest of us, and where only a small percentage of the work actually adds value to our society anyway? We should have a much smaller workweek by now to free us up to live happier and more fulfilling lives, but creating a more empowered citizenry scares the fuck out of the establishment, doesn't it?!"

An echo of agreement swept through the audience.

Adam took a long breath, like he hadn't taken one for a little too long. "There is a simple answer though. Both individuals and communities need to start growing their own food and hemp, period".

"Hemp?", someone queried.

"Yes, hemp. It's a variety of Cannabis that has low levels of THC and can be used to create so many of the products we use. Paper. Plastic. Bio-fuel. Building materials. A form of concrete, which they call Hempcrete. Fibre for clothing. Paint. Soap. Rope. Shit, what else? Ah yes, foods for cooking.

Carpet. The list goes on. There are literally thousands of ways we can use it. And the most amazing aspect is that it can increase our independence by not needing to rely on the petro-chemical and other monopolised industries. Therefore, it is environmentally responsible too".

"And Cannabis is a medicine!", Nazim yelled from the crowd.

"That's right Nazim, it is clinically established. We have an endocannabinoid system in our bodies that is designed to absorb the healing agents of this plant, which is why it's so effective in treating and curing so many diseases. Who knows of Permaculture?"

Around three quarters of the crowd replied yes or put their hands up.

"As you know, Permaculture is simply an environmental design science based in philosophy and ethics. It's a state of mind and heart, which translates into action. You work with nature to benefit yourself, your family and your community, as well as the environment itself. It's a super-win on all levels. But back to the point, there's a concept in Permaculture called companion planting. It probably didn't originate there, but that's where I learned it. Essentially it means that certain plants work well together. Some help to repel pests for others or they might put a compound in the soil that the other plant needs. Regardless, there are benefits to the relationship that might be one-way or two-way. That's why it's wise to understand those relationships and plant accordingly, because it makes growing food so much easier and effective".

Adam stopped to wipe the sweat off his brow and take a sip of his beer.

"So cannabis is one of humanity's companion plants", he explained. "Not just for all the amazing materials it can provide, but for the medical benefits too. And that's why it was prohibited for so long. Cannabis is a symbol of sovereignty, and big money couldn't have that. The petrochemical and pharmaceutical monopolies would have never got anywhere near the size they are today if Cannabis wasn't made illegal".

"Scumbags!", someone commented, vehemently.

"Wow", Gary said to himself. "That is fucked up".

"So that's what we at least need to do for ourselves, especially when it isn't happening on a widespread scale. We need to increase our independence to not just survive if the shit hits the fan, but to live a more natural and self-governing life too".

Getting thirsty again, he consumed more of his drink, finishing it. Bobby replaced it whilst Adam continued.

"Now, where was I? That's right. There are many types of events that could set a societal breakdown in motion. In fact, it's inevitable. Everything works in cycles, from economics to nature and everything in between, however to what extreme it unfolds really is up to us. I'll give you the perfect example. Sun cycles have associated climate cycles. There are small cycles and larger ones too, and they drive changes in our weather. They can impact earth so much that we could experience a mini ice-age, or even a large one. Now, if we're prepared, we'll be fine. If we're not, we won't".

The crowd sat still and in silence, holding onto Adam's every word.

"And that's something we're experiencing right now, too. The sun is effecting our weather in extraordinary ways. It might even be impacting 'The Schuman's Resonance', which measures the earth's electromagnetic heartbeat, because it has spiked to levels never recorded before".

"Think about it as various frequencies of consciousness", added Nazim.

"Exactly", noted Adam. "So anyway, historical examples which trigger chaos include war, economic collapse, disease, natural disasters; that sort of thing. But in the modern age we are at an unprecedented level of vulnerability, simply because most of us rely on the power grid. Back before the twentieth century we had systems which were much more self-reliant, but now if the grid goes down it is estimated that within a year or so over three quarters of population would have perished".

"And they call us mad for prepping", yelled someone from the audience.

"It's crazy", approved Adam. "We have never been so heavily reliant on system processes continuing, and that reliance is so toxic that most people would die if it were to shut down. And all it would take is the malfunction of the electricity grid. Trucks would stop, meaning food, medicine and fuel would run out very quickly, especially because of the 'just-in-time' inventory and delivery systems. That means there isn't months of supplies stored locally, they're being shipped from all over the country and the world just as they're required".

Adam opened his new beer, had another sip and continued: "It's not too unrealistic to think that the grid could be taken down for a prolonged period of time either. There are several ways this could occur. One is natural, such as a via a solar storm or a cataclysmic terrestrial event, including an erupting supervolcano. Then of course there is the potential for a terrorist attack, a cyber-attack, an EMP or even nuclear war. It's all this which separates us from previous disasters in our civilised history".

"Holy hell", Gary muttered to himself. "I never realised how fragile our way of life is. But then again, it wasn't long ago we had economic depressions and world wars. I guess they were more prepared back then too".

"Many people mock us because society has been relatively stable for a while", persisted Adam. "But those who personally experienced wars and problems with the economy know too well what is possible".

This made Gary laugh with a hint of humble pride. "I'm getting the hang of this", he thought.

"Well, the newer generations have been poorly educated on our history. They know little of the struggles of civilisation. They know little of the struggles of the people. They only know their own individual struggles, their own mental sickness and their own existential crisis. They need to take responsibility for their own choices, but we can't blame them entirely either. The indoctrination camps they call schools have churned out little minions who turn a blind eye to the realities of our stolen world".

This reminded Gary of the lecture that John gave to James. "It all sounds so dire", he thought. "Why am I only experiencing negative stuff? Surely there's more to life than just doom and gloom!"

At that instant the crowd's attention was averted to a jet flying high over them. It was racing towards the city. They all ran out to the front, to watch its activities. As they arrived to the best position to look down the valley, the jet did a 180 degree turn over the ocean and headed back towards them.

"What the fuck's that?", someone screamed, pointing at something falling out of the sky.

"Get to the bunkers!", Adam yelled. But it was too late. The explosion was magnificent. Gary watched the entire city centre erupt in a giant fireball, right before everyone covered their eyes and faces. Once again time slowed down. "Please don't make me feel this", he said to himself.

It went dark momentarily, until Gary watched Adam's hands burn to a crisp in front of his face. Adam dropped to his knees, whilst Gary had a clear view of around ten people turning to charcoal. His perspective turned into a bright white, but only for a split second. Then it went dark.

And suddenly, Gary was gone.

CHAPTER 6

Feeler

As Gary's consciousness came streaming back, he immediately recognised the familiar surroundings. He was in his parent's house, where they'd lived for at least the last decade or so. He sat up on the lounge that he remembered playing on as a child, the one he wouldn't let them throw out. His parents actually had it refabricated to accommodate his request.

"Was that all a dream?", was his next thought.

He stood up and walked over to the foyer. On the right to the entrance was a thin table with some flowers and a bowl, with various things in it. He reached in and pulled out a set of keys. As he began to head towards the front door, he got a glimpse of himself in the mirror.

"It's me", he acknowledged. "But fuck I look older".

He attempted to stop walking towards the door to take a better look at himself, but wasn't able to control himself. "What the hell? I'm still in the game", he concluded. "I must be experiencing an older version of myself".

As he moved across the front veranda and walked down

the stairs, he noticed that the neighbourhood surroundings had changed dramatically. New houses had replaced a few old ones, whilst the park across the road had essentially doubled because the neighbouring house had been demolished, with the land absorbed into it. He felt an instant sadness because some of his favourite trees were missing, however new ones had been planted too. Overall it looked generally cleaner and better manicured.

He walked into the garage and opened up the boot of his father's old, but stunningly restored Monaro. Pulling out a small unmarked box and holding it under one arm, he closed the boot and walked back inside. He strolled down the hall and then entered the dining room, placing the keys and box on the table. As sounds of laughter filtered through the back window, he looked into the backyard and saw his father, mother and little brother walking towards the back door.

"Gary! Gary!", yelled his brother. "I just got a hole in one!", he exclaimed.

"Nice work", both Gary's replied, one in thought and one verbally.

Real-Gary studied his brother, Simon, as he walked through the kitchen. He noticed he was around 13 or 14 years old, which was around seven or eight years older than he remembered him. Gary was an only child up until 25, when his parents had accidently fallen pregnant for the second time. As Gary was born when his father was 17 and his mother was 16, they decided to give parenting another shot.

This was because they'd spent the first ten years of Gary's life struggling to keep their heads above water, so when Gary's father hit a masterstroke by inventing an app for smartphones which helped parents connect with local babysitting, coaching and other services, they made a lot of money which enabled them to live more comfortably, travel and take better care of their own lives. His parents believed that Simon was an opportunity to go back to their roots, and they loved the idea of expanding their family unit too.

Simon ran up to Gary and motioned for a high five. He lifted his hand and met it with strong force. Laughing in what seemed a slightly painful way, Simon said, "Got me again you punk".

"Let's head into the lounge room and relax for a while", said Sophia, Gary's mother. His father, Gerald, agreed with a nod of approval.

They all walked in except for Simon, who ran towards his favourite seat. "Shotgun", he yelled.

"He remembered", Sophia murmured to Gerald.

"No one ever wants that seat beside you anyway", chuckled Gary. "Especially when your smelly self sits there all the time", he continued, cheekily.

They all giggled to themselves.

Sitting down, Gary noticed the setting sun glistening through the splits in the vertical blinds. It shed an amber light through the room, which almost looked like an orange fog. "Reverent", he thought.

"Remember when we used to play Monopoly every Sunday night", Sophia remarked nostalgically. "Gary would come over almost every week. Couldn't resist the Sunday roast, could you?"

"That and I just wanted to hang out with you guys. Plus,

I wouldn't have seen my little brother growing up into a big pain in the ass", Gary joked.

"I had a good teacher", Simon reacted wittily, giving him a wink.

Real-Gary was quite impressed with Simon's development. "He's got poise", he thought.

"It was so much fun. We used to have so much fun, didn't we?!", Sophia asked, almost rhetorically.

"We still do", Gerald whispered to Sophia whilst giving her a light pinch on her thigh.

"Eewww, get a room", sniggered Gary.

Real-Gary looked at his parents to critique how they'd aged. They looked pretty healthy, but were clearly showing grey hairs and wrinkles. They looked happy too, but there was also a bit of spark missing. It was more of a feeling for him though, rather than an observation.

"Do you remember what we need to fix on the go-cart Simon?", asked Gerald.

Both Gary and Sophia looked at Gerald with a strange stare.

"Yeah Dad, how could I forget. Pretty much the whole thing. You crashed it bad, remember? I was even in hospital for a night. You were so worried about me doing that, and then you went and did it with me on your lap!", he cackled, very loudly.

"What are you talking about", Sophia directed towards Gerald.

"You remember Mum, I know you do. You were really worried cos' you didn't want us to get hurt", said Simon, before Gerald could speak.

"It's probably a bit blurry for her", Gerald interrupted. "Remind her".

"Well, Dad and I had just finished so we took it up to the top of Silver Hill. It was so hard pushing it up to the top. It took ages. We stopped like twice, or three times. We thought it was going to be so much fun. It's a massive hill, so I was pretty scared, I think". Simon stopped for a moment, looking like he was lost in thought.

"You were scared", reinforced Gerald. "You begged me to go first".

"Yeah, that's right", Simon continued. "It was sooo big! Longer than a handball field".

"It's almost as long as two, but they're called football fields", interjected Gary.

Real-Gary had no recall of any of this.

"Yeah, you were so lucky Dad", endured Simon. "Not like me. I had concussion".

"I didn't mean to, it was an accident", frowned Gerald.

"I know Dad. So we got it to the top and I asked Dad to go first", Simon continued, diverting his attention towards his mother. "That's right, I was so scared but you said we'd do it together. So you got in and I hopped on your lap. You pushed us forward with your hands and we went so fast, so quick. I remember screaming. It was fun, but I was still scared. Then you tried to slow down but the brakes wouldn't work. I remember you told me to hold onto you as tight as I could".

"That's right", Gerald said solemnly, whilst sneaking a look at Sophia. She subtly shook her head in disapproval.

"That's when we went straight into the bushes. I remember crashing, but that's it. Then I woke up in the hospital", finished Simon, with his voice trailing off at the end.

"You're a soldier", admired Gerald.

"Yes, you're our brave little man", Sophia concurred.

"So, you do remember?", asked Simon, quite shyly.

"Of course I do, well, I do now", Sophia responded. "It was a few years ago after all".

Real-Gary was feeling good after hearing this story, even though he hadn't heard it before. It made him think back to other memories of his childhood.

One of the first was of the front yard cricket they used to play. They would get the recycling bin and use it as stumps. They had so many old cricket bats and balls, and everyone had their favourite bat. They would invite the neighbours over, both the parents and the kids, and they would spend the afternoon playing cricket and listening to music. The neighbours would bring over foldout chairs and esky's, and they'd drink and talk and laugh.

Navigating this memory reminded him of his younger childhood. They lived in an area that was subsidised for the poor. The police were always there, nearly every second or third night. People fought all the time, especially because of the gangs. "That place was crazy", he said out loud, almost involuntarily.

This triggered his memories of how much his parents were good to him. They always said they wanted him to feel strong, to feel like he knew himself. He was rarely spanked, or even grounded that much either. Gerald and Sophia had an open communication with him from an early age, so when he had done something wrong they would talk to him about it, and try to help him understand why it was wrong and how he could grow from it. He learned a lot from them, especially because he didn't feel like they were being unfair to him. He felt respected, which ensured he respected them back. He really admired them as a child, and still does.

He then recollected the time that his father magically appeared at the convenience store when he was being picked on by the school bullies. By age eleven, Gary and his parents had already moved out of their old neighbourhood, but Gary was finishing up his final year of primary school. They were preparing to home-school him, instead of sending him to a high school where they didn't feel he was going to get a great education. They did end up schooling him for a couple of years themselves, but eventually Gary insisted he go back because he wanted to socialise more.

He had already spoken to Gerald about the bullying in the past too, particularly because he had come home with a black eye and multiple bruises. He had been bashed on several occasions by this group, particularly by a kid called Rich. So it was little surprise to Gerald as he walked around the corner and witnessed three boys circling Gary, whilst mocking and taunting him.

One of the kids yelled out to Rich. "There's Gary's dad. Run!"

"No need to run boys", Gerald stated quickly, stopping them in their tracks. "Gary can take care of himself", he continued, whilst giving a secret nod with his eyes to his son.

With noticeable confusion the boys stopped and look at each other, as well as Gary and Gerald. Gary's back straightened a little whilst he turned directly to Rich.

"Yeah, I can take care of myself. I'm sick of this shit", he said confidently, whilst pointing at Rich. "I'm done with you picking on me. You need your little girl mates to protect you. You need them, because you're weak. If you've got a problem with me, why don't you try and sort it out yourself!"

"What, you want to fight?", Rich replied, somewhat modestly. "You're just a pussy", he continued, with a bit more confidence.

"No, I don't want to fight you", Gary countered. "But I will if I have to. I will fight all of you if you don't leave me alone. I'm over you picking on me. You're all just scared little bullies!", Gary escalated, trying to instil some fear into their hearts.

"Fight him!", encouraged one of Rich's friends.

And without missing a beat, like his entire identity depended on it, Rich swang a roundhouse with his right fist. Gary ducked it and followed through with an awkward uppercut to his stomach. This not only stunned Rich, but winded him a little too. "You little cheat", he yelled, whilst running at him.

As they collided Gary grabbed him by the shirt with two hands, and fell backwards. He let Rich roll on top of him whilst embedding his left foot into his stomach. In a smooth action he used the momentum that Rich provided and flipped him over his head as he rolled onto his back. Rich flew through the air and landed with a thud.

"Aww, you got pumped Rich", said his other mate. "Don't take that. Get him!"

With teary eyes, Rich got up and once again ran at Gary, this time a little more cautiously. He was growling in pure rage, scaring Gary into action. He lifted his clenched fists and delivered a straight right shot, colliding with Rich's jaw. He fell to his knees and rolled onto his side.

"That's right", Gary said in a surprised voice, looking at Rich's mates. "You come near me again and the same will happen to you".

One of them raised his fists and threw a punch at Gary, hitting him on the left shoulder as he tried to move out of the way. Gary stumbled a little but regained his footing, just as he was approached for the second time. "One-two", suddenly captured Gary's mind, which was some of the basic training his Dad had given him. And in almost perfect unison Gary threw a jab-straight combination that sent the boy crashing to the floor.

Rich and his two mates were in shock, with the one that just got hit sobbing under his breath. Rich had just climbed to his feet when Gary walked up to him. Firmly but softly, Gary said, "Now leave me alone Rich. You ever try to hurt me again and I'll make sure you'll regret it".

Without saying a word, the three boys almost ran in a fast walk towards their homes. Gerald walked up to Gary and gave him a fist bump. He then ran his hand up his spine to the back of his neck and gave it a nurturing squeeze. "Like I keep saying to you, I don't ever want you to start a fight. Ever. But if you need to defend yourself, do it. No one else is going to do it for you, so I want you to know that it's perfectly okay to protect yourself and your friends and family. I'm proud of you mate, you were fucking awesome".

Gary hadn't thought about this memory for many years. In fact, it was almost like he'd completely forgotten it until it was revitalised by his current experience. Because he had rarely been in a fight since that moment, he assumed he had no need. "My god, my Dad is awesome. This probably saved me so much pain because it filled me with the confidence to properly care for myself".

Snapping back to his parent's lounge room he realised he was sitting with Simon alone, watching something on the television. Simon looked distracted, which both Gary's became aware of. Gary got up and almost snuck off towards the dining room where he had placed the box earlier. He picked it up and walked towards the staircase, and quietly ascended it.

"Okay, hold on Gary, there's got to be some great lessons coming up", thought Real-Gary, excitedly.

As Gary reached the top, he turned to the left and walked along the hall. As he neared the end he could hear his mother speaking angrily, like she was upset. He stopped to listen to their conversation. "It's just too much", Sophia sobbed.

"I'm sorry Sofe, I shouldn't have asked him", apologised Gerald. "I just wanted to know what he could remember. They said they would be able to make it a smooth transition, and they clearly have".

"Yes, but why did you do it in front of me! I love him Gerald. I love him too much. That was so painful to go through, I almost broke down in the middle of it. He was such a special boy, with so much life. He was my new soul, my new baby. This whole thing just feels so fake".

"He will continue to evolve, just like normal. You know they said his body will still grow like a normal child. He will grow into an adult who loves his family and his life. It really is amazing, Sofe", Gerald said, upliftingly.

"How do you know? How do they know?!", she reacted swiftly. "It's never been done before. Anything could go wrong. In the meantime, here we are knowing all this, scared that something could go wrong. It feels like torture Gerald, it feels like we're putting ourselves through abuse. And for what? To help the industry experiment? We're not their Guinee pigs Gerald, and neither is Simon!"

"I know we're not", Gerald replied, putting his head into his chest.

"There is something seriously wrong. I can feel it. I feel like we're doing something to his soul. I feel like we're hurting him. When you asked him that question, I felt it straight away. My heart was in my throat Gerald. I almost threw up".

"I really didn't want to upset you. I didn't want to upset anyone, including Simon", Gerald pleaded.

Gary opened the ajar door of the room. "You can't upset him Dad, it's not Simon. He's not human. You know they've replaced most of his brain with a bio-computer".

"What the fuck?!", Real-Gary blurted out in shock.

"Yes, I know, I know. But I feel like he's still there. I feel like Simon's spirit is still there", Gerald cried, very softly.

"It's not Dad. He's a robot", stated Gary, firmly but softly too. "It's artificial intelligence. Ever since he went into the coma he's been gone. He's with Nan and Pop and Shirley. We shouldn't have kept him like that for two years. We shouldn't have used him for this experiment. You know I was very vocal about it because of exactly this reason. It's going to bring back so many bad memories and keep us stuck in the past".

Real-Gary started weeping emotionally. "How can this be? This can't be real. There's no way that this could be my future. There's no way that this technology will be available in only a few years. Oh my god Simon, I hope you're okay! I fucking love you bro".

Feeling heartbroken, his attention snapped back to the scene as Sophia slightly raised her voice. "I told you I didn't feel right about this. I told you it didn't feel right", she wailed deeply, dropping her face into her hands.

As she continued to sob wildly, Gary put down the box next to the bed as he and Gerald both wrapped their arms around her. "We can end this now if we want", he uttered.

"End this now? What is that meant to mean?", contemplated Real-Gary.

"There's a kill-switch in the box", continued Gary. "I had a mate make it for me. They're going to be super pissed if we do it, but that's they're problem. This technology is so new, nobody knows the consequences. But think about it. It's like being in a fake version of reality. He's not there, I don't see any of Simon in his eyes. He seems lifeless. He really comes across as a robot. You can see the glitches too. I've seen it happen so many times. It's just programming. We'll never have Simon back. We need to accept it".

Sophia burst out with deeper weeping, startling all of them.

"What do you think Sofe, is that what you want to do?", asked Gerald, after she calmed a little.

"I don't know hon, I just don't know", she replied, gaining more composure. "I need to think about it some more. I need to…"

Before Sophia could finish her sentence, a small piece of metal sliced through the bedroom window and pierced her left temple, followed by a muffled gunshot sound rolling through the air. It sprayed blood onto Gary's face, including in his eyes. Almost simultaneously the bedroom door flung open and three men dressed in black suits opened fire. Real-Gary was just able to see his father get hit at least two times in the head and two in the chest, although he was unsure where he was shot as he slumped onto the bed and fell to the ground.

And suddenly, Gary was gone.

CHAPTER 7

Knower

"Oh my God, oh my God, oh my God", Gary gasped, as he regained awareness.

Whilst he began to process that he just watched his parents be killed, he tried to make note of his surroundings. The first aspect he noticed is that it all seemed so much brighter. And colourful. He had taken magic mushrooms quite a few times before, so it instantly reminded him of those experiences. He was in a forest which was a mix of temperate and tropical plants. He could hear the sound of crows and other birdlife bellowing overhead, which balanced out the insects which were humming at near eardrum-piercing levels.

He was sitting in a camping chair, with a fire two metres in front of him. It was really cold with condensation almost engulfing his face when he breathed out. He couldn't tell if it was morning or afternoon, although it was obvious it was one of them because of the vivid colours he could see in the sky through the breaks in the canopy.

"How's the shrooms going?", he heard a soft, feminine

voice ask. This cracked up Gary, making him momentarily forget about his previous experience.

A woman in her early-twenties walked around to his right and sat on his lap. As she leaned in to kiss him, Gary observed that she had brunette hair with a slight red tinge. There was a blue streak in it too, which kind of looked punk rock. She was slim in the face and had a piercing on her lip, where an iconic beauty spot would reside. And she smelled of erotic perfume.

The girl kissed deep and long, playing with his tongue and lips with her teeth. As she nibbled on his neck, Gary's body replied. "They're so good".

Gary realised in that moment that he was in a woman's body, because of the tone of her voice. "They're soo fucking good Lucinda", she repeated.

Lucinda went in for another kiss, which ended quickly. "Damn", Gary reacted unconsciously.

She got up and walked over to the fire. Picking up a few logs of choice, she buried one deep into the hot coals and delicately placed the others on top. Then she sat down in her own chair and pulled out a pack of rollies. "I could do this forever, Laya", she said, almost cosmically.

"There is only the forever now", replied Laya. "This is the stuff of dreams. You're the stuff of dreams Lucinda, especially your hot little body", giving her a flirty wink.

Lucinda finished rolling her cigarette and passed them to Laya. As she started to roll her own, she felt the mushroom magic really kicking in. This was not isolated to her either, as Gary felt like his feelings and visuals were amplifying as well.

"How can I be tripping?", he thought, as his mind began to wander into itself.

Laya sparked her smoke and stood up from her chair. She walked over to the tent, which was a very simple setup. Gary observed a blue ute parked just behind it, with the passenger window almost fully down.

"Oh shit", she muttered to herself. Gary assumed that she had noticed the same thing because she changed direction towards the car.

"What Malaya?", enquired Lucinda.

"Just the window", she explained.

As she opened the door and manually wound it up, Gary could see into the car which was filled with various bags and other equipment. "Grab the second mattress and blanket", suggested Lucinda.

"Where are they?", Laya replied, without receiving an answer.

She closed the passenger door and opened the one behind it. As she moved some gear to the side Lucinda walked up behind her and gave her a cheeky slap to her ass. "Yum", she teased.

Lucinda grabbed Laya by the shoulder and guided her out of the way. She climbed into the back of the car with her ass raised high in the air, making Laya and Gary feel rapidly horny. As she reached behind the driver's seat, Laya grabbed her bum with both hands, which Gary strangely felt, as if he was Lucinda. Laya then bent down and buried her face right into her where her holes were and took a long whiff, which Gary also felt.

"Now that's luscious", Laya said, seductively.

As Lucinda backed out of the car she had with her an

uninflated air mattress and large woolly blanket. "Let's go lie down on the edge and watch the stars come out to play", she suggested. "Grab our big jackets too, Malaya".

Laya walked to the front of the tent and unzipped it along the bottom. She reached to the right and pulled out two snow jackets. Zipping the tent back up she looked across to see where Lucinda was, who was still puffing on her smoke whilst slowly walking towards a trail to the right. Laya reached a slow jog to catch up with her, but did it as quiet as she could. As she snuck up behind her she put her smoke in her mouth, dropped the jackets and slid her right hand down the front of her crotch and her left hand onto Lucinda's left breast.

"Ecstasy", Lucinda moaned, as her body shook a little. Gary once again experienced this touch, further confusing him.

After rubbing her pussy and nipple for another few seconds, Laya kissed her on the back of her neck and whispered in her ear. "Love you sexy bish".

She bent over towards the jackets and picked them up, as she started a slow jog. She turned to face Lucinda whilst walking backwards and blew her a kiss with the hand that held her cigarette.

The girls walked along a track that meandered a little before beginning a slight decline. "Forgot the bloody torch", Lucinda remembered. "Ah well, I'm sure we'll be right", she giggled.

The track opened up to a large clearing after about fifty metres, which brought more light with it too. Gary was taken aback from the dying sunset and the valley that dropped hundreds of metres below. Everything appeared so surreal, so artistic. The colours, although fading, were a rich tapestry of pinks, purples, oranges and blues.

They chose a spot close to the edge of the cliff where there were no trees above them which would block their view of the emerging stars. It was getting dark very quickly as the girls took turns in pumping up the mattress with their foot. There was a pump embedded into the mattress itself, so it was easy enough to activate. After three or four minutes of taking turns filling it up, as well as taking the opportunity to touch each other both sensually and sexually, the mattress was ready to go.

By this stage Gary was flying. He watched Lucinda put on her jacket, lay out the blanket, and sit on top of it in a kind of psychedelic haze. As she brushed her hair from her face it looked fiery and alive, with her hands emitting what looked like an energetic charge. Laya zipped up too, then joined her.

By this time an orange glow dominated the air-scape. "It's so fucking gorgeous", thought Gary. "I wish this entire game could be like this", he continued, trying to block out the memory of his last experience.

Laya pulled out the smokes and slightly struggled to roll two fresh ones, whilst they both sat in silence. After sparking one she handed it to Lucinda, and then repeated again for herself. Then they laid down on their backs and gazed into the increasingly night sky.

"Last weekend when I took LSD, I felt like I reached the stars", commenced Laya. "I remember wishing you were there. I really wanted to have that experience with you".

"We can have it right now", Lucinda proposed.

"Yes, we can", continued Laya. "I've read that people

say they had an ego death, but that's not what it was for me. My sense of self, my Malaya-ness, certainly melted into the universe, but there was still a part of myself that was there. It was still me having an experience. The experiencer and the experience. Even though I was freed from my normality, my normal ego perception, I was still me, just a more expanded version. I remember losing some sensations from my body, like taste and touch and smell. I could still see though, but it was a strange visualisation. Like I kind of dissolved into the stars or something. After a while I noticed that my eyes were closed and that my perspective was more like another sense that I didn't even know I had. It was so fucking cool. I had never experienced anything like that, baby".

"How did you feel?", Lucinda asked lightly.

"It's hard to say. It's hard to put into words. At first I did feel awe and wonder, and actually when I think about it that never left. But after a while I felt like I was the stars. Like I was everything else. I remember making jokes about it, like calling myself God. I was laughing at times and then blissed out at others. I had a story going on in my mind, which is why I always felt like me. I was analysing it in a sense, playing with it in another, even though I didn't feel like I had the normal five senses. I had lost my body, but I hadn't lost my mind".

"I'm starting to feel like that now", whispered Lucinda.

"Me too", thought Gary and Laya at the same time.

"Actually, now that I think about it even more, I did lose consciousness at one point. I remember coming out of it, after what felt like half an hour. I could remember a lot of it, including the storyline that was unfolding in my mind, but I only became aware of it once I'd grounded myself a bit more. It's like I was conscious of my basic connection with the universe, of my connection with everything else, at least on one level, even though I was still having an individual experience. My ego was still there, experiencing, even though that experience was more connected than what normal waking life feels like. That's why I walked away thinking that my job is to enlighten my ego, or my sense of self. To heal it. To grow it. Empower and expand it. Not treat it like it's my enemy. Fuck being my own enemy", she concluded, with a chuckle.

Gary was really beginning to directly encounter what was being described. It was immense. He felt like he wasn't just more connected to everything, but personally with Lucinda as well. As she began to speak, Gary sensed it like he did with Laya.

"My father says something similar. He tells me when he meditates he goes through different levels. I think it's beta, alpha, delta, theta. Wait, no; theta, delta. That's it. He says that when he hits an alpha state he feels more focused and less busy in his mind. But as he goes into theta, he begins to lose the sensations of his body. Once he goes deeper he said it's like he's floating in space, like he's weightless. He says it's a challenge to maintain a delta state if he actually reaches it, but he knows when he's there because it's like he connects with the cosmic mind. And he says the same too, that he feels like he's still himself, but that his understanding has been enlarged to encompass more of reality".

"That's exactly what it was like", Laya declared enthusiastically.

"That's what this whole experience has felt like", Gary

thought in near unison with Laya. "I feel like I'm still Gary, but more than that too".

As Lucinda continued to talk, Gary's perspective begin to split into two distinct dimensions. He could see through the minds of both Laya and Lucinda.

"Yeah I love feeling connected to everything", Lucinda affirmed. "Consciousness really does feel like it's the bridge between all of us. I mean, that's the only experience we ever have, right? I've never experienced anything but being conscious. There's some philosophies that say this too. That mind or consciousness is the basis of reality and that matter is more the expression or constructs of consciousness".

"Idealism vs materialism, yeah?", quizzed Laya.

"Yeah, that's it", maintained Lucinda. "But it feels like it's more than just one mind too. Some people believe that only their mind exists, that everything and everyone else is a part of their imagination or their mind. Their dream. I don't feel that way though. I believe that you exist just as much as I do, meaning we're not just one connected thing, we're many things connected. Do you know what I mean?"

"We're not just one consciousness, we're also the minds of consciousness", Laya proposed.

"Exactly. That describes it perfectly. And it makes sense that I'm connected to everything else, even though it doesn't usually feel that way. Especially when I've experienced all that weird stuff".

"Yeah, we've talked about this before a little bit, but I want to hear more. Give me some examples that you haven't already", Laya suggested, eagerly.

"Well, as you know sometimes I can feel other people's feelings, even when they're really far away", explained

Lucinda. "I never told you this, but when you found out your dog died last week I felt really sad just before you called. I actually felt like I was going to throw up for a second. I didn't want to tell you at the time because you were so upset, but it was a really clear feeling. Then as we started talking it went away".

"That's so cool. Fuck we're connected. What else?"

Another perspective was beginning to cultivate in Gary, although he wasn't quite sure what to make of it. This third perspective quickly became as prominent as the other two. He could clearly see through Laya looking at the stars and through Lucinda looking at Laya, as well as his own view floating above them, looking at the stars too. "This is mind-blowing", he thought, before laughing at his unintended pun.

"What's one of your big ones?", Laya delved softly.

"Well, this is a little embarrassing, but before I met you I was walking down main street, feeling a little unloved. You know I was a bit sad then. So I remember thinking that I shouldn't need anyone to make me happy and that if I didn't start loving myself and my life more then why would anyone love me anyway? Because I was so lost in thought I wasn't watching where I was going properly, and next minute I bumped into a little old lady who then crashed into a shop window".

"Oh my God, was she okay?", Laya queried, with genuine concern.

"Yeah, she was fine", reassured Lucinda. "She had a little laugh. I was super embarrassed, and just kept apologising. She brushed it off and told me not to worry about it".

"So what was the big connection?", probed Laya.

"Before she left, I introduced myself. And you wouldn't believe what she said to me", Lucinda teased. "She said, 'Hello Lucinda, I'm Malaya".

"Okay, so wh.."

Before Laya could finish her sentence, Lucinda interrupted. "Wait Laya, its coming. So as she walked away I looked at the window to make sure it was okay. That's when I realised I was standing in front of the toy shop. And exactly where I had knocked her into the window, there was a care bear staring right at me".

"Wait, don't tell me. There was a name badge pinned to it with the name Malaya?", Laya kidded.

With a loud laugh, Lucinda confirmed her cheeky prediction. "Oh my god, can't believe you guessed that!"

They both laughed, rolling to face each other. "No way!", resisted Laya.

"Yes way", Lucinda insisted. "I laughed about it for days. I joked to myself that this little old lady was a shapeshifting care bear. I totally forgot about the monologue I was having before it happened, until a week later you came crashing from the clouds like a drunk care bear".

The girls cracked up laughing as hard as they ever had together before.

"That is sooo fucking cute!", thundered Laya. "How come you've never told me this? It's such a wonderful story babe, that makes me feel even more connected to you".

"Well, I'm not going to tell that to someone I've just met, am I?", chuckled Lucinda.

"No of course not", Laya said, still laughing. "We have been together for nearly a year though".

"Yes, well, I'm telling you now baby. I guess this is the

right timing. Just like the timing was right when I was just thinking about loving myself more and then that happened. It was like I had to have that realisation before I met you, to make sure I was doing the right thing by myself. And you. And that's what my connections have been like, both big and small. They're patterns or themes that emerge in my experience. It's like they're screaming 'look at me, look at me, there is meaning in this world'. So once I started being open to them, they seemed to happen more. Maybe they were always there and I just rarely noticed, or maybe once you become aware that they exist you become stronger or more powerful in making them happen. I don't know, but it's magical".

"You're fucking magical Lucinda", Laya said seductively, as she leaned in to kiss her.

As the girls embraced each other in a passionate blend of their lips and tongues, Gary felt like he was kissing himself, which made him laugh hysterically. "This just keeps getting better", he clowned.

The girls rolled onto their backs, in pure bliss. "God we're synchronised", Laya said lovingly. "That's what it's like for me, the connection I have with the world. It feels like I have experiences that are synchronised. They're not coincidences, they're not random chance. They're synchronicities that have meaning to them. It's like they represent information that if I'm conscious enough, I can come to understand".

"Just like symbolism", suggested Lucinda.

"Yes. Right on", continued Laya. "It's like they're symbolic of something much deeper. People, animals, numbers, concepts; it's all part of it. Sometimes I come to a more profound understanding of what they represent, sometimes I don't. And I used to get frustrated, like really, really frustrated when I couldn't comprehend the significance, but now I just let them go and if it's seriously important, I believe it will come back in another way".

"I still have that, actually", Lucinda confided. "These bizarre things happen and I have no idea what I'm meant to learn from them, which sometimes pisses me off. I want to know more. I want to experience it more".

"Yeah, I feel ya", validated Laya. "I just find it funny now. Just hold on for the ride. There's no destination; just more learning, more healing, and more growth. Then hopefully we can be more wise too", she joked.

As the girls giggled to themselves, they squeezed each other in a tight embrace. They blended seamlessly into each other, like two fires uniting.

Gary was deep in thought, at this point. With no distractions by the girls, he contemplated the discussion. "I've always felt connected but never properly acknowledged it. My relationship is the epitome of it, but so often I've seen and felt patterns that I've just passed off as coincidence. How foolish of me. But it feels so simple now. I am so much more than just an individual human. There is an ocean of energy that connects all of our islands".

With that thought an image of three islands came to the forefront of his awareness. He could feel the triangle of connection between all of them, with each island representing the symbiosis between mind, body and soul. He could almost see how it was entangled, and the more he concentrated on it, the more it came clear in his vision.

It first appeared as three points of perception that formed an equilateral triangle. As this geometric shape formed in his mind's eye, a fractal pattern spread out to what felt like infinity. Then, the three perspectives began to merge. They folded onto each other, and into each other. They became one again.

And suddenly, Gary was gone.

CHAPTER 8

Driver

"I feel so much more powerful", was Gary's first thought as he regained perspective. As his blurry vision clarified into a crystal clear image, he saw one of the most beautiful trees he had ever seen, towering above him. It looked over fifty metres high, with lush green foliage that symbolised health and vitality.

"Be the tree", he heard himself say, even though it didn't feel like he was the one who said it.

"Be the tree?", he repeated to himself. "What's that meant to mean?" As he contemplated the question, he remembered the conversation between Laya and Lucinda about symbolism. "Okay, so every object, or every construct of consciousness innately represents specific information, and how we relate to that information has meaning. So what does the tree symbolise and what meaning does it have for me?", he asked himself.

Before Gary could further his introspection the vehicle he was embodying looked down into their lap and began packing away the remnants from their lunch. Gary believed it was a man based solely on his attire. He picked up bits of plastic and scraps and placed them in a plastic box, which he then put into a small carry bag. As he motioned to stand from the chair he was sitting in, Gary felt frustrated as he was wanted to gaze deeper into the majesty of the tree.

"No, SIT DOWN!", he commanded, almost unconsciously.

In response, the man sat back down and moved his right hand to his stomach. Gary had the slight feeling that he was nauseous, indicating to him that the man he was in felt a little sick. "Wow", he thought. "Did I just create that sickness so I could look at the tree?"

As the man put his bag back on his lap, he pulled out a small box, a cup, a spoon and some water. Gary took the opportunity to observe more of the tree from the edge of the man's perspective. It had small flowers throughout, as well as papery bark covering the entire trunk and its branches. It was perfectly balanced from bottom to top, like a perfect cone. It looked as if it was designed that way. There were a variety of bird species playing in different areas, most of which were up high and hard to identify. And the roots around the trunk danced along the grass until they disappeared completely into the earth.

"It really is just so natural, so untainted", Gary thought, in awe. "It's so mystical too".

"Hey Buzz", shouted a voice from around ten metres behind where they were sitting.

Gary had only just noticed the ruggedness of his hands and the deep black hairs on them, indicating that he was definitely in a male. The man turned around to look at who had spoken to him, and before he was able to see the person he replied, "Warwick, what's up my man?"

Warwick walked the opposite side of how Buzz had turned his head, so he flung it around to greet him as he passed next to him. He put the water onto his lap and between his legs, so he could give him a fist bump as he moved in front of him. He then sat to his left.

"Are you drinking Coke?", he joked, referring to the white powder he had deposited in the cup.

Before he could respond, he let out a laugh. "Nah, not till later. It's bicarb soda mate. It works bloody wonders for my indigestion".

"Bicarb?", Warwick laughed. "I thought that was for cooking and cleaning?"

"Mate, this stuff is a miracle substance. Yeah I've heard it's good for cleaning and whatnot, even for cleaning your teeth. But I was put onto it by an ex. She reckons it's an alkaloid and helps balance out the pH of our body, especially with all the acidic crap in our diet. You know, processed and fast food. That sort of thing".

"Speak for yourself mate, I don't eat that shit", chuckled Warwick. "Nothing but organic food for me. Except pizza. I still fucking crave pizza man, haven't been able to kick that yet".

"Yeah my diet isn't so bad these days", reflected Buzz. "Still indulge in crap every now and again though. But this bicarb, I use it all the time mate. Phenomenal. Heartburn, indigestion, colds, flus, hangovers.. you name it and I'll use it. Saves so much dosh too not buying all the pharma shit".

This conversation was all too familiar to Gary as his parents had been using it since he was a little kid.

"Serious. How does it work again?", queried Warwick.

"From what I understand the human body is like a fish tank or pool or whatever. It has an optimum pH level, like soil for plants. If it gets too acidic then the immune system struggles to fight off toxins or bacteria or whatever. So using bicarb puts the body back into the right balance, so the immune system can get on with dealing with whatever it needs to. Pretty simple, but amazing stuff. Apparently it can even help to slow tumour growth in cancer patients too".

"No shit, hey. I've actually got a bit of heartburn right now. Let me try some", Warwick asked, with curiosity.

Buzz poured some water into the cup and stirred it for five seconds. He let it settle for another five and then handed it to him. "One teaspoon is all you need".

Warwick skulled it down and handed the cup back to him. "Fucking hell mate, tastes like cum!", he hooted.

"Doesn't surprise me that you know what cum tastes like mate", Buzz said wittily.

"Shit, I set myself up for that one", Warwick conceded, whilst still laughing.

Buzz pulled out another teaspoon of bicarb and made his own health potion. As he drank it Warwick continued the conversation. "Yeah, it doesn't taste the best, but I can feel it working almost instantly. Good stuff. So you heading back to the office soon?"

Buzz nodded his head whilst finishing off his cup. Gary's slight feeling of sickness had essentially dissolved by this point, so he was feeling really good again.

"Yeah sweet, I'll come with you", Warwick continued. "Before we go though, I've got some fucking awesome news. I've been trying to talk with you about it. You know how

Chaz wants to run the pilot for 'Blow the Mind'? He said he'll consider us for the writers".

"Fucking oath", said Buzz enthusiastically. "I really need to get out of this suit for a while. It's just not me. Plus, I'm sick of being imprisoned by Mr. Fuckstick's bullshit. He has no idea what he's doing, I have no idea how he even got the job. He's fucking hopeless".

"Yeah I know, right", Warwick agreed, whilst having a little chuckle. "I'm keen too. Chaz was having a meeting this morning so we might even find out today. I've been trying to call you about it all morning".

"Yeah I left my phone at home and I've been in meetings all morning. Haven't even checked my emails either", explained Buzz.

As he was finishing his sentence, Warwick's phone rang. "Awesome, this is him now. Hang on a sec".

Warwick stood up, pulled his phone out of his right pocket, looked at Buzz with a hopeful smile and pressed a button on the phone. "Chaz mate, we were just talking about you". Warwick looked up into the distance while nodding his head slightly to what Chaz was saying to him. "Yeah, I'm with him now".

Gary and Buzz could slightly hear Chaz's voice, but couldn't make out the words.

"Okay, we'll be there in five. Thanks mate". Warwick hung up from the call, put his phone in his pocket and gave a large, impressive smile to Buzz. "Alright, get your shit together, we've got a pilot to write". As he completed his sentence, he gestured for Buzz to give him a high five, which they did in a perfectly aligned meeting of the hands.

"What, now?", Buzz asked, slightly confused.

"Yes, now. It's between Chaz and Mort. We need to get together an ad hoc list of ideas for the producers. See how we respond under pressure. We need to get them something in the next hour or two. Come on, let's fucking go", he said with sheer happiness.

"Well this sounds like fun", thought Gary. "Puts a bit more balance to all that crazy shit at the start".

Buzz threw the remaining items into his bag and got up in a hurry. They walked at almost a slow jog to the taxi rank, around twenty five metres away. "Fuck that bicarb did the trick", confirmed Warwick.

"Told ya mate, miracle substance", Buzz replied, assertively.

They hopped in the first taxi in the line and closed the doors. "Gnosis Tower on 12th", instructed Warwick.

As the taxi pulled out into the street, Gary noticed the taxi driver had an ornament of a horse stuck to his dashboard. "I wonder what the horse energy symbolises?", he thought to himself.

Warwick's phone beeped, interrupting Gary's thought. "That's probably the mandate", Warwick said hopefully. He reached into his pocket again and pulled out his phone. "Nope, it's the missus. She wants to go to dinner tonight. If we score this role, I'm gonna make it an epic celebration!"

As he was putting it away, it beeped again. He look at the screen which made him take a deep breath. "Alright, this is it", he authenticated. "Okay, so let's start now. May as well use the five minutes. The pilot is called 'Blow the Mind'. It's likely to be a ten or so part series that explores weird or different points of view in the world. We need to come up with at least ten ideas for the episodes. The major concepts, as well as subthemes".

"Well I've got a few ideas", laughed Gary.

"Okay, so my first thought is.." Buzz was cut off by Warwick before he could continue.

"WAIT, wait, Buzz. Let's record it, so we don't miss anything. I'll get Elle to type it out when we get back".

"Oh my God, another Elle. Fuck I miss you. I want to make love to you baby", vented both Gary and Buzz instantaneously.

"You want to fuck Elle?", Warwick asked, a bit confused. "Yeah she's hot, but what about your woman?"

"Fuck, I don't know what just happened, must have been in deep thought", Buzz laughed, awkwardly.

Gary only just cottoned on to what just happened. "Okay, so I must have some control on what Buzz says", Gary thought to himself, very softly. "If I do it like this, without emotion or passion, it doesn't seem to work?", he asked himself, waiting to see if it influences Buzz.

"Anyway, my idea I had was about sex", Buzz continued. This established to Gary that it didn't have any effect.

"Go on", said Warwick, as he pressed record on his audio app.

"Think about all the crazy attractions that people have these days. I know it's been done before to an extent, but instead of capturing the strange things that people are attracted to, we could tell the narrative of people who identify as having no sex at all".

"Okay, I like that. The transgender thing is really popular right now. There's so much attention on it, so we could get inside the minds of those people who feel disconnected from being a male or female and how that relates to who or what they're attracted to. Good stuff. But yeah, the whole 'I want to marry my goat' thing really is bat-shit crazy", ridiculed Warwick.

"Or how about 'I want to fuck the exhaust pipe on my car'" joked Gary, with the intention of making Buzz say it. He waited to see if it worked.

With both Buzz and Warwick both in laughter, Warwick responded. "Yeah I love my convertible, but making love to it just doesn't seem right. Plus, my dick wouldn't fit anyway", he messed around further, guaranteeing they kept laughing for a few more seconds.

"Okay, let's see what I can do here", thought Gary.

"So what I was thinking for another episode is how some people..."

"Wait, let this flow", interrupted Gary, through Buzz. "Let's flip the switch. Instead of only identifying those who think differently, let's analyse those who think what is considered normal. So for example, think about the millions, if not billions of people who continue to vote for their favoured political party. Doesn't matter if it's left or right, just the fact that all these people relentlessly support their side but they rarely get the change they're actually looking for. So for some they've been voting for decades, but they still don't realise that it doesn't matter who they vote for, big money interests are way more likely to have their preferences enacted over and above the will of the majority. This is evidenced in a research paper that analysed the recent history of policy decisions by the government. They asked varying financial classes what their preferences were over a twenty year period and the results were way more in favour of the wealthy, rather than the rest of the people. The result? We have an oligarchy, not a democracy, but people still continue to vote anyway".

"Holy fuck, that's genius!", Warwick responded animatedly. "I've actually never thought about it like that. Fuck, I'm one of those people! And I even know the research you're talking about too. I'm doing something considered normal, but it's nonsensical. It's crazy. It doesn't work, but I continue to do it anyway. What did Einstein say about this again?"

"Actually, Einstein never said that apparently. But I'm pretty sure what you're referring to is that 'Insanity is continually repeating the same thing expecting to get different results'. I'm glad you like it", articulated Buzz, without any input from Gary.

"Well, we're a network which challenges the mainstream crap anyway. I think they're gonna love it!", Warwick glowed with conviction.

Gary knew it was his time to chime in again. "One of the biggest hypocrisies in our world today is people who condemn illegal drugs like pot and psychedelics and stuff, but they're addicted to sugar, food, alcohol, pharmaceuticals, sex, TV, their own emotional bullshit, their own bigotry, all that crap that shows how fucking hypocritical they are. Yet they won't do the research to understand that certain psychotropics such as DMT, MDMA, psilocybin and so many others have actually been clinically proven through so many scientific studies to not just help cure addiction, but many other mental issues too. It's un-fucking-believable that so many people in society still think that these drugs are bad, when they can actually be a great thing if used properly".

"I'm hearing ya Buzz", backed Warwick.

"No, you're hearing me", laughed Gary.

"That's what I said", chuckled Warwick.

"Whoops", thought Gary, trying to not put any emotion into it.

He then deliberated for a moment about what to say next. Before he could talk, Buzz continued the chat. "I didn't even know I had these ideas. I feel like I'm channelling them".

"Not too far off", mocked Gary.

"Yeah, they're great Buzzman. Keep em' coming", approved Warwick.

Gary wasn't sure what to say next, but began speaking anyway. "So another one is how all these surveys continue to illustrate that public trust in media has been declining for a couple of decades. It's at all-time lows. Yet, so many people still watch these channels and believe their version of events. It's like people have little memory. News has been exposed as fake so many times, on really important life and death matters mind you, but the masses continue to lap that shit up like it's gospel. I mean, if they put their money where their mind is, the media monopolies would collapse. Very few people would watch their shit, so they wouldn't get advertising because it wouldn't be selling much. And you'd see an explosion in independent media, especially networks like ours".

This surprised Gary, because he had never seen these surveys before. He wondered if he was channelling someone else too.

"Yes. YES! I fucking love it. Chaz will love it. This could really put us on the map. So many people are rejecting the official narratives and are looking for channels which tell the truth. This is BRILLIANT", Warwick exploded in passion, before grabbing Buzz's head and laying a big creepy kiss on his forehead.

"That's my reward?", provoked Buzz.

"What else you got", Warwick pleaded.

"How about that people love to hate things about others, but are so far removed from their own bullshit that they don't see that they more or less do the same thing too", voiced Gary and Buzz.

"Betcha that's us as well", smirked Warwick.

"Yep, no doubt", agreed Gary. "Or what about when people condemn other parents because of whatever their child or they did, yet they've got such poor relationships with their own children?"

"That might be hard to capture, but I getcha", mused Warwick.

"Then there's the belief that certain corporations and multinationals are unethical, yet they still trust the toxic shit they put in mainstream medicine, as well as the food and water supply in general", persisted Gary.

"And they keep quiet about cheap and natural medicines too", Warwick expanded.

"Exactly", continued Gary. "Bicarb is the perfect example".

The taxi came to a grinding halt, particularly because the brake pads were on their last days. "Four Twenty", directed the driver. Warwick handed over his corporate card and the driver waved it over the electronic gadget. He handed the card back to Warwick, along with a receipt, which he placed in his wallet.

As Buzz and Warwick exited the vehicle, Gary noticed an owl perched on a ledge four metres above his head, which was followed by another metaphorical light bulb going off. "Or how's this one, and this is big. For all of our so-called civilised history we've had a ruling class of some kind, like kings and queens. Yet in this day and age not only do many people believe they don't exist, or that even if they do, they're effectively obsolete".

Buzz and Warwick swiftly entered through the revolving doors to the foyer of their building, scanned through the security gates and headed towards the elevator.

"Yeah you mentioned the oligarchy versus democracy", reminded Warwick.

"Yes, but now they're disguised by the banking and other transnational monopolies", detailed the Buzz and Gary combination. "I mean seriously, the gap between the rich and poor has raced into the stratosphere, the common man pays up to and sometimes over half of their wages in taxes and we're still being told what to do and how to think by these slimy asses".

A little old couple hopped into the elevator at the same time with the boys, with the woman giving Buzz a cheeky nod of approval. Warwick hit the level 22 button.

"So why aren't people putting two and two together and realising that they're not free, they're slaves to a debt-based monetary system, they're slaves to the dominant dogmas and they're slaves to the aristocracy that sit in their ivory tower having a good old fucking laugh at us!", Gary said passionately, even though he wasn't sure if it was actually him saying it in the first place.

"Amen!", agreed the little old lady.

Both the boys cracked up laughing. "See, even this sweet elderly woman knows she's getting fucked", Buzz continued, without Gary's input.

"Yes, you're right mate", consented Warwick. "We have the right to govern ourselves, but we don't. Now that's pretty insane if you ask me. That would make some great material if done right".

The elevator came to a stop, with the elderly couple motioning to get out. "Good luck with taking back your sovereignty", said the old fella. "We've been trying to achieve it for eons", he chuckled to himself, as he and his girl strolled into their desired location.

As the elevator reached their level, Warwick turned to Buzz. "This is gold material mate. This is exactly what we stand for as an independent media outlet. This is why I'm here, and why so many others are too".

They both hopped off the elevator and took a right towards Warwick's office.

"Have you thought of any others Buzz?"

"Just one", confirmed Gary. "This has no doubt been done before, but it's important to highlight. Given there's so many religions, I really don't know how so many people can still believe that their one is the right one. Don't get me wrong, religion has its benefits in some ways, and there's no doubt truth that permeates them all, whether it's literal or symbolic. But why don't more people see that religion is just different attempts at explaining the unexplainable and that organised religion stifles that goal? Why do they continue to delude themselves by believing that out of all the realities, out of all the civilisations, out of all the ideologies, that they've found the ultimate answer to life in a couple of books? Do they realise how fucking stupid that sounds?"

By this stage Warwick had already opened the door to his office and both of them had walked through. "Yep, nail on the head again Buzz". They sat down in the lounge section and Warwick reached into a draw on the coffee table. "Speaking of Buzzes, you want one?"

He pulled out a thin metal case and opened it up for Buzz and Gary to see some cocaine and a metal straw. "Nah, I'm good", replied Gary. "In a bit. Want to finish this line of thought", he joked, intending the pun.

"Suit yourself", chuckled Warwick. He leaned over and snorted two big lines, one with each nostril. He then placed the container back in the draw and reached over to the phone. He picked it up and pressed a button, which was obviously a number shortcut.

"Hi Wick", responded a female voice, broken by a bad connection.

"Elle, I need you to come get my phone and transcribe our recent conversation", ordered Warwick, with an obvious strain resulting from the coke.

"Be right there", she confirmed.

"Okay, so yes, religion", recollected Warwick. "All the wars, all the fighting. What a joke. They might have some things right, they might not. But the hide of people who think they have all the answers".

"There's another one actually", said Buzz, independent of Gary. "The new religion known as science. Don't get me wrong again, the scientific method and much of its exploration is fantastic, but there are so many dogmas that have hijacked the orthodoxy too. The primary example is scientific materialism, which has hardened into a commonly believed assumption when the evidence is pointing in an entirely different direction".

"Everything in my previous incarnation was way beyond that belief system", Gary thought quietly, making sure not to trigger Buzz into action.

"I've taken acid enough times to know that materialism is a load of shit", laughed Warwick.

"What's that saying?", injected Gary rhetorically. "Spirituality is an individual relationship with the divine and religion is crowd control?"

"Yeah, sounds about right", agreed Warwick, with a slight laugh.

"Well, we can add science to that list too", Buzz said disappointingly. "It's such a bloody shame, because it's an amazingly powerful tool. But just like everything else it's been tainted by money".

Warwick's door opened slightly and a head poked around it. "Knock knock".

"You're right, come in Elle", guided Warwick.

As she walked into the office, Gary's heart exploded. "Holy fuck, Elle!", he yelled.

"Whoa", Warwick said in surprise.

"Yes, Buzz, you okay?", she replied suspiciously.

Gary tried to keep his calm as he weighed in on what just happened. His woman, his beautiful Elle, had just walked into the room. His heart was melting. He missed her so much. It felt like an eternity since he's seen her.

"Shit, sorry, I've been feeling a bit crazy today", reasoned

Buzz. "Guess that's the balance to channelling all these awesome ideas, hey mate", Buzz said to Warwick, looking for reassurance.

"It's all good brother", he replied kindly. "Well, I have a feeling this is going to be the start of something very special. They might not buy all of our ideas, but they will no doubt love our out of the box tactics. This could be a game changer".

"I look forward to hearing about it", Elle said pleasantly.

"Oh my god, she's so gorgeous", Gary thought, with the intention of keeping it to himself. It must have worked, because he noticed that Buzz and Warwick were talking amongst themselves. "I miss you baby. I want to hold you. I need to hold you".

Gary's attention was only focused on Elle. She was taking the phone out of Warwick's hand, with a big luscious smile on her pure face. As Gary got further lost in the aura of Elle, a look of horror crossed her face. She pointed to the window and screamed something that he didn't make out.

As Buzz got to his feet in a rush, Gary looked to the left to see the owl sitting on the windowsill and a small yellow plane heading straight for the office building. Within half a second it had entered the building accompanied by a fireworks of sparks, glass and fire.

And suddenly, Gary was gone.

CHAPTER 9
Lover

"Gary? GARY!", yelled Elle.

He slowly began regaining his consciousness. He was in another body, laying on the grass looking up at the clouds. "I'm here! Well, I'm somewhere", he reassured her.

"Come back to the island", she requested.

Gary's perspective quickly dissolved in front of his eyes, until it re-emerged on the magnificent island they created together. "This is off the charts crazy", Gary exclaimed, whilst hugging her tightly.

"What have you been doing?", asked Elle.

"I've been in the bodies of other people. I've been experiencing what they're experiencing. I've been in potential futures, I think. Or parallel existences. It all feels so real. It's not like a dream where things don't make sense, they're all very real experiences".

"Have you figured out what you're meant to do? It's been over an hour, Gary. Your vitals are deteriorating. It's like your fading", she said in a disturbed manner.

"I think I need to learn", he said unconfidently. "Actually,

124

I know I need to learn. To evolve. The experiences have been really interesting. Scary too. Most of the bodies I'm in either die or get hurt. But the information, the conversations, they're really thought-provoking. I feel like I've learned more than in the past ten years".

"Let's try and exit together", she suggested.

He nodded and they both closed their eyes. Both of them attempted to exit, but Gary failed. He opened his eyes and Elle was nowhere to be seen.

"EXIT!", he repeated loudly. He stood alone on the beach. "Reset", he pleaded more softly. Still no change.

Gary stood still on the sand, wondering what to do. "I get the feeling I need to understand myself somehow", he thought. "I get the feeling I need to be stronger".

He looked around and took in the relaxed atmosphere. "Maybe I should stay here for a little while and think", he said out loud. "I need to process what's happened so far. There's got to be some clues I haven't noticed yet".

He remanifested the same cabin from earlier, entered the bedroom and laid on the bed. "I'm going to try some meditation", he thought to himself. "I need to at least try to figure this out whilst I'm myself".

He closed his eyes and recycled through his recent memories. "I was getting stronger. I was gaining capability to possess another body", he said to himself, whilst thinking of the experience with Buzz.

"Are you still here?", Elle's voice came out of nowhere, stunning him a little.

"Yeah, inside", Gary said without hesitation. He sat up and watched Elle walk through the open door. She sat down on the bed next to him.

"You need to work this out baby. This is scaring the shit out of me".

"I'm trying. Me too. But I'm feeling strangely confident, like part of me knows it's all going to be okay. I definitely know this much though, I know I fucking love you so much Elle. You're the best thing that has ever happened to my life. I feel so lucky that you love me", he said, looking deeply into her brown-coloured eyes.

"Aww honey, me too", agreed Elle, with a loving look on her face. "You've always been the man of my dreams. I used to dream we were going to be married one day. I was over the moon when you asked me to go to our first festival together".

Gary leaned in to kiss her. They gave each other a passionate, open-mouthed kiss and fell into the sheets wrapped in each other's love. They kissed each other's face and neck, giggling like teenagers. Slowly their hands begun exploring their bodies. Gary ran his right hand down Elle's waste until he had reached her backside. He gave it a tight squeeze and then guided it back up her tummy and under her shirt. He began to caress her breasts, which made her moan.

"What are we doing?", Elle said, somewhat annoyed at herself.

"We're making love", replied Gary, whilst climbing on top of her.

With no resistance, he pulled up her top and unhooked her bra from behind her back. Lifting it over her breasts he took them both in his hands and licked her left nipple. As soon as it was rock hard he manoeuvred to her right nipple and did the same. He gently but deeply massaged her boobs at the same time, grinding his swelling cock into her watering pussy. Feeling her whole body beginning to tremble, he licked his way up her neck and began kissing her again. It was a slow, long kiss that got lost in time.

"I am so in love with you baby", he whispered. "You're the most amazing woman".

Elle directed Gary's head down towards her crotch. Kissing his way down her stomach, he undid her jeans and pulled them off, making sure her panties went with them too. He stood up and threw them across the room, and then pulled off his own shirt and pants. Throwing them in the same direction, he climbed completely naked up onto the bed and stood over her. With a mischievous look on his face he started waving his penis in circles, which ended with both of them lost in a deep belly laugh.

"Get down here, you fool", giggled Elle.

Still laughing, he dropped to his knees and buried his face deep between her legs. "You taste like my favourite dessert", he said lustfully, after licking her all over. He played with her pussy with his tongue, biting into her softly, which made her body squirm. He then focused on her clit, licking it and flicking it. This tease was too much for Elle, and she quickly began to pant.

"Oh my God, I'm cumming baby, I'm cumming", she squealed in delight. Elle spent the next thirty seconds in deep orgasm. She wriggled her hips, almost violently, but Gary had a firm grip on her which ensured his mouth never left her pussy. Just as her orgasm was ending, Gary lifted her hips and plunged his tongue deep into her hole. He then licked back up to her clit and pushed his tongue firmly against it.

"Fucking yes baby. FUCK! I'm cumming again!", she moaned.

Her second orgasm was quicker than her first. Feeling more than satisfied, she pushed Gary's head up so that he kneeled above her. She sat up onto her knees and removed her top, fully exposing her soft, sweaty breasts. She then grabbed Gary's penis with her left hand, and slapped it with her right. "Alright, your turn my sexy man".

Elle bent over to take Gary's cock into her mouth. He closed his eyes and raised his head in deep pleasure, as he let out an involuntary moan. When he reopened his eyes he looked at Elle's ass in the air, with her curved hips leading down to her toned body. As Gary looked down to watch his woman suck on his manhood, she looked up. Their eyes met in total desire. Still looking up at him, she licked up his shaft, under his knob and then gently spat some saliva which ran down his cock.

"You are deliciously divine", Gary chanted.

For the next couple of minutes they were both lost in ecstasy. Gary was so entranced that he didn't notice he was about to cum, which jolted him back quick enough to stop Elle before she put him over the edge. Lifting her head up to meet hers, he kissed her on the mouth, biting at her lips. He slowly guided her onto her back, still kissing her, and then penetrated her wet pussy.

"Mmmm ... mmm", Elle said softly, almost unconsciously. "You are a real man. You're my real man" she continued, as he slowly moved in and out of her. They ran their hands all over their bodies, kissing and biting and licking. They moved onto their side, back to the middle and to the other side. They rocked with each other, almost in perfect synchronisation. They made love, with increasing velocity.

As Gary thrust in and out of her, Elle was getting more saturated between her legs. She grabbed him by the top of his arms and turned him over, whilst he was still inside of her. On top she rode him like she never had before, making his penis hit all angles within her. With sweat running down her body, she could feel her G-spot getting massaged, which only increased the flow of juice running down his shaft and onto his balls.

Their sex had never been so lubricated.

Elle pulled Gary forward so they sat upright together. His cock was as deep as it could go. He could feel wetness tickling his entire sex, which only forced more pre-cum inside her aching vagina.

Kissing, touching, tasting, feeling. Swaying, shaking, bending, breathing. They were about to be released. They were about to cum as one.

Looking profoundly into each other's eyes, their vision blurred. "Now this almost feels like a dream", Gary whispered. Their energy was so entwined, their fire was so hot, that they felt like they had merged in trance.

"My tantra", gasped Elle, not making complete sense.

And with that comment, their moans exploded in unison. They wailed in a frenzy. "Fuck me Gaz, fuck me", Elle roared, unleashing the next gear in Gary's drive.

Gary had passed the tipping point, and so had Elle. Time slowed a little for the final stages, giving them the precious gift of a longer orgasm. As Gary began unloading his cum inside of her, Elle squealed is absolute bliss.

And suddenly, Gary was gone.

He awoke back in the body staring at the clouds. He was still mid-orgasm, releasing his final throws inside another person. "God damnit", he yelled, whilst still unleashing the excess energy. Gary watched the guy he was in uncomfortably reshuffle his penis in his pants. "You can't be feeling as awkward as me", Gary said jokingly, to bring a little humour to what just happened.

As Gary came back to a normal state of consciousness, well as normal as he could be in this situation, it dawned on him: "Did he just touch his cock because I was finishing my orgasm inside of him?"

Gary started instantly cackling, thinking about the way he had just structured his thought. After a few seconds of almost hysterical laughing, he navigated back to his original question. "Or could it be I manifested in this body because he was already feeling sexual, which aligned our consciousness? Wait, but I was in his body first, before Elle and I were having sex. Shit, this is so confusing".

The man stood up, which clicked Gary back to the experience. As he walked towards a lit up area, Gary took in the beautiful scenery. The sun was setting to his left, illustrating there wasn't much light set aside for the evening. There were a few people here and there, but not many. There were birds still flying and fighting between the large, healthy trees. The lawn was perfectly manicured, almost looking like a golf course. There were flowers and shrubs, and even some fruit trees, which looked like they were oranges or mandarins. It was difficult to see over the trees and into the distance, but some buildings were just tall enough to rise above them.

"It feels just like my old suburb", Gary thought.

The man walked over to the toilets. Walking in, he went straight to the basin and turned on the tap. Looking down he washed his hands and then splashed his face with water.

Gary looked inquisitively at the person he was in. He was a middle-aged man, maybe mid-forties. He looked tanned and relatively healthy, although he had a very noticeable pot belly. He was dressed nicely with a collared shirt and jeans. He wore sunnies on his head, which held back his slightly balding hair. He watched the man look into his own eyes, staring himself in the mirror.

"You need to do this", the man said to himself.

"This could be exciting", Gary said to himself.

The man pulled out his wallet and looked at a family photo that was wedged in behind a plastic shield. Gary managed to get a quick glimpse at the name on his license, but he couldn't make it out in time before the man shut his wallet and replaced it in his pocket. Hastily the man exited the toilet block, and walked towards a lit up area about fifty metres away.

"It's so beautiful", Gary thought, admiring the sunset.

As he sat on a park bench, the man pulled a book from his pocket. He opened it up and began reading. "Do what?", Gary thought. "Read a book?", he joked.

The man repeatedly looked up towards a playground and back to the book, only moving his head slightly. Gary wondered what he kept looking at. Around twenty metres nearly square in front, was a playground with swings, a slippery dip and other entertainment for the children. There were only four kids, of about seven years old.

"What the fuck?", detected Gary. "YOU BETTER NOT TRY ANYTHING YOU FUCKING CREEP!"

The man began to cough violently, which ended with him clearing his throat from some excess phlegm and spitting it to the ground. He pounded his chest a couple of times and re-cleared his throat.

The man watched the children saying their goodbyes. Three walked to their left, whilst the fourth walked back towards the toilets. The light had almost completely disappeared by this point, and the park was empty. The man slowly rose to his feet and began following the boy to his right. Walking around twenty metres behind him, he increased his speed. The toilet block was getting close, and the boy seemed to heading towards a dark area to the right of it.

Gary quickly reflected on the amazing sex he just had. "I can't believe I'm here experiencing this after what just happened. But if I was still with Elle I wouldn't be able to at least try and help this kid", he concluded.

He refocused his attention and noticed the man was much closer than before. "Don't walk in that direction boy, he's got cover there. He'll fucking get you. Please stop!", cried Gary.

The boy clearly heard nothing, because he continued on his trajectory. The man continued to follow, while the child seemed to sing something to himself. As they got closer, Gary confirmed that he was around eight years old. He had a school bag on and was in school uniform. He looked so vulnerable and innocent.

"Don't do this, mate!", Gary yelled. "How could you hurt a child? Why would you want to hurt anyone?!"

The man coughed again, which drew the attention of

the boy. As he turned around, the man was about five metres from him. "Excuse me boy", asked the man, kindly.

"Yes sir?"

"I'm looking for the toilets?" said the man, still walking towards him.

"They're right there", pointed the young lad.

"Yeah I know, they're locked though", he lied. "What school do you go to?", he asked, walking in the direction the boy was already headed in.

"Don't fucking answer, just run boy, RUN!", Gary screeched, almost scaring himself. He was getting more and more anxious that he wasn't able to control the actions of this man.

"I'm not meant to talk to strangers", stated the child, whilst still walking next to him.

"That's fair enough", said the man. "One more question though, do you know where there are any other toilets?", he continued, whilst secretly pulling out a handkerchief and a small, brown bottle from his pocket.

As the man covertly poured a little of the substance into the cloth, the boy replied. "At the petrol station down the road", he said proudly.

By this stage the two had entered into the dark area of the park. Without indecision the man speedily wrapped his handkerchief around the boy's face, compelling him to fall limp.

"NOOOOOO!", Gary screamed.

The man dragged the boy in between some small shrubs, into a cove-like clearing.

"I'M NOT GOING TO LET YOU DO THIS!",

shouted Gary. "THIS IS NOT GOING TO HAPPEN ON MY WATCH!"

The man pulled down the pants of the unconscious child. As he lay there completely immobilised, the man undid his belt and jeans, shifting them over his thighs. He spat on his hand and started to stroke his penis. This made Gary feel like he spewed in his own mouth.

"I WILL NOT LET THIS HAPPEN", Gary erupted. The fire in his heart was vicious. He felt like he was turning into something else, like he was transforming into the Hulk. "I WILL NOT LET THIS HAPPEN!!", he thundered again.

Gary began to feel a strength that he's never felt before. As the man prepared to enter the boy Gary was fuming in rage. "I WILL NOT LET THIS HAPPEN", he screamed again. That's when Gary began to take control of the man's body. He threw the man to the floor, away from the child. The man got onto his knees, indicating he was moving back towards the boy.

"This is the end", he said assertively, but calmly to the man. Gary looked towards the dark ground but was still able to make out a large rock sticking up though the undercover. The man's head went hurtling towards the rock, resulting with a massive cracking sound. The man's head lifted up and repeated the action.

Two hits.

Three hits.

Four hits.

And suddenly, Gary was gone.

CHAPTER 10

Changer

"I'm getting stronger", was Gary's first thought, as his awareness came flooding back. "Well, actually, I'm not sure. I had the power to speak through Buzz, but I couldn't through that pedophile. I was eventually able to control his actions though. Fuck, this is so complicated".

Distracting himself from his uncertainty, he started to get a grip on his surroundings. As he noticed he was in a playground, he wondered if it was the same one as his last experience. Looking for more details, he recalled the exact same layout, acknowledging that it was. The body he was in squatted below a railing and commenced sliding down a slippery slide. "Weeeee!", said his body.

"Oh shit, I might be that little kid now", Gary speculated.

The child ran towards two adults waiting on the edge of the sand. "You ready to go", said the man.

"Sure am, Dad", he replied. "Thanks for letting me have a bit more fun".

"Of course Simon", he returned with a glaring smile.

Gary felt like his heart was beating outside of his chest,

even though he didn't have his one. "It's my family", he said lovingly. "And how is it that I feel like I've got my own body, when I'm in someone else's? This is totally crazy. I'm probably in a mental institution somewhere".

"BE THE TREE", echoed the voice again. Gary had completely forgotten about this experience.

As Simon manoeuvred in between his parents he grabbed both of their hands. He began talking about what he did in the playground, which gave Gary an opportunity to reflect on his memory of the tree. He remembered how powerful it looked, how alive it looked. He remembered that it was an independent entity, but that it was also connected with other life around it.

Gary had his attention directed back to Simon's perspective because of his question to Sophia: "Mum, when's Gary coming home?", he asked vulnerably.

"I'm so sorry Simon, you know he can't come back. He's in heaven now", she reminded sincerely.

"I'm dead?", queried Gary. "Is this what's happening? But I only saw Elle not long ago. This can't all be an afterlife experience, can it? It all feels so real. It all feels so alive". He felt more confused than ever.

"But I miss him. Why did God have to take him? Why does God do bad things?", Simon asked, innocently.

Sophia looked at Gerald with a sad look. "God isn't a person like us, Simon. God is everything. God can't choose to bring Gary back, because God doesn't make choices. God is life, God is creation, with all the bad and all the good that comes with it. And without the bad, we couldn't experience the good. We wouldn't know what it means to feel good if we didn't understand what it means to feel bad", spoke

Gerald, as slow and as articulate as he could. "Do you know what I mean, son?"

"Do you mean that if I didn't know what it was like to be sad, I wouldn't know what it's like to be happy?", Simon responded, intelligently.

"Yes, exactly", Gerald confirmed with pride.

"But my friends still have their brothers and sisters, why did God choose to make me sad by taking Gary?", he specified selfishly.

"Like I said son, God didn't choose anything", reinforced his father. "We'll never know why it happened, why he died. But Gary's gone now. It's just part of life. I wish he didn't go so early too, Simon. We all do. But we can't change it, God can't change it, nothing can. We have to live with it and try to find happiness in other ways".

"But it's not fair!", cried Simon.

"I know it's hard to understand, but everyone goes through hard times. People die at times. It's hard to take, and it's completely okay to feel sad. But there's so much other goodness too, isn't there?", continued Gerald, trying to inspire him.

"Yeah, I guess so. I love you. And my friends. And my toys."

"What else do you love?", asked his mother.

Before Simon could answer, Gary's spiralling consciousness crystallised around fifty metres ahead of them. It was the exact same tree that he examined when he was in Buzz's body. "I love climbing trees", Gary said through Simon's voice box. "I want to climb that tree", he continued, whilst pointing at it.

"Do we have time?", Gerald directed to Sophia.

"Another fifteen minutes won't hurt", sanctioned Sophia.

"Yes!", said Simon, excitedly.

"Awesome", Gary said to himself. "Fuck being all down and sad, if I'm dead, I'm going to make the most of this".

At that moment Gary decided to see if he could take control of Simon's body. He let go of his parents' hands and starting running towards the tree. "Wow, this is just amazing", he thought.

As he approached the tree he pondered on the realisation that he was in the same park – the same playground – as two of his other experiences. "Is it a metaphor for life?", he questioned to himself. "We're all playing in a playground of experience?"

He immediately recognised the park bench that Buzz and Warwick were previously sitting at. He had come from basically the opposite direction, which is why he hadn't noticed a rope ladder on the base of the tree. At about a height of four metres the branches begun, with little space between each higher tier of limbs. Gary grabbed the ladder and almost flew up it, like he was a possum going home to nest.

He reached the first branch, flung himself up and looked down towards Mum and Dad. "Don't go too high", Gerald ordered.

'The Gary/Simon show' looked up and was taken aback at how high it reached. It was an entangled web of branches and foliage that made for very easy climbing. He began the ascent like he was a professional at it, hopping and skipping in a fluent motion. As he reached a particular limb he noticed that there was an army of small ants carrying what seemed to be remnants of a piece of bread.

He finessed around them without disturbing them, and continued his mount.

"BE THE TREE!", the voice returned, almost with a vengeance.

Gary continued to climb as he thought about what this meant. He began to focus on the texture of the tree on his hands, which filled him with an energetic sensation that ran up his spine. "Dad's going to get a coffee, Simon. I'll be sitting on that bench", Sophia yelled, interrupting Gary's concentration.

"Okay Mum", Simon responded, without input from Gary.

Gary redirected his attention back to the combination of smoothness and coarseness of the bark. As he moved his hands to different limbs, a fine papery dust floated in the air around him. He thought back to his original thoughts, when he was Buzz. "What were the main points? 'Flowers', 'balance', 'birds', 'roots', 'natural' and 'mystical'?" These were the keywords that stuck out in his memory.

"So the smooth and rough dichotomy of the bark must represent duality. But it's connected too. It is the one thing. The tree. The flowers might represent beauty, or attraction. Actually, it probably represents growth too because they turn into fruit and contain the seed. So they symbolise rebirth as well."

Gary continued climbing, making sure that he was out of sight of his mother.

"Okay, balance. Would that mean duality too? Or maybe harmony? The entire structure of the tree is mathematically ordered. It illustrates geometric principles. It's like it's saying that it's designed according to the laws of nature."

Gary was around fifteen metres above the ground at this stage.

"So birds, or animals?", he pondered. "That's got to mean interconnection, right? I mean, if it wasn't for the birds and the bees…"

Gary interrupted himself, momentarily thinking about his sex session with Elle.

"Birds and bees. Birds and bees", he re-interrupted himself, trying to refocus. "If it wasn't for them it would be very difficult for it to reproduce. Well, it couldn't, if it wasn't self-pollinating. But even if it could, the seeds might drop next to the tree, but that would drown itself out. So it needs animals to survive. The bees spread its pollen, igniting the creation of the fruit and seed. Then birds and other animals eat the fruit, spreading it away from the tree itself. Then there's animals that eat other animals, so if a tree gets infested with one species that could be harmful to it, other animals come in to balance it out."

"SIMON?", investigated Sophia.

"Yeah, I'm here Mum", responded Simon, not Gary.

"So it's not just interconnection, but interdependence. The tree needs the animals and animals need the tree. It's a beautiful, symbiotic relationship", thought Gary, with increasing reverence.

"Now to the roots. They enter the earth, the soil, and gain sustenance from it. It grounds the tree. It keeps it stable and able to survive. The roots also go deep into the earth and absorb water".

"And nutrients", said the eerie voice.

"Oh shit, you can hear me? Who are you?", interrogated Gary. He didn't receive a response.

"Nutrients, hey?", he said to both himself and the mystery voice. "Okay, so from what I understand soil is alive with an abundance of life. Well, it should be anyway. Fuck the industrial agriculture model, relying on synthetic fertilisers for their monoculture crops which ensures so much of our soil is devoid of life".

Gary momentarily laughed at his inner activist who was emerging because of this entire experience.

"These microorganisms or microbes play an important role, especially in providing all the right ingredients for the plants, which in turn provide all the right nutrients for us when we eat them. So once again life supports life. These organisms in the soil decompose organic matter and plants get nutrients and minerals from this process".

"Keep digging", said the voice again.

"Nice pun", Gary reacted cheekily.

As he thought a little deeper about it, Gary noticed he had climbed another ten metres. He looked down and felt an adrenaline hit, and then looked up to see how far he was from the top. In that moment he was briefly blinded by the setting sun through a small opening in the vegetation.

"Light!", he exclaimed. "All life needs light, not just photosynthesis for the plants, but for warmth and vitamins and other biochemical activity in the bodies of animals. We are so dependent on it that sometimes we take it for granted!", he revered.

"Exactly", agreed the voice.

"So, what was the next one?", Gary asked to himself. "Natural. Nature is just so pure. It is pristine. It is a reflection of how the laws of the universe create order, including life".

In that moment Gary's consciousness began to blur.

The boundaries of Simon's body loosened. He developed an additional perspective which exited the body of Simon, as though he was looking at him from the outside. His original perspective entered into the blood of Simon's eyes, and began a journey as a white blood cell into the veins of his brain, attacking foreign invaders with martial art expertise. His outer perspective watched it travel into his neck and down his arm whilst the inner viewpoint blew apart harmful bacteria with a single touch.

"What a fucking ride", exhilarated Gary.

The inner view hit the wall of the fingertip, navigated through the skins cells and came to the division between Simon's body and the tree. The vision proceeded into the bark cells of the tree, whilst Gary's outer consciousness watched it begin a rollercoaster ride to the outer reaches of a branch. It twisted and turned, it sidestepped and flipped. It travelled through flowers, through leaves, through microorganisms on the surface and even through a shiny red lady beetle cleaning itself on the undercover of a leaf.

"This is phenomenal", celebrated Gary.

It then shot rapidly back towards the trunk and navigated through the network of veins that transport water throughout the tree. It headed straight down into the roots, and then into the soil, with Gary's outer perspective following the trip. It bounced and banged, it took sharp turns and reversed. This pinpoint of awareness was on an unknown mission.

It made it deep into the earth, at the edge of the roots, and then danced with the surrounding life. It met face to face with fungi, with bacteria, with microbes and with algae, as well as small bugs and rodents. It was like this awareness was alive and celebrating the wonders of life that existed underneath the surface. It relished and delighted in its experience by whirling and spinning and twirling.

As it hit an underground stream of water, it took a deep dive through the wealth of life all around it. It then dissolved into the atomic structure of the water and observed its memory, before reliquefying and shooting out of the water like it had refreshed itself with a rebirth. It then shook itself off, like an excited dog exiting an ocean.

"Am I just still on holiday with Elle tripping on Mushrooms?", wondered Gary in amusement.

As the inner image cleansed itself it bulleted back through the soil, into the roots of the tree and voyaged up the trunk like a firecracker fulfilling its purpose. It reached the very tip of a leaf at the very top of the tree and entered the air like it had just bounced on the world's largest trampoline.

As it did a backflip with perfect fluency, the experience slowed to a near stop. Molecules and other lifeforms in the air danced around it. The outer consciousness then raced up beside it and merged as the vision re-entered the tree. The two perspectives were one again.

They were the consciousness of the tree.

Gary could again see multiple perspectives all at once. From a birds eye view, the tree was glowing with auric energy. He could also see as if he was the roots, the trunk, the branches, the leaves and the flowers. He could feel the web of activity electrifying him. He felt the coolness of the water flowing through his veins. He could feel the life of countless microscopic organisms. He could feel the tree's pulse, vibrating in resonance with the earth. And he could feel the life energy of the tree itself, in all its majesty.

"The tree is conscious!", rejoiced Gary. "The animals on it are conscious, the cells are conscious, the molecules are conscious, hell, even the atoms are conscious! All things have some form of consciousness, even if they don't have self-awareness. This is the mystical! This is the magic!"

"Now we're talking", said the voice, getting more uplifting with each emergence.

"BE THE TREE. I GET IT", announced Gary. "I am the tree. On one level I am an individual expression of life, but on another I'm interconnected and interdependent with all other forms of life. I am connected through the grand awareness, but I am my own spirit as well. Everything has spirit. Life is so much more than just plants and animals, life is everything and everything is life. Even though I am Gary, I am everything else, just as everything else is me!"

As this realisation hit Gary like a supernova erupting in his soul, his multiple angles of consciousness collapsed into themselves and then circled like a whirlpool to re-enter the body of Simon. At the point of arrival Gary became aware that Simon was at the highest possible point he could climb.

The slight breeze, although refreshing on his face, was swinging the much thinner trunk to and fro. Gary had to hold on tight, as he realised it was easy to slip and fall to his death. "Well, Simon would die", he clarified to himself. "Even more accurate, Game-Simon would", he continued, before remembering the previous conversation between Simon and his parents.

Gary was stuck between alternate potentials of what was going on. Was he dead? Was he in a game? Was he having a psychedelic trip? "Be the tree", he repeated to regather himself. "Be me, but be everything".

And with that thought Simon let go of the branch, out of the control of Gary. He fell gracefully and silently towards the earth. The visions he had during this experience came flooding back, as if it was a tribute to itself. Time slowed once again as all the perspectives concocted into one.

"I told you to be me", said the tree.

Gary wasn't sure what he was seeing, but it was like he could see sound. It was a bright white with colours that danced as he heard the voice of the tree. "You're a tree?", he questioned.

"I'm the tree, I'm the life force of the tree, I'm you, I'm all of it", was the response. "This is so critical for your species to understand. It teaches respect for all living things, for Mother Nature, and for physical and non-physical life. You're hurting your earth, you're desecrating your natural systems, which in turn hurts yourself. Humans are very good at being self-abusive, that's for sure. But when it's leading to your own demise, it's time for you to finally realise".

"Is that why I'm here? To help fix humanity's destructive behaviour?" But there was no answer in return.

And suddenly, Gary was gone.

CHAPTER 11

Adjudicator

An amber from a fire frolicked in front of Gary's face, landing gently on the middle of his forehead. It stung for a split second, waking him into complete lucidity. "I can feel the body", he acknowledged to himself.

The figure he was in stood next to the fire, smoking a thick bunch of wrapped leaves and blowing the smoke in what seemed a purposeful manner. Dancing around him was a chaotically ordered circle of men and women. Some of them were wearing animal skins, which looked like kangaroo and possum, and others were more or less naked. They were holding and swinging various objects, such as spears, sticks and other items Gary couldn't quite make out.

Their faces and bodies were painted with splashes of red, white, black, brown and yellow. The patterns took many forms, including stripes, spots and circles. The way they were singing felt illustrious to Gary, although he had never heard it before. "This must be the original peoples of Australia", he hypothesised. "They all look so happy, so full of life".

In the background there was drumming, chanting,

knocking and clapping, but Gary couldn't see exactly where it was coming from. It was near pitch black in the distance, illuminated only by a full moon hovering directly overhead.

The energy of the experience was nearly too overwhelming for Gary and he started to feel like he was back with Laya and Lucinda in a shared state of altered consciousness. "Meditation in action?", he ruminated, as he felt increasingly high. "I've heard that drumming and dancing can have similar affects as psychedelics".

"Hello Gary", said a voice that delivered an abrupt piercing to his heart.

"Is that you tree?", he asked confidently.

The voice broke out into laughter, before settling into a soothing hum.

"Don't mock me!", Gary enforced.

"I'm not mocking you", the voice reassured gently. "I'm connecting with you. I am the tree of your memory, but I am much more than that. I am you, but I am more than that too. Right now I am the shaman that you're currently embodying. My name in your language is Wildfire".

"Okay Wildfire, how can I help you?"

Responding with another deep laugh, Wildfire continued. "That's a great question, and I'm so happy you asked. Help me to help you, is your answer".

The chanting around them increased in volume, shattering Gary's consciousness further. It was like one dimension was merging into another, causing multiple distortions in his perspective.

"How can you help me?", Gary asked rhetorically. "You can help by guiding me towards the truth".

"Another great response, my kindred spirit. That's what

this ceremony is designed to do. To guide you towards the truth, to guide us all towards the truth. For it is in the truth that we will find more truth, and we will find solace. For it is in ourselves we will find new layers of the self, and we will find new paths".

Gary thought to himself how poetic it sounded, but was confused by it more than anything. "Feel free to elaborate", he replied cheekily.

"You are a man of humour, I like that about you", laughed Wildfire. "Deep down you know that it is in the smile that healing begins. And once again you've led me to our path. For if we are not free, what are we?"

"A slave", Gary answered, matter of fact.

This gave Wildfire another tickle to his soul. "Yes, you are right", he chuckled. "We can choose to be a slave to others, or a slave to ourselves. We can also choose to be a slave to that which does not serve us. And regardless of what we choose, freedom is a prerequisite to make that choice. But decisions always have boundaries. They are themselves, boundaries".

This sent Gary into reflection. The image that manifested in his mind's eye was of a mirror, with his face staring back at itself. Instantly it shattered into what Gary could only describe as an infinite number of pieces.

"What do you desire Gary?", tested Wildfire, bringing Gary back to the moment.

"I want to go home, I want to get back to Elle", he answered, almost automatically.

"Is that what you really want, deep down in the pursuit of your soul?", he tested again.

Thinking back to the conversation with David, Gary

considered once again that maybe he needed to have this experience, regardless of whether he wanted it or not.

"I really don't know what I want, or need", he confessed, solemnly.

At that moment the fire erupted with extreme intensity, only for a second or two. The dancing and chanting increased in potency to match it.

"Yes you do Gary, it exists in you somewhere", Wildfire honoured. "But if it makes you feel better, nobody knows the whole truth. Not you, not me, nor our souls. We are on this journey to not just learn the truth, but to create it too. For the truth evolves if only at the whim of creation itself, but that doesn't mean we needn't create it for ourselves as well".

It did make Gary feel a bit better.

"And that's what freedom stands for, Gary", he continued. "To be free is to create who we want to be inside of our perception. If we're courageous enough, if we're focused enough, nothing can stop us. But we are bound too, and that we must learn to live with".

The light from the fire flickered in a mind warping haze, generating a feeling of pure bliss.

"Bound by what?", quizzed Gary.

"We are constrained by the laws of reality, Gary. By our bodies, by Natural-law. And we are also guided by the impulse of our soul, compelling us to live our destiny".

"I'm not constrained by my body now", Gary countered.

"Aren't you? How do you know? Is your body only physical, or is it more?"

"I'm not sure", Gary admitted.

"Listen Gary, we have arrived at a crux. Freedom is not

just about having no rulers. No one can actually rule you unless you consent in mind, in heart and in spirit. They can even threaten your physical body, but you still have a choice to obey or not. To be able to make that choice, that is freedom. Yet even if you don't consent, it doesn't mean there aren't rules. And one of the greatest rules we live by is that of our individual and collective destiny".

"I'm not sure I believe in destiny", Gary retorted honestly. "It seems so whimsical".

Again, Wildfire gushed laughter. "Don't you, Gary?"

Without letting Gary speak, he continued. "Destiny is growth. But freewill exists too, meaning our shared destiny is the map towards our collective evolution and your personal destiny is the map towards your individual evolution. It is your guide for creation. It is the growth of your mind, the growth of your soul. Your destiny is the path you must choose to take to become the next manifestation of yourself. It is natural, not contrived. It is pure, not tainted".

"So how can I be free if I have to live my destiny?", puzzled Gary.

"Ahh, and we've arrived at the heart of our next riddle. You are free Gary, free to accept or reject your destiny. You can choose to live it as efficient as you like, or you can also choose to fight it and live very little of it. But you'll always be attracted to your destiny and your destiny will always be attracted to you, because it is you. If you choose to distance yourself from it, it will come crashing back like a tsunami of truth. The further you move away from it, the more force it has when it hits. It is beyond any power that a mortal mind can summon Gary. It created the boundaries of your existence, the foundation of your experience".

"What a mindfuck", Gary thought to himself, as his consciousness danced to the beat of the drums.

"Yes, what a mindfuck", laughed Wildfire. "Don't ever forget you are free to play and dance and sing and love, to all of your heart's desire. And you can freely choose to co-manifest your destiny, if you open yourself to it".

"Co-manifest with what?", asked Gary, with deepening interest.

"With your soul, Gary. The self-aware mind is a powerful force, more impressive than what any one person truly understands. But it is still subject to its blueprint, its spirit. It's also subject to its unconscious programming, including all its traumas, dysfunctions and self-appointed boundaries. The vibration that manifested you is another level of you, and it has its own agenda. And the deep recesses of your wiring has its own agenda as well. So not only are we shaped by all of those boundaries, we are bound by our choices too. And it is in this knowledge we can choose to cleanse our minds and bodies to more powerfully live our destiny".

"So how do we know which choices align with our destiny?", Gary asked, inquisitively.

"Wisdom, Gary. It's translating the knowledge you gain from your experience into wise thoughts, wise feelings and wise behaviours. You will align sometimes, and other times you won't. You can also choose to fall to the whims of the impersonal, or you can deflect that which is dissonant. You are the adjudicator, Gary. You are the mind of your soul".

"So what if I make poor choices, isn't my destiny going to be affected?"

"Your destiny is a direct path towards new levels of you.

It is the evolutionary desire of your soul. It doesn't change in essence Gary, only in its expression. Its first manifestation is the conception of your human form and then as you begin to empower your mind it adapts to your choices, giving your Self the opportunity to embrace it and live it", Wildfire clarified.

"It's really confusing", Gary declared.

"Think about it like this. We are not just awareness in and of itself, we are also awareness looking back on itself. We are not just pure awareness, we are also self-awareness. That's the dual nature of existence".

Gary reflected on the same concept Lucinda had explained, as his mind wandered into the atmosphere.

Wildfire continued, drawing Gary back into the present. "Self-awareness is a game of growth, Gary. When you make choices, be it in thought or behaviour, it is an expression, a presentation to yourself and creation itself. Our choices emit a force and attract similar frequencies back, determining our ongoing experience. That's why the consequences of our choices – which are subject to the boundaries of Natural-law – guide how our destiny unfolds, because we've transmitted particular frequencies into the field of God. But that doesn't change our destiny because it's just naturally there, manifesting in alignment with our choices, giving us the opportunity to fully live it or not".

"Hang on, so destiny isn't a fixed experience in a fixed time?"

Wildfire let out a cheeky laugh. "Destiny can be lived in an infinite number of ways", he continued, whilst still chuckling. "It is primarily evolution, not experience. And that evolution occurs from simply embodying the lessons of your experience. If you fail to honour your destiny in one moment, then that isn't your last chance. There is no last chance. It will come back in another form – in another experience – and the opportunity will once again be at the forefront of your mind".

"Wow, I think I understand", pronounced Gary. "I remember so many times when the same lesson kept popping up in different disguises, until I eventually learned it. And even when I did, it would come back every now and again just to make sure I'd properly embodied it. The perfect example is when I finally learned how to love myself, with all my strengths and weaknesses. I remember feeling more free than ever before and that's when my relationship with Elle really hit the next level".

"Yes, you do understand", Wildfire harmonised. "Our destiny is first expressed naturally as an infant, and then it adapts to our choices. It becomes a mixture. It will show itself in one way or another and our role is to recognise it and then live it".

Gary was really beginning to feel beyond himself by this point. He felt larger, like he was connecting to other aspects of himself that his self-awareness had not previously recognised. His consciousness was one perspective, but it was spread across the experience in a way that he wouldn't have been able to explain with words.

He could see himself dancing and chanting through the shaman, as well as observing the tribe and the activity of the whole village from a birds eye view. He could see auric-like energy connecting each member of the tribe, as well as the huts and surrounding forest. It also touched upon fields that looked like crops.

"I didn't think they farmed like that", Gary's left-brained logic chimed in.

The entire scene was magnificent. It was like a real-life painting in motion. There were vivid colours and energetic winds playing and swaying in accordance with the vibrations of the tribe.

He zoned in on the shaman who was looking up into the sky, directly at him. "You enjoying yourself, Gary?", smirked Wildfire.

"This is beyond what I would usually define as fun", he responded, as his multiple angles folded from a spider web shape into the shaman's perspective. "I feel like I am living my destiny right now, Wildfire. I feel like I didn't have a choice to experience this, but I do have a choice to make the most of it by learning, or discard it by closing my mind and heart to it. It's like we cannot permanently escape our destiny, we can only avoid it temporarily. Run, but can't hide sort of thing. What bothers me though is that most of our experience seems so random, like there is no order or design to it. Major experiences happen sometimes that feel totally synchronised, but the rest of it feels so disconnected and isolated".

"That's the nature of duality, Gary, that's the nature of co-creation", Wildfire responded, without missing a beat. "Your self-awareness is just one version of an infinite variety. Your spirit is in relationship with other spirits. It is true that you are separate, Gary, because you are a unique co-creator. But so is your mother and father and family and friends. So is every other lifeform. Together we are co-creating our collective experience, which means experiences seem random on the surface. But they are not; nothing is random, everything is the co-creative result of destiny and choice".

"So just because I'm not conscious enough to understand how a particular experience manifested doesn't mean it's just a randomly generated event?", Gary asked, more to himself.

"That's right, Gary. Experience manifests in accordance with all of our collective energy. And that's our purpose; to keep opening our awareness so we can grow in accordance with our destiny and circumvent that which is predominately for others".

"So let me get this straight", Gary begun, which resulted with a cheeky giggle by Wildfire. "It is my destiny, it is everyone's destiny, to learn and grow. Not just as a human, but as a soul or energy or whatever. Our destiny manifests as experiences that give us the opportunity to grow. Do we choose to learn and grow, or do we not? If we don't, then that opportunity will manifest later in another way. But if we do make the choice to expand ourselves, then it reverberates into the depths of our soul, ensuring it expands as well".

"Couldn't have said it better myself", laughed Wildfire.

"There's another thing that bothers me though. I said before that I wasn't sure if I believed in destiny, but now that I've reflected on it I feel like I was destined to be with Elle. Yet if it can manifest in an infinite amount of ways, then that mustn't be true".

"Didn't you make the choice to be with Elle after the opportunity naturally manifested?", Wildfire rebutted.

"Yes, I did. I think get it. It makes sense now. I didn't make the choice to meet Elle, but I made the choice to be with her, and she's given me more opportunities to grow. She helps me to live my purpose and vice versa".

"Precisely", Wildfire confirmed. "The deeper layers of Elle and you obviously resonated for each other's growth, but you didn't have to choose it once the opportunity materialised. That's freedom, even though the choice you made was right for you".

"But what happens if we break up later?", Gary asked, with a slight frequency of paranoia.

"Then you've made another choice, which may or may not align with your next stage of growth".

This sent Gary's consciousness spiralling into the archives of his memory with Elle. He reminisced about when they first began their relationship. He was 22 and she was close to turning 19. They had known each other for several years prior, however, as they had met through family. Gary had always known that Elle had a crush on him, which he had secretly towards her too. Given she was nearly four years younger than him though, he felt socially pressured not to court her.

That didn't stop him thinking about her though. He had other girlfriends who he wished were Elle. Sometimes he even had sex with them thinking about her, and would regularly masturbate about her too.

They hadn't seen each other for over a year when they ran into each other one sunny afternoon in the full heat of summer. Originally he thought it was a random occurrence, but given his recent experiences, that had changed.

He remembered the moment vividly. She had her hair tied back in a ponytail and was slightly sweating all over her body. She was wearing short black shorts and a cute pink singlet. Her top slightly exposed her boobs on the side and her shorts showed off her luscious ass and curves, so blood began to uncomfortably pump into his pants.

He recalled how good it all felt though.

She acted confidently, but Gary could see she was a little nervous. This gave him a little more assurance as he was feeling slightly nervous too. He teased her about a fake tattoo that she got from a children's party she attended the previous day. He made her feel sexy in his eyes as well by commenting on her cute smile, which only increased her attraction to him.

The timing was perfect because one of Gary's mates had just pulled out of a music festival planned for the following day, leaving him to see if he could sell the ticket. Gary asked her if she wanted to join him and his mates. She said she was stoked because she already wanted to go, but it had sold out before she could get a ticket. Gary was cheering inside, but he tried to stay as cool as he possibly could.

The next day they went to the festival and ended up alone for the last set in the dance tent. They had taken some ecstasy a couple of hours earlier, ensuring they were feeling loose and free and high. They danced with each other, like they'd been doing it forever. It was in hot unison, rubbing against each other's bodies and sliding in each other's erotic sweat.

Gary and Elle's first kiss aligned with a laser and smoke show that filled the atmosphere with a hallucinatory feeling. They were locked into the greatest kiss of their lives. They ran their hands all over their bodies, trying to stay conscious of not getting too sexual in front of so many people. They lent back and gazed into each other's eyes whilst continuing to slowly dance, with their hips locked into each other. That's when Elle said something that Gary will never forget.

"About time", she said with a sexy smile. Gary's heart exploded in a plethora of feelings.

"You're a lucky girl", he responded, with a cheeky grin. Elle laughed and gave him a whack to his chest, before grabbing him roughly and giving him another long, passionate pash.

The next eleven years were filled with so much love, lust and adventure. They had their bad moments too, including learning to cope with living with each other and accepting their annoying differences. They fought just like any other couple, which even escalated to verbal and emotional abuse at times. Elle had physically attacked him on one occasion too.

None of these challenges were enough to drift them apart, though. Sometimes they would go a little backwards, but they would just rein it in and capitalise on it by becoming closer than ever before. They really admired and respected each other, even with their weaknesses. They were just purely in love and nothing was going to get in their way, especially themselves.

"Oh my God, you are the best", Gary muttered to himself.

"Yes, she is a beautiful soul", agreed Wildfire.

"Oh fuck, did you just experience that entire thing", Gary asked, a little embarrassed.

"There's no need to be ashamed", responded Wildfire. "It was beautiful to witness the memory of your connection with her. Your love is one for the ages, one that all souls admire".

"I need to live my destiny", devised Gary. "I need to succeed at learning what I need to, so I can get back to her".

"Who says that your destiny will return you to her?", queried Wildfire, in a slightly distorted tone.

And suddenly, Gary was gone.

CHAPTER 12

Completer

"I say it's my destiny!", raged Gary, as he became conscious once more. "I choose to be with Elle!", he continued, with fierce love and conviction.

He looked around and immediately recognised his surroundings. He was back on the island, which gave him a sigh of relief. "I want to exit the game", he said in a demanding fashion. No change. "Exit Game", he stated, in a surprisingly calmer manner. But there he stood, alone on the island.

"Reset", he commanded, trying a different angle. The breeze had a momentary gust, but that was the only alteration in his experience.

Attempting one more approach, he called for Elle. "You there babe?", he asked. But there was no answer.

"Fuck, what am I meant to do now?", he said out loud to himself. Looking around was a little depressing but inspiring at the same time. He missed Elle, but he also felt empowered that he was back to being himself.

Thinking back to the experience with Wildfire, the

words that stood out were when he said to him t.
'choose' to be a slave, including to that which doesn'
us. This reminded him of his experience with Lez and F
particularly because Feddy chose to be a slave to the Cr
regardless if he didn't understand it.

Besides his family, this was the first time that Gary
fond of someone in his game experience. "Lez was a leger
I wonder what happened with the virus?", he thoug
sentimentally.

And suddenly, Gary was gone.

Instantly he was aware again, floating in what appeared
as space. He had no physical body and could see in every
direction. There was no sun or moon in sight, leaving the
stars as the only source of light. They were in abundance
too, littering the backdrop with an intense array of sparks
and glitters.

As he started to get completely lost in the reverence
of the experience, his perspective suddenly snapped into
a normal third dimensional point of view. "Gary, what
is your next choice", echoed a friendly Voice. "You can
choose whatever you want, but remember, all decisions have
boundaries".

In that moment a face was birthed out of the light of
the stars, and immediately Gary recognised it as his own.
It wasn't vivid in a third dimensional sense; it was more of
a two dimensional sculpture made of pinpoints of light and
dark.

"I'm assuming it's out of the question to return to Elle",
Gary joked, "but I'm gonna try anyway. I want to return to
the game store".

"Nice try", said the Voice, with a chuckle.

"I'm taking you're not just the tree, nor are you just Wildfire?", Gary questioned.

"Good to see you're learning", it remarked. "I am whatever you want me to be, Gary".

This spun Gary into deep thought. "Whatever I want it to be", he repeated to himself with the intention of not letting it hear him. "Did you hear me then?", he asked.

"What do you mean, Gary?", it replied quickly.

"Good, I'm getting stronger", Gary narrated to himself. "I don't know if I trust it. How do I know that it wants the best for me? After all, it indicated that I might not be going back to Elle, and it's implying I can't right now because my choices have boundaries. But how do I know that's true? I could be speaking to an evil spirit or alien, for all I fucking know".

And with that thought an idea came to his mind. "Nothing, just thinking to myself", he said, answering the previous question. "I've got a plan. I want you to share with me what resulted after my previous experiences", he said, with unrelenting self-assurance.

Without a word, the face rapidly took a third dimensional form and approached him at speed, which led to it engulfing Gary's perspective and sucking his consciousness through his mouth. As he passed through a door that resembled a flyscreen, a layer of his self was divided from him. He then travelled through a wormhole at lightening speed, slicing layers off his egoic filter with each screen that he passed through.

After eleven energetic bodies had been ripped into separate perspectives, Gary found himself in a white space that felt infinitely large. He could still see through each

of his twelve layers, the most prominent views being his original one back in space and the version of himself in the bright light. He concentrated on his new found awareness, and spoke.

"Are you here? What do I call you?", he said, with an even greater level of confidence.

"Call me Gary", it laughed, telepathically.

Gary wasn't amused. Even though he was literally blown apart by the experience, he wanted answers. "Show yourself", he demanded, also telepathically. "And I'm not calling you Gary, Voice".

The telepathic nature of the exchange took Gary aback a little, particularly because the method of communication was so alien to him. "It really is amazing", he thought to himself, not wanting the Voice to hear.

"Lighten up, Gary", teased the Voice. "You needn't take things so seriously here", it continued, with a slow, deep chuckle. "I do want to help".

As the Voice materialised before Gary, he reinforced to himself that the Voice couldn't hear thoughts that he intended as private. He then examined it carefully, immediately recognising it as a perfect circle that appeared to have no edge. Inside was a filmy liquid, which reminded Gary of an interdimensional portal in a sci-fi movie. It was colourless, like it blended into the light around it. It was a distinctly obvious, but transparent entity.

"Wildfire told me that the truth would lead to more truth and that understanding more of myself would lead to new paths", Gary announced. "I want to know what happened in those realities or visions or whatever the fuck they were. I want to learn more from them so that I can understand myself better, so I know the path or paths that I need to take".

"You're on fire!", stated the Voice, which coincided with an explosion of colourful geometric shapes and symbols dancing in the circle. "Let's start with the Breakaways".

Gary's perspective melted into a kaleidoscope of bright colours. It had multiple circles turning within a larger circle, which seemed like a giant puzzle. Out of the centre a picture emerged and grew until Gary's vision had switched to a bird's eye view of the planet, like he was looking at it standing on the moon. The thing that struck him most was that earth looked different to what he'd seen in photos. He didn't recognise some of the shapes of land mass, and right at the top of the North Pole it appeared as if a giant eye of a storm hovered over it.

"The virus worked, Gary", said the Voice. As Gary's perspective shot like a bullet through space, into the atmosphere, through the clouds and onto the earth, the Voice continued. "This is twenty years afterwards. The Creeps were mostly destroyed once their AI systems were disintegrated. They were vulnerable to attack by a much larger force put forward by the Peeps, so it was unavoidable for them to be defeated".

Gary flew through the wall of a large building which reminded him of a prestige meeting place for public officials. In the foyer was a five metre tall statue made of what looked like gold and silver. It was a sculpture of Lez, indicating it was a tribute to the hero who sacrificed his own life to save his people.

"Lez gave his life for them Gary, but unfortunately all it did was buy some time", explained the Voice. "They have already divided into socioeconomic classes. Monopolies run amok and conflict is commonplace. Very similar parameters are in place for a very similar future to unfold, Gary. They simply haven't changed the right fundamentals of the social system".

"What fundamentals?", Gary asked.

"That's your job to ascertain", it replied succinctly.

"Alright, I want to see what happened to Brittney", progressed Gary.

His perspective immediately re-entered the kaleidoscope, which was abuzz with more colourful movement. Out of the psychedelia emerged a picture of Brittney, who looked healthy, happy and strong.

"Brittney evolved well, Gary. The conversation with David really opened her eyes to how she was behaving. She tossed out a huge portion of her wardrobe along with other cosmetic paraphernalia. Her self-esteem was restored by a mentoring program she engaged with, also resulting in a reality check regarding her out-of-control vanity. She went on to study social work, specialising in mentoring young women".

"That's inspiring", remarked Gary. "A feel-good story is definitely welcome among all this mess. Clearly she took seriously being attacked by those women. It was great timing for her actually, when you think about it. She was being given golden information on a silver platter just as she had some sense knocked into her".

This made Gary laugh a little, given the irony of it all. "Alright, let's check in on James".

The kaleidoscope immediately remanifested and the circles moved into a specific arrangement, reminding him of a combination safe lock. An image consumed his view, which was of a desecrated city. It bluntly reminded Gary of a zombie apocalypse movie.

"Here we go", Gary said with a little despair, shaking his non-existent head. "I'm taking the economy collapsed?"

"Yes, it did", replied the Voice. "It escalated out of control. First the stock prices went to near zero, sending everyone into a panic. Banks froze because of the mass withdrawals, which led to a credit crunch. Nobody could pay for anything as the majority of money was wiped from the system, leading to mass strikes and protests. Many people just packed up what they could and tried to find a safezone, particularly away from cities. Within a month or so all the trucks and ships had stopped, bringing the food supply to a halt, which was followed shortly by the failure of the electricity grid and therefore the water supply".

Gary had an image flash before him of James and Carol running in fear, making him feel instantly sad. Before he could say anything, the Voice continued. "The men and women behind the curtain didn't plan it that way, as they wanted to keep society more or less functioning so they could increase their technological prowess and enter into the transhumanist future they dreamed of. It was too late before they realised that their greed and inhumane behaviour wasn't just a major setback for humanity, but themselves too".

"How many survived?", Gary asked with concern.

"Not many", truthbombed the Voice. "Less than twenty per cent were alive a year later because very few people were prepared with the knowledge and the materials to take care of themselves. This created three separate groups of people, the previously wealthy who had all the equipment they needed, those who had made at least some preparations, and then the rest. Whilst there were communities created by good people, bad ones were too. The next several decades was characterised by a lot of violence although there were also many places which were highly functional and productive, which were emblematic of the human spirit to love and cooperate with each other".

"What happened in the end?", probed Gary.

"There is no end, Gary. But for the record, humanity survived this ordeal. After all, they've been through worse. But it was ultimately an unproductive path because it undermined all the progress they'd made, ensuring that they'd have to go through so much of it again".

"I feel sick", Gary commented. "Let's move on. Hmm, I've drawn a blank. What happened next?"

The kaleidoscope reappeared, did its little dance, and unlocked a picture of Annie. "She survived!", Gary yelled, quite happily.

"Yes, she did. The bullets missed all her vitals. I'll let you in on a little secret; she planned it this way on an energetic level."

"You mean her soul?!", Gary questioned, but said it more as a statement.

"Energy, soul, Annie", the Voice listed. "They're all just words to describe her individual snapshot of infinite spirit. But yes, it was designed that way, to give her the opportunity to grow into the next stage of her destiny. And she did. She continued the plight to unite the people, including those who did the bidding of the virus-makers. She was very successful too. The collective immunity to the virus reached critical mass, and it died out. They exposed the agenda to the world and the people worked together to have them dethroned".

"Then what happened?", Gary asked enthusiastically.

"To be decided", replied the Voice.

"Next stop, nuclear fallout", directed Gary. An array of colours swirled amongst the circles which resulted with a picture of a ravaged planet.

"The nuclear program was a foolish materialisation", updated the Voice. "It didn't take long for humanity to die out completely. The people behind it thought they were going to be safe in their underground cities, but that was just wishful thinking. All organisms, except for some living in the depths of the earth and ocean, perished. It was a near complete extinction, an event that is one of the foulest failures by self-aware lifeforms".

"What about planet earth?", was Gary's immediate question.

"Absolutely fine. A scratch, really. The time it takes for it to heal is relative to how long it would take a human to heal. The real tragedy was the demise of the organisms of the planet".

"God fucking damnit", yelled Gary. "And now I've got to deal with my dead family", he continued sadly, but aggressively.

Colours. Circles. Consciousness. Out of it emerged a picture of the lifeless city that was Gary's first experience.

"What's going on?", Gary whispered sombrely.

"This is the result of the technology Gary. They took your brother's body and replicated it. Instead of relying on humans to do their bidding, those at the top of the power structure inserted bio-computers into newborn babies and turned the human population into mindless zombies".

"And I had the power to stop it", Gary said, guiltily.

"If the kill-switch was activated then it would have set them back long enough for more conscious people to stop it ever being realised".

"I caused it?", Gary whimpered, in a state of shock.

"No, of course not", laughed the Voice. "You can't take responsibility for other's actions, you can only take responsibility for your own".

"I don't know what's so fucking funny, but if I made the choice there and then, like I should have, then none of this would have happened".

"If you haven't noticed by now there are an infinite number of splits, of timelines. This is but one. You were also watching another version of you, so it wasn't you who did or didn't make the decision. So don't you think that it is a little funny that you're so emotionally invested in it, Gary?"

"When it puts it like that, I guess it is", Gary chuckled to himself.

"Yes, fair enough", he continued, slightly laughing to the Voice. Gary thought about what the lesson might be here, but drew a blank.

"You ready?", asked the Voice.

"Sure, let's do it".

The colours seemed even more intense this time, reminding Gary of the Mushrooms that Laya and Lucinda took. Once the picture emerged, Gary felt immediately uncomfortable.

"You manifested a scene where the girls are in a

sixty-nine with each other?", he accused the Voice in an inquisitive manner.

"No, Gary. You did. This is your experience, after all".

"Oops, now that's an epic Freudian slip", he joked. "Okay, this is a great scene and all, but I really don't want to feel horny right now. What's going on with the girls?"

"They're great. After that night, it was like they fell in love all over again", the Voice reported, almost romantically. "They had a rebirth as individuals, and as a relationship. Their connection with each other increased, which increased their awareness of their connection with reality. They became stronger. They became more caring. They became wiser. They're using their abilities to do good for their world, not just practically, but on an energetic level too."

"Looks like they're having more fun in the sack too", Gary said cheekily. "Alright, enough sex for now. Let's head to the see how Buzz and Warwick faired. Oh wait, fuck, that's right, the plane. Elle too. What's the point of returning to this one?", Gary stated unhappily.

"Well, haven't I got a surprise for you", snickered the Voice.

This made Gary feel very animated. "Hurry the fuck up, colours", he said light-heartedly.

The scene manifested as Gary looking down from a staircase into a large living room. Sitting on the couch was Buzz, Warwick and Elle. They were chatting and laughing.

"Who would have thought?", toasted Buzz.

"What the hell? I thought they all perished?", Gary directed to the Voice, anxious for an answer.

"No, that was you again", it said, throwing a massive spanner in the works. "There was an unconscious part of you that knew you had to leave, so instead of torturing yourself over Elle you created the vision so that you journeyed to your next destination".

"Wow", laughed Gary. "Can't even trust the fake reality to be real", he continued, before deliberating the silliness of what he had just said.

As Gary's consciousness floated towards them, their voices became much clearer, snapping him back to the experience. "You are the man, Buzzman!", responded Warwick.

"It was pretty genius", agreed Elle.

Gary acknowledged that she looked more beautiful than ever, even though she looked more or less the same. There were slight variations, such as her hair colour and clothing style. But she was glowing. Her soft skin and sensual eyes begged him to hold her.

"WE nailed it", detailed Buzz. "It was a team effort. I told you those ideas came from my angel or spirit guide or something like that. Or the universe had its own agenda. Who the fuck knows. Whatever it was, I'm glad it happened, because not only are we the highest performing independent network in the world, but we've started to change the game with this show. The media monopolies are in demise, people are waking up in droves and the harsh realities of this world are now becoming matters of public debate, meaning meaningful change is on the horizon. This is the time that we can choose a more honourable path for humanity!", he celebrated.

"He's right", confirmed the Voice. "Your choices, your input, has brought this reality towards the tipping point it needs to bring about truth and justice in their world. In that one tiny experience, you gave so much to the people in this world, including yourself".

At that moment a person walked through an open door that led to a kitchen. "Fuck, that's me", identified Gary. "What am I doing here?"

As he walked from the kitchen he was near juggling a tray with various drinks on it. "A scotch for you Buzz", he said whilst handing it to him. "Rum", he continued, giving it to Warwick. "And a Pina Colada for my sexy-ass woman", he said smoothly, passing it to Elle.

"Now, let's have a cheers. To start, I want to thank you for bringing me on board this project", Gary said, beginning the speech.

"Couldn't have done it without you", interjected Warwick.

"Well regardless, it's been an honour", Gary continued. "Working with such an amazing team doing something amazing for the world. It doesn't get much better. But out of nowhere, it did. Elle, you're the icing on the cake, the pineapple on the works burger".

Everybody broke out in laughter.

"But seriously, you are amazing Elle, you all are. We deserve to celebrate this with all the hard work that we put into the first season. And it's only going to get better. With Season 2 under development, the people are more excited than ever. And they should be. There is a media platform that is actually doing their job for a change".

"Here, here", agreed Buzz.

"So everybody, I'd like you to raise your glass and cheers to not just our future success, but the future success of humanity", wrapped up Gary, with a sparkle in his eye.

"Cheers!", responded everybody at once.

Gary sat on the lounge next to Elle and hugged her with his left arm, whilst everybody took a large skull of their drink. "Now for a shot of Sambuca!", Gary yelled.

The real Gary, if he could call himself that, spoke to the Voice. "This is one of the most amazing experiences I've ever had. To see Elle and me together in another life, just reaffirms our love and connection. I'm a little bit jealous that they've been so successful in something so profoundly life-changing for their society, but I'm so proud of them. Thank you Voice for helping me to see this".

"The pleasure is all yours", it replied, cheekily.

Without any notification, the colours returned with the wheel and it rolled into action. Gary was still lost deep in thought as he realised the next scene had already manifested.

"You crushed his skull so severely that he died on route to the hospital", the Voice informed him. "The little boy ran for help when he came to. He didn't remember anything, including how he got there. He just woke up, saw the man covered in blood and screamed for help".

"It's probably best he died", Gary said cautiously.

"You did what you thought was right, Gary. The man was very sick. He had been raped as a child, repeatedly by both men and women. His parents sold him for sex from a very early age. He had been programmed to think it was okay to behave like that".

"That doesn't mean he shouldn't be punished!", fumed Gary. "He was taking advantage of children. He stripped away their innocence, hurting them for his own pleasure. He did not honour their sovereignty. Surely he knew that what he was doing was wrong!", he continued, with utter conviction.

"Everything you say is true, Gary. Unfortunately this type of behaviour is rampant. It is not just created by people behaving this way, but it's also amplified by the energetic programming expelled by dark occultists. It's a serious issue that needs to come to mass awareness. It needs to see the light of day so that it can be healed. It is such a crucial area for humanity to collectively acknowledge".

"You mean this goes to the top?", Gary enquired.

"It is at the very top, and it goes all the way through to the bottom. It is widespread and always has been", the Voice established.

"It is crucial to acknowledge", reiterated Gary. "There is no middle ground when it comes to the rape of children. You're either for it, or against it. Nobody can sit on the fence with this, meaning that once it is exposed it is a powerful mechanism for the masses to unite to bring truth and justice to our world".

"Yes", the Voice concurred, without elaborating.

"Oh no!", cried Gary. "Now I've got to visit Mum and Dad. They've lost both their sons".

Immediately the wheels spun which ignited the cascade of colours. It was first time that Gary acknowledged that there were some colours that he hadn't ever seen before.

The visualisation that transpired was immediately identifiable. He was back at his parents' house. They were sitting on the same lounge, looking like the same people. However, next to them were three children, two girls and a boy, and one was a different ethnicity.

"Who are they?", explored Gary.

"They're the children your parents adopted", answered the Voice. "Your parents were distraught, and hated themselves for many moons. They couldn't believe that they'd let Simon climb that tree".

"Another fucking failure", Gary grilled himself.

"Was it, Gary? Or did it end in growth?"

"You tell me?", Gary reacted, somewhat aggressively.

"What has your experience been?", the Voice asked.

"Well, fuck, I've grown dramatically, at least I think I have. But I'm still lost in a fucking virtual reality game!", he continued, with increasing rage. "I mean, I'm talking to some fucking circle that looks like a gateway to a parallel universe! I'm probably in an insane asylum, for all I know".

"Wouldn't that mean none of this happened, so there's no point beating yourself up anyway?"

Gary calmed himself and looked at his parents. "It feels so real", he said, softly.

"Your parents have become more advanced versions of themselves" the Voice advised him. "They did behave self-abusively for some time, but they also shook it off and tried to make amends. They became more appreciative of their life, and the life of others. After they first discussed it, it was an easy decision for them to adopt, because they knew there were children who deserved a better life and they knew they had the capacity to provide it. They've been great parents, not just to you boys, but also their new children. They treat them as if they were their very own, ensuring they have a loving and supportive family".

"What are their names?"

"Kathy, Shinta and Jasen", the Voice said swiftly. "They've been living with your parents for two, three and four years respectively. It's been six years since Simon fell out of the tree".

"You mean I fell out of the tree", grumbled Gary.

"Technically it wasn't you who let go", the Voice reminded him.

Instead of furthering the discussion, Gary looked in admiration at his parents. They were so special, so sweet. They were sitting on the couch just talking, with no distraction from the television or anything else. They really seemed happy, and so did the kids.

After a few minutes of observing them, Gary begin to feel tremendously homesick. "Let's get the fuck out of here, I've got work to do", he announced.

This time Gary felt like he was attached to one of the spinning wheels, to the point he was getting dizzy. He laughed at the sheer joy of feeling like he was on a theme park ride, but whilst he had taken a psychedelic. After what felt like a short time, he was once again hovering over the tribal village.

"Well, I know what happens here. Colonialism. The destructive imperialist machine", Gary condemned.

"The tribes from this region survived for another fifty thousand years, Gary. They were already close to that age too. They had an amazing run, but all things must eventually change. And for the record too, you were right. They were farmers who practiced agriculture".

"I thought that's what I saw, but you're seriously not defending the decimation of this beautiful people, are you?", Gary responded in a stunned tone.

"The treatment of all the peoples of this earth by the colonial expansion was cold-hearted, Gary. It is a deep wound on the collective psyche of humanity. Nobody deserves to have their people slaughtered, their sovereignty trampled and their health annihilated", the Voice elucidated.

"So what did you mean then?"

"Humanity was reaching a new era", explained the Voice. "Technology was nearing the point of instantaneous communication from all over the planet, meaning the collective consciousness of humanity was about to go into hyper-drive. Love it or hate it, the world was changing. And no stone would be left unturned on this expansion".

"Yes, but it could have happened more humanely".

"I'm not disagreeing with you Gary. Humanity has a poor track record when it comes to conflict. So much death, so much destruction, so much suffering. This is why the next epoch is necessary. Humanity has to face its shadow head on and rise above the violence of its past. It's been imbalanced for too long, Gary. There will never only be positivity in the construct of duality, but the ratio between light and dark has long been skewed".

This was actually making sense to Gary.

"There needed to be a platform for direct information sharing across your planet", the Voice continued, unabated. "This is the purpose of the internet. It connects people from every corner, from under every rock, ensuring that a planetary tribe can be birthed. The culture of humanity is well under development and it is in finding some commonality with each other that humanity will be able to save itself".

"From what?", Gary asked with deep concern.

"From itself, Gary. Humanity is not yet an advanced species. It is not yet advanced in mind, in heart and in spirit. But it can be. In fact, it needs to be to survive. Connecting the people on earth was a necessary step in this evolution, even though so much unnecessary suffering occurred. And that was humanity's choice, Gary. But it doesn't need to continue this way".

"I really can't see how everyone is going to get along. We're so divided, so hateful at times too".

"You don't all have to get along with everyone, Gary. You don't have to think the same, you don't have to be the same. You can all have your differences, and that should be honoured and celebrated. After all, it fosters so much creativity, and even fun".

"Okay, I'm hearing ya", Gary conceded.

"It's really simple, Gary. All you have to do is accept that you're part of the same human family and that you need to work with each other for the benefit of all of you, regardless of whatever small or large differences that you might have".

"But what happens when different cultures or even people disagree on the way to move forward?"

"Great question, Gary. What is the one principle that can unite all the people of the world, regardless of race, creed, age or sex?"

"FREEDOM!", immediately yelled Gary, in a pure state of passion. "If everybody learns to respect not just everyone else's Sovereignty, but their own too, then there is absolutely no reason for conflict to arise".

And suddenly, Gary was gone.

CHAPTER 13

Organiser

"WAKE THE FUCK UP GARY, YOU NEED TO GET ACTIVE", yelled a voice who sounded just like Elle, whilst Gary felt like he was being slapped across his face. But when he opened his virtual eyes with a startled intensity, it wasn't what he anticipated.

He began to make note of his unexpected surroundings, first noticing an organ of great magnitude. "I must be in a church", he said to himself, after looking across the bench seats which filled most of the large room. The pews were almost completely filled with what seemed an excited bunch of people. Enclosing the room were murals, paintings, mosaics of stained glass and carvings in the walls that looked decades, if not centuries old.

Lit candles littered the room, mostly along the edges. Gary was inside a woman sitting at the organ, which he was able to notice because of the reflection in various areas of the metal. Just as he began to get a grip on his location, the woman started playing.

To his left was a choir made up of both younger and

older people. They were dressed in purple and black robes, and layered in height because of the stepped platform they were standing on. They began singing in beautiful harmony with each other, feeding and absorbing the energy from the sounds of the organ.

Gary made out a few of the words, including 'Jesus', 'love' and 'sin'. "Here we go", laughed Gary. "Same old story, submit to Jesus or burn in hell", he thought to himself, sarcastically.

As the song drew to a close, a person who was obviously a Priest walked from behind the front section of the church and up to the podium. An individual singer in the choir was finalising the song with a high, drawn out note. The woman had stopped playing the organ by this stage, and the singer's voice was softening. The Priest began to clap in admiration, which incited the churchgoers to do the same.

As the applause reached its peak, the Priest began to talk into the microphone. "Okay, okay, now wasn't that wonderful!", he shouted, with a wide, uplifting smile.

A surge of celebratory energy engulfed the crowd for the final time.

"What a day! This is so special in so many ways!", the Priest proclaimed.

By this stage the crowd was settling towards silence. The Priest looked throughout the assembly with an excited energy that attracted the audience into his stare. All noise finally came to an abrupt halt and the air was so clear from sound that it reminded Gary of when his consciousness flowered in the womb of the cosmos.

"In just under half an hour, our beloved Pope will make his speech to the world!", the Priest affirmed. "It is for this reason that today our sermon was a short one. We have set up a projector in the common room in the adjacent building, which can fit up to fifty people. But for those who wish to take the trip home, we're now going to bring this gathering to a close".

Gary felt an itch arise from his soul, although he didn't know how to scratch it.

"Instead of passing around the donation boxes, we've left them at the doors as you exit", continued the Priest. "Please donate what you can; every bit helps. God bless, my brothers and sisters".

As the woman started playing the organ in a soft and soothing melody, the crowd began to make their way towards the back doors. "The pope's address to the world, hey", thought Gary. "Now that would be a great opportunity to..."

And suddenly, Gary was gone.

He became self-aware in an amazingly decorated room that was saturated with religious art and traditional design. High ceiling windows immersed the space in abundant light. Through the windows Gary could see a large crowd gathered in a city square. "There are tens of thousands people out there", he acknowledged, delicately.

The room was buzzing with activity. Maids and butlers hustled in their jobs, and to the right was a long table that had over two dozen chairs. At least half of the chairs were being used by both men and women. They were chatting amongst themselves, and some of them were taking notes. The table was lined with gourmet food and sparkly jugs containing various liquids.

"Pope Thomas", a woman said to Gary's left. "Please follow me. The elders are waiting for you".

"Yes, my child", replied the Pope.

Gary was feeling very excited that he had travelled into the body of the Pope, but it dawned on him at the same time that his mission must be to speak to the world. "I don't think I have the knowledge or confidence to do this", he said to himself, careful not to engage the body of the Pope.

They walked through a door to their right and down a long corridor. There were amazing works of art perfectly placed along the walls, none of which Gary had seen before. It was a magnificent sight, for a hallway. Gary wondered what all the other rooms would look like, both for public and private viewing. It was at that point that Gary decided to try if he had any control over the Pope, but in a subtle way. He attempted to make his hand clench and then move it to his mouth to cough into it.

"Success", Gary celebrated to himself.

They reached the end of the hall, which split off in both directions. In front of them was an overly sized entrance to another room that had two large but closed wooden doors. The woman knocked three times on the door, in a very deliberate fashion. The left one swung open almost immediately and they both entered.

"Sit down, Thomas", said a man at the very end of another large, long table. There were at least fifteen people sitting, most of them men. Gary observed at least four women, mostly of an older age. The entire group were either wearing suits or other professional attire, which radiated an intense atmosphere of power and control. The Pope made his way to the closest seat and sat down, which was at the opposite end of the man who had just directed him.

"We want to make sure we're on the same page", he elaborated to the Pope.

"Well, this is getting juicy", Gary quietly thought to himself. He was super conscious of not affecting the Pope in any weird way.

"As you know Thomas, we've found it very difficult to trust you. We have said very clearly that certain keywords and concepts are not allowed, and others are absolutely essential, but you have broken our rules twice before. We know that you don't trust us either, that you don't trust our agenda. But what we do and why we do it is none of your business. If you fuck us again Thomas we will expose you for having sex with those underage girls and then kill you. We have the video footage and we will release it if we need to".

"Holy fuck", Gary thought to himself, pulling back his emotion as he reached the middle of his thinking. This also gave him a light giggle too, given the unintended pun in his reaction.

"You drugged me and forced me to do it", exclaimed the Pope. "I have lived a mostly pure life and you tried to corrupt me. My service has long been to God and to humanity".

"Your service is to us, Thomas!", interrupted the man, simultaneously smacking the table with extreme force. "We have controlled the church for centuries. We own you. We own the people. They are slaves to the real God Thomas. You know how this world works, a little too much actually. You did well to trick us into believing you were part of our order, but we know now. We know you don't want to serve your real ruler, but you have no choice. As above, so below".

"Real ruler?", thought Gary.

"I just want what's best for this world", the Pope responded, sullenly.

"You don't know what's best for this world, Thomas. We do! We've been controlling this shitfest for longer than you'll ever know. You need to trust us, you need to put aside your doubts and follow your orders. It's what's best for all of us".

The Pope's head fell to his chest. Gary felt a tear rolling down his left cheek. "It's hard to trust you, after what you did to me", he explained.

"It's standard operating procedure, Thomas. We do it with all high profile public figures who are not already compromised, you know that. We cannot let anyone or anything get in the way of our mission. I know it's hard to understand, but you need to trust us", reassured the man, almost compassionately.

"Okay", he conceded. "What do you want me to do?"

"Just follow the script. Follow our direction. Don't question it, don't question us. Just engage the people as planned so we can get on with the mission".

In an unspoken pact, the Pope nodded his head. "You're excused", said the man.

The Pope rose from his chair and the woman who had guided him to the room raised her hand and motioned to the door. A servant opened the right one and they exited.

Gary wasn't sure what to do. The idea of another ruler circulated his thoughts. "Is there something important that I'm missing", he deliberated. "Is it the right thing to speak up, to organise the audience into greater clarity?"

"You with us?", asked the woman.

"Yes", the Pope answered. "I am. Now I must attend the bathroom".

Halfway down the hall the woman stopped at a door on the left. She opened it and walked in, in front of the Pope. He followed her and as she stopped he continued walking to another door on the far right. He entered, approached the toilet, lifted the seat, drew his robe to the side and pulled out his penis.

Gary was a little amused. "Taking a piss with the Pope, who would have thought?!"

As the Pope urinated, Gary began contemplating again about what he should do. He thought back to when his brother's body was hijacked by the technocrats. "There was a decision that should have been made, but it wasn't. But that doesn't mean that this is the same circumstance", he thought, confusingly to himself.

The Pope repositioned his penis and robe, flushed the toilet and proceeded out the door. "He didn't even wash his hands. Typical male!", Gary laughed, before acknowledging it as a sex stereotype.

The Pope walked past the woman and out into the hallway. "Don't let us down", she said chillingly.

As they re-entered the original room a voice gained the attention of its occupants. "All rise for his Holiness".

Everybody stood as he walked through the doors. He greeted everyone with a smile and a nod of his head. The woman followed close next to him, directing him towards a door near the very far corner of the room, past the table. The woman rushed a little ahead of the Pope, opened it, and they both walked in.

Before she closed the door she spoke to a man that was standing not far from the doorway. He stood very still, with his hands folded into each other, down to his front. "I'll call the rest in five". The man nodded his head and she closed the door.

"Okay, you've got ten minutes until go-time. I want you to go over your speech again, but make it quick. You've had plenty of time to memorise it", she explicated, whilst handing him some sheets of paper. "You'll be taking this with you in case you get lost. We want every single word, every single sentence, to be conveyed. There are too many symbols that need to be represented for the entire program to be engaged. This is so important for the mission, Thomas, so don't fuck it up!"

As she finished her sentence, the door opened. The man that was standing outside of it entered.

"I said I'll call you in when we're ready!", shouted the woman.

"Yes, I know, but it's important", he replied.

"What the fuck do you want?", she reacted angrily.

He walked over to both of them sitting on the couch. "I need to tell you both something".

As he was ending the sentence he rapidly moved his right hand and grabbed her violently around her neck, followed by his left hand which covered her nose and mouth with a white cloth. He held it in position whilst she kicked and punched wildly, but it lasted only several seconds before she fell to a slump.

"Go you good thing", cheered Gary, ensuring he kept it to himself.

"Are you ready, Sir", the man gently said to the Pope.

"Yes", he replied.

"Okay, everything is ready to go. They're expecting you in nine minutes, so it will be a total surprise. Everything is set up, all you have to do is switch on the microphone which is on the front of it. We're guarding the electronics, so nothing can be tampered with. I'm proud of you, Sir. I'll walk you out".

The man helped the Pope rise to his feet and then walked over to two large bay doors, opening them without any indecision. The crowd increased a little in volume, but not in a way that indicated they were expecting to see the Pope. The man moved to the side, pointed towards the microphone on a little table and nodded his head.

As Gary and the Pope walked out onto the veranda, the gathering erupted in immense cheers, clapping and whistling. Gary had never heard anything so loud. "The energy is phenomenal", he narrated to himself.

The Pope waved to them whilst flashing a quick smile, but then raised his hands and motioned for them to quiet down. As they followed suit and quickly came to a penetrating silence, a large dragonfly hovered right in front of the Pope's face, did a little circular dance, and flew down into the crowd. The Pope picked up the microphone, switched it on and held it close to his mouth.

"Hello", he said, in a welcoming manner.

The crowd re-erupted, leading the Pope to calm them with a gesture from his right hand. "I have some bad and good news for you today", he began. "I have information that will shock you, that might even scare you, but I also have information that will inspire you with hope and purpose".

The crowd stayed eerily silent.

"This is going to be awesome", Gary thought. "At least I don't have to do it, that way I can't fuck it up", he chuckled to himself.

"There are people who control the Church that don't have your best interests in mind. They infiltrated our organisation a long, long time ago, and have been calling the shots ever since. They forced me to do things that I am not proud of, however I must take responsibility for all my actions. And so should they, which is why I am going to expose it all to you".

The crowd was a mixture of cheers, talking and silence.

"Please listen to me. God knows I am telling the truth, so please allow your hearts to know that I'm telling the truth. These people don't worship our God, they worship something else. They have used the Church to do their bidding for centuries. They believe that they have turned you into slaves for their ruler, and that I cannot allow to continue. I don't know their deepest agendas because they keep them a guarded secret, but I do know they murder, they pillage and they keep the truth from the world. Just now I came from a room in which some of them are located. There are over a dozen of them in our sacred building right now".

The audience let out a bellowing boo that echoed throughout the plaza, sending a shiver through Gary's soul.

"Listen, my children. Today they wanted me to tell you that we need a one world religion, one that will secretly ensure they increase their power and control".

More boos filled the air.

"Whilst I recognise that all the religions have both parallel and contradicting beliefs throughout, I also recognise they aim to tell a story of something greater than us. A story of God. I believe that it's important to come together and work together, but that doesn't mean we need to have the same way of explaining God. For God is a hero, and he should be a hero to all of us. He can save us, regardless of the culture we were born into".

"Listen, we need to honour both our similarities and our differences. We need to accept that we're the same in some ways but unique in others", Gary accidently blurted out through the Pope.

He had started to get uninspired by the Pope's speech, so he unconsciously decided to take full control.

"I want to honour all of you who stand up for what's right. I want to celebrate all of you who nurture morality in your heart and mind. And I want to praise all of you who love your fellow men and women, regardless of any difference in race or creed".

Gary lifted the Pope's arms which sent the crowd into a frenzy of festivity.

"But there are some dark truths that we must accept, including that there are secret groups who run our world behind the scenes", Gary continued. "They haven't just taken over our Church, but our governments and institutions too. They own the money, they own the media, they own the medicine and therefore they own the power. They are treating you as slaves and you haven't even acknowledged it!", he yelled passionately, wondering if he went too far.

The crowd remained mostly silent.

"Your freedom is being stolen from you", he continued anyway. "You are told what to think and how to behave. And you happily do it, because you have a misplaced trust in so-called authority. But they don't deserve your trust. They are desecrating our beautiful planet, they are killing innocent people in their wars, they are stealing our shared resources and they are disempowering you so you are easier to control".

You could have heard a butterfly flap its wings, it was that quiet.

"Religion inspires people to do the right thing, but it is only the tip of the iceberg. God is not a man in the sky, God is everything, including you and I. It is the mother, and the child. It is the universe, and the earth. It is the creator, and the created!"

"It's also the penis, and the pussy", Gary laughed privately to himself.

"I encourage you to have a personal experience with the divine, beyond the teachings of our religion, of all religion", he continued. "For hundreds of years the wisdom of the Church has been restricted by those who secretly control it. They have kept knowledge for themselves, without sharing it with the people. They have purposely led you astray so they have more power, so they have more control. I implore you to find the wisdom that is scattered throughout the teachings of the Church, but at the same time find the wisdom that exists inside all of you".

Gary took a deep breath and continued, even though he felt like something else was influencing what he said. "You deserve to be more empowered, to be more enlightened. The teachings of all religions can only take you so far before you must set off on your own journey of self-discovery. You must peel back the conditioning to find the deeper layers of the self. You must navigate through metaphysical enquiry to connect with your innate power. And you must enter into esoterica to open the doors of your consciousness and connect with spirit".

The energy of the gathering took on a confused frequency, so Gary retook the reins to keep it a little simpler.

"There is so much more to what religion has taught us, to what the institutions have taught us. Never accept that the official stories are entirely true. Just take a look at the world around you to see the proof. There is so much suffering, so much pain. Our world could be so much better, so much fairer. But it's not. The reason why we haven't brought more justice, love and peace to our world is simply because of the way it has been designed. And not by God, but by the people who control it".

He took another deep breath before continuing. "It is our job to make this world a better place. We shouldn't rely on governments or religions to do it, because they've clearly failed. All of us need to take responsibility for ourselves, our families and our future generations. We need to take responsibility as a human family".

The crowd's vitality increased dramatically, almost like they were energetically compelled to feel more empowered, to feel more comfortable with the truth.

"We need to unite under the banner of freedom", Gary perpetuated. "Everybody has a right to be free, everybody has a right for their sovereignty to be respected. We should be free to do whatever we want in life, as long as we don't cause harm and impose ourselves on other people's freedom. Free to think how we want. Free to feel how we want. Free to act how we want. As long as we honour that in everyone else too, then we will finally rise to the next level of humanity's evolution!"

This sent waves of roars thundering through the air.

"And whilst we're talking about Sovereignty, I pledge

to change three things in the Church. First, I will purge it of its evil controllers who do all this harm. Second, I vow to allow women to be Priestesses. And third, I pledge to rid the Church of pedophilia and any other actions that hurt others".

As the noise from the crowd exploded into an unprecedented decibel range, the bullet heading for the Pope's skull remained audibly undetectable. Once again time slowed down for Gary, giving him a telepathic opportunity to feel it careering towards him. With an unwavering fervour, he tossed himself back through the doors, ensuring the bullet only grazed the back of his scalp. As he hit the ground the Pope's frail neck was not strong enough to restrict the movement of his head, which ended in his forehead solidly hitting the slate floor.

And suddenly, Gary was gone.

CHAPTER 14

Experimenter

"What do you want to do now?", asked the Voice. As Gary realised he was back in the cosmos with his starlit face staring back at him, the memory of his recent experience came flooding back. "What happened with the Pope?", he said in a troubled manner.

"Does it matter, Gary? You're experiencing different timelines. You can create anything that you feel is right".

"Alright, let me think for a moment". Gary once again intended his thoughts to be private. He considered what lessons he could take away from his last encounter. "The focus was freedom, but what comes next?" The result of his reflection on the Peeps came to memory. "The social system".

Whilst navigating his memory he decided to see if an answer could manifest itself organically, so he began to meditate by attempting to clear his mind of all its activity. The moment he felt free of his own thoughts a recollection came crashing into his consciousness: "What we really should be doing is decentralising our governmental apparatus, migrating from the cities back into smaller communities and re-empowering society to be more self-reliant and self-governing".

"Adam, you fucking legend", Gary thought enthusiastically.

He then turned his attention back to the Voice. "Okay Voice, I think I know what the next step is. I want to create an experiment".

"And what experiment would that be?", it replied.

"I want to create my own world. Actually, I don't care what you say, I want to return to the previous one with the Pope and understand what happened afterwards. Then I want to change it as I see fit. I want you to explain to me what impact my choices have so I can modify them accordingly".

The image of the spinning wheels manifested immediately, accompanied by a burst of colours that looked as magical as ever. The image that protruded from the centre encircled Gary's perspective until he was flying in the air looking over the plaza where the Pope had spoken.

"Your speech confused a huge portion of the population, Gary. Many people supported the Pope, but many condemned him too. In some ways, it fuelled the division of the people. Those who were in support demanded that the secret order be held accountable, but the corruption ran so deep that all they had to do was hang a few people out to dry which resulted with little disruption to their sect".

"Did many people follow the advice?", enquired Gary.

"A small percentage took it seriously by delving into the depths of their deception, but most people realised little change. Programming is really difficult to overcome, Gary.

The power of the subconscious and its neurological wiring is phenomenal. It takes so much introspection and a repetitive shift in behaviours to actually create sustained change".

"Hmm. Okay. Now it's time to manifest my ideas. Well, they're not my ideas but you get what I mean. I want all the governments of the world to be smaller and decentralised. I want policy decisions to be made at a local level wherever possible. I want people to gradually migrate out of cities to live more self-reliantly in smaller communities, including growing their own food and hemp".

"Done", said the Voice.

And suddenly, Gary was gone.

"What the fuck, I didn't ask for this?", Gary said, startled from the unexpected shift.

Looking around, it didn't take him long to realise that he was in an unfamiliar small town. The next realisation was that he was fully in control of his body. "I feel normal", he said out loud.

"Good to hear, Gary", a male voice said behind him, sarcastically.

Gary swung around to greet him. It was a man he had never seen before, of about his age. "Hey Albert", his body said warmly. "Not sure what happened, a thought must have escaped through the filter", he laughed.

Real-Gary realised that he was in another virtual self that must have been very different to his own version of reality. He decided to take a passive role and learn about this Gary's life.

"You know I don't like Albert", he responded with fake anger. "I only get called that when I'm in trouble off the mother, or the missus", he chuckled.

"Sure thing, Albert", Gary cheekily replied.

"Fuck you, man", he said with an ongoing laugh. "Hey, we're heading in for a pick. You coming?"

"Yeah, in about an hour Al. I've got a session with one of the young fellas now. See ya in a bit, mate".

Gary picked up a bag, tapped Al on the shoulder and made his way towards a series of buildings that were next to a large, open area that looked like a sporting field. As he walked quickly to his destination, Real-Gary absorbed the surroundings. The homes were scattered in almost an unplanned way. In every direction forest encircled him. Because he was on a flat bit of land he wasn't able to see into the distance to ascertain what existed outside of it, except for the mountain ranges that illustrated he was in a valley.

The place, the feeling, was really beautiful. As Real-Gary had grown up in suburbia, his experience being immersed in nature was restricted to travel, so it felt really good for him to be here even though it was quite cold. The sun was not too far above the horizon, indicating it was late afternoon. He could smell the crispness of the fresh air, which was a refreshing experience. There were all types of sounds coming from various birds and bugs, with a subtle humming of cicadas forming a foundation to the natural orchestra.

As Gary arrived at a large building made from wood and concrete, Real-Gary admired the unique look to it. A woman of about fifty years of age greeted him as she walked out through the front doors. "Hey Gaz", she said affectionately. "Apollo is in there waiting for you".

"Another Apollo", Real-Gary thought with light-hearted suspicion, careful not to invoke the action of Gary.

"Great, thanks Dacey. Have an awesome day", he replied.

He walked through the doors and said hello to several people, before proceeding down a hallway and into a room on the far right. "Hi Apollo", he said welcomely, before sitting on a chair behind a desk.

As Gary unpacked some paperwork from his backpack, Real-Gary took in the cosy feeling that radiated from the room. Apollo, who seemed about sixteen, was sitting on one of two comfortable looking lounges that were in the far corner. There was a wooden coffee table placed in front of them, with various books on it. A couple of beanbags sat in the corner across from the desk, next to a large bookcase filled to the brim with books. There were also little statues and ornaments scattered across the room, including an incense burner that was emitting a rosy smell into the air.

"I'll be with you in a tick", Gary informed Apollo.

He sorted through some of the paperwork, pulling a file out and holding it his right hand as he joined Apollo on the couches. "Let me see where we were up to", he said, whilst opening it. "That's right, strategies for the anxiety. Have they made any difference for you?", he asked, a little too clinically.

"A mentor, hey", concluded Real-Gary. "Didn't see that coming".

"Yeah, they have", Apollo replied happily. "The last session was really helpful, Gary. I really appreciate it. I'm nowhere near as anxious and I followed your suggestion to really take the time to connect with myself and why I might feel that way. I think I figured more of it out, actually".

"I'm all ears", Gary said, much more engagingly.

"Well, you know how we talked about the migration and that I miss seeing my friends?"

Gary nodded his head in validation. "I don't think it's just that", Apollo continued. "I think in a sense I don't know who I am without them. It's like I lack an identity in some ways. Like, who am I?"

"And who are you?", Gary replied, giving him the opportunity to explore his own question.

"I know I've only been here a year so I'm still settling in like you said, but I keep thinking back to when you told me that we have certain things about ourselves that are either created, or natural to who we are, such as genetics and family and being human and stuff".

"And our own, unique energy", Gary expanded.

"Yeah, exactly. This might sound weird, but I feel like I'm meant to be me, even though I don't really know who 'me' is", he said bashfully, using his fingers to accentuate the quotation marks. "I mean, I like sports and games and stuff, and doing nice things for people. I love looking after the animals too. But I just feel like I'm not sure who I am under all that stuff".

"Once we begin to look deeper than the way we've been influenced by our environment, we start to connect with other parts of ourselves. Our essence. It doesn't happen overnight, though. In fact, it's a lifelong journey. You'll get used to it, you'll even look forward to discovering new aspects to yourself", Gary reassured him. "And never forget, you're not alone Apollo. After 'The Great Relocation' began huge amounts of people have been feeling lost and confused. I used to, and still do in some ways. We were all so used to the roles we played in our career and society as a whole, especially as a cog in the consumerist culture. So we had to recreate ourselves without much guidance, including learning new life skills".

"Hmm, 'The Great Relocation'. It's got a ring to it", Real-Gary said proudly to himself.

Gary picked up the jug of water on the table and poured out two glasses, before continuing to verbalise his thinking. "Many people miss their old circumstances, which is fair enough in some ways, but totally ridiculous in others".

"Why ridiculous?", Apollo asked, sounding a little self-conscious.

"Well, many people left their previous lives where a lot of baggage had been created, such as depression or stress or even a deeply embedded existential crisis, but part of them still wanted to return".

"Exi-what?", asked Apollo, inquisitively.

"Existential crisis. It means they felt confused about their existence, regardless if they were conscious of it or not. Lack of purpose and meaning, that sort of thing. So they wanted to go back because they probably felt it was easier. They missed their comfort, their schedule. Their lives were a habit. They had their nine to five job, they came home and watched TV or got drunk or played out whatever vice they had for escapism, saw their family and friends every now and again, bought some new stuff, then repeated again and again".

Gary paused for a moment as his heart skipped a beat in a flood of compassion. "Laziness was so entrenched into their lives that it was like they were on auto-pilot. Very little creativity and passion. And drive, except of course to make more money and be successful in a job that a lot of them ironically hated. There was very little learning too, except for mundane shit of course. Who did what down the street, what happened on the latest TV show, the latest phone just released, blah blah. All this translated into hardly any growth for them. They were stuck in Groundhog Day, in a groundhog version of themselves, but they still missed being like that because it was predictable. They knew what to expect, so they had some sort of security in their lives even though they were miserable. The sad thing is though, there's a lot who have slipped into similar patterns after they relocated".

"That's kind of what Mum says, why she wanted to leave", Apollo added.

"It was one of the major drivers, Apollo. A lot of people were fed up with their lives. They felt like slaves to the system. They were getting sick, and for what? They just felt like there was so much more to life".

"My issues are so little, compared to theirs", Apollo said, guiltily.

"There is absolutely nothing wrong with wanting to feel good, mate", he replied with soft conviction.

Gary picked up a glass of water and skulled it, which prompted Apollo to take a sip from his.

"I am happy", said Apollo, after spilling a little bit on his shirt. "I do miss my old life in some ways though".

"What do you miss?"

"Mostly my friends, even though I've made heaps more here. I miss the beach too. And the waterslides. Oh, and travelling, that was always fun".

"There were always going to be sacrifices, I guess you're gonna have work out whether they're worth it or not. Weigh it all up Apollo, to see if this place has more advantages. And yes, travel is a big one for many people. Since we began to decentralise our social systems and spread more out too, overseas and even domestic travel became much harder. This is especially true for communities who developed their own currencies, because a lot of places won't convert it to the standard. The relocation effected many industries too, including automobiles and aviation. They're still going through their reset, especially as more and more of society convert to bio-fuels made from hemp and other plants".

Gary looked like he was in deep reflection for a moment.

"There are many hiccups to what happened and we've still got so much to work out, especially because it wasn't planned from the start. But with so many people who just put their hands up and said 'that's it, we've had enough', the world had no option but to adapt. There is something big missing though, like it could be done so much better. I mean, we've got so much great technology that we're not using, such as 3D printing and other robotics and automation equipment. We've definitely done more right by ourselves and the environment, and people are working together so much more and helping each other out, but it's like we had to go back to more traditional living to achieve it. There's got to be a way to have the best of both worlds, including being able to travel wherever we want and get good access to the latest technologies that actually help us function better. It's just that we haven't figured it out yet".

Real-Gary felt a little deflated after hearing that something important was still missing.

"I'd love to go to India one day", Apollo reflected. "I hope we can work it out soon, at least before I'm older.

But you're right, there's lots of great things about moving here. School is so much more fun and I actually get to do different stuff nearly every day! I even know over 100 species of plants, now. I get to talk to lots of interesting people and I love the gatherings we have too. I guess I'm just a little scared which makes me feel a bit stressed. But you're helping me a lot".

"I'm very happy I can, mate. I'm new at this, so I'm still a little nervous. I've got lots to learn, but when I talk to people like you I feel that we're both learning something together".

They continued chatting which led into family-related stuff. Real-Gary took the opportunity to do his own reflecting. "Something big missing", he repeated. "It really seems to be going well, but I guess the situation is more complex than what I hoped, especially when we look at it from a planetary perspective".

He continued looking back through his memory to see if the answer was somewhere in there. He thought about his encounter with Wildfire, especially that they lived for tens of thousands of years in a sustainable way. "They might not have had all the technology and fancy comforts, but they really seemed happy. There's got to be something that I can learn from them?", he proposed to himself.

After mulling over his memories for quite some time, he was provoked out of it by Gary saying his goodbyes to Apollo. "Just let admin know whenever you want to see me again mate. Anytime you like, as long as I'm free".

"Thanks", Apollo replied, gratefully.

He exited the room whilst Gary packed up his stuff. Once he finished, he walked out past the front desk, letting them know to call him whenever he's needed. He proceeded back to where he ran into Al and hopped into a medium sized ute. He started it, which sounded to Real-Gary just like a normal car.

"I wonder if this is running on Hemp?", he thought.

As Gary began to pull out, a white cat slowly walked in front of the car, forcing him to wait until it was out of the way. They then drove for about five minutes on both cement and dirt roads. Real-Gary observed that the landscape was a mix of cleared land, crops and forest, with houses scattered amongst the vegetation. He could see lots of fruit on various trees, some of which were planted in well-established bush.

Real-Gary then thought of Elle, his parents and family, wondering if they were here in this area too. "I can't wait to see them all once I get out of this crazy fucking game", he said hopefully to himself.

As the car turned a corner, another small town appeared. The houses were much more spread out than suburbia and there was a lot more vegetation too. Real-Gary was struck by the lack of lawns and the abundant garden beds that surrounded the homes. It definitely looked the picture of a town that took care of itself.

They took a right turn, leading to a large opening in the trees. There were dozens of cars parked around what looked like one giant garden bed, about the size of a football field. There were greenhouses covering about half of it, as well as people all over the place. Some were talking and laughing, and others were working together or by themselves.

Pulling in to park, Al exited through an opening in a hedge with another man of about their age. "Perfect timing,

Gaz", yelled Al. "Change of plans. We've just had a new arrival, so let's go have a beer".

Al and his new mate walked over to Gary's window, as he wound it fully down. "Gary, Rex. Rex, Gary."

Rex held out his hand to shake it as Gary did the same through his window. "Nice to meet you Rex. Welcome to 'The Web'. Hop in".

"You too Gary. Cheers", replied Rex, in a humble tone.

Rex hopped in the back behind the driver's seat, whilst Al moved around the front and hopped in the passenger seat. "To the pub?", Al suggested.

"Sounds good", replied Gary. He reversed out and headed away from his original location. "Where'd you come from Rex?"

"My wife and I moved from the City. We've been there all our lives, so we're a little excited about the venture", he replied.

The boys continued with some chit chat. After around 100 metres, they took a turn to the right, along the side of the community garden. After another 100 metres he took a winding left and pulled up when they'd travelled fifty metres or so.

"Alright, this is 'The Hub'. My shout", laughed Al.

"What's so funny?", asked Rex.

"It's the community pub", answered Gary. "All the beer and spirits are made locally from our shared resources, which means it's all free. We have volunteers who run it".

"That's so fucking cool", thought Real-Gary.

As they entered through the front doors, they were hit with the sounds of a place busting with life. It was a very large open room, with pool and table tennis tables, as well as lots of types of seating. There were beanbags, lounges and short and long tables. Real-Gary noticed that he couldn't see any poker machines.

"Hey Drew, what's the latest brew?", Al chuckled to the bartender, as he approached the bar.

"It never gets old for you, does it", Drew smirked in return. "We've just got the next batch of Pale Ale hooked up. You'll love it".

"Okay, make it three", Al ordered, without consulting the other two.

They received their beers, and Al led them to the back courtyard. "I'm keen for a smoke too", he advised them.

Out the back was lots of seating amongst plentiful greenery. There were lush rainforest plants mixed in various herbs, vegetables and fruits. "Hey boys", Al shot across to a group playing some poker. Both Gary and Rex nodded their heads and tilted their glass towards them as a nonverbal hello, which the boys did in return.

Al sat down in the cane chair section, which encouraged Gary and Rex to mirror. He took a metal cigarette container out of a pocket inside his jacket and opened it up. Inside were manually rolled smokes that looked like joints. He took one out and sparked it, filling the air with a sweet cannabis smell.

Rex initiated a new conversation. "So I did a heap of research about this place before we moved, but there's still so much I don't understand, obviously. I mean, free alcohol. If I knew that I probably would have moved here a long time ago", he said with a smirk.

"Yeah, so many benefits", Al responded with a cheeky grin, after taking a long draw of his joint. "It's amazing. I've been here for nearly five years and it's been a blast. The food is healthy and the community is supportive. There's still a fair bit of bickering and small-mindedness that goes on, but it's a great place to live".

As Al passed the spliff to Rex, Real-Gary decided he wanted to hear how it all came about, so he took over for a short moment. "It's amazing how it all started", he said, using reverse psychology.

Rex had a perplexed look, which prompted Al. "Do you know how it happened?"

"Sort of, not really", Rex answered.

"Nailed it", thought Real-Gary.

"It was after the infamous Pope speech", Al began. "The discussion on freedom and what it actually meant became really common. There was a widespread movement to make individuals in power accountable for the harmful impacts imposed by contract and corporate law, such as the health detriments of forced medications, electromagnetic pollution and even the money-creation process itself. It led to many people understanding how the legal and government systems actually worked, including that governments were literally corporations. Plus, they knew it was all fake money. This generally resulted in them in changing their lives, including quitting their shitty jobs, eliminating their contracts with the system and working with local, ethical businesses. There was an increasing shame towards those who hoarded money and resources too. More people in society were saying 'serious the fuck, don't you want to live your life with a bit of respect for yourselves, your human family and your environment?' So a big catalyst was when people who had made a fair bit of money throughout their lives started to buy their own land to get back to a more natural lifestyle in smaller communities".

"Like Drew's father, Ben", elaborated Gary. "He was one of the first who came to The Web. He made a fuckload of cash in real estate and stocks, then sold it all to help build here. He helped set up the first cooperative, as well as the pub and the gardens. He's a living legend around here".

"It was people like Ben who really got the ball rolling", continued Al. "Don't get me wrong, it had been building for decades, but when big money began to do it, suddenly more people paid attention. Permaculture actually ended up becoming a fad, in a sense. Grow your own food, become more self-reliant, disconnect from the control mechanisms and connect with nature and community instead. It really took off. As more and more people realised they had enough money to do the same, they did. Then it seriously snowballed. It was funny actually, because it became cool to get away from the rat race and create an abundance of health and love and purpose in your life. So sad, really, because that's how it always should have been. At the end of the day though it was one of the best trends that ever happened".

"Awesome, I wonder how many people live in cities now?", Real-Gary pondered to himself.

"It's unstoppable now", Al continued, like he had read Gary's thought. "I think the latest figures are that on average city populations have shrunk over half their size, which isn't bad since it's only been a decade since it all began. The younger generations are still going there to make some money, which softens the blow a bit, although many of them get fed up with it after a short time. I love how many senseless jobs disappeared too, forcing people to leave. They were lucky, really. All those new communities being built, so they needed help".

"They were also welcomed into established places that were fairly self-organised and could care for them, like this one", added Gary.

"Best thing that could have happened to them", perpetuated Al. "Imagine working your whole life in a job that you hate just to be a debt-slave to the banks to pay off an overpriced mortgage. Fuck that. They're lucky the workforce was purged of all those junk roles".

"It really couldn't have happened without three key ingredients" included Gary. "Number one was the localised food systems and second was hemp making such a colossal comeback. The third which came later was the expansion of cryptoservices and community currencies and banks. Those three processes really helped to make each community much more independent. They didn't have to rely on the global economy, at least nowhere near as much. If only we could sort out the energy issue, we'd be basically free from external control".

"Yeah the energy challenge is definitely a big one. Plus, the open-source revolution deserves a mention too", added Al. "It was really integral that everybody have better access to the information required to cheaply build and repair the infrastructure and machinery we desperately needed to supply our own resources".

"I love all the community gardens and street food", joined in Rex. "No multinational chains shipping money overseas, just healthy, organic food in abundance. Love it!"

"Yeah, everyone gets free food and we sell the surplus to the city. It helps fund more projects and programs. You've seen the big garden here, but there's at least four other ones too", identified Gary.

"So Al was saying", replied Rex. "It all seems a little surreal, actually. I remember when it first started. The media and government were mocking it, calling it Hippie 2.0. That's why I never really figured out what the catalyst was. They pushed their propaganda to keep us from understanding it. But with so many people making the transition, they couldn't hide it from those who were interested. It drove a lot of people to engage with the independent media, actually. That's what I did, at least a little".

Rex scratched behind his ear and then continued. "My sister, who lives at the end of the valley, was huge in helping me to understand what was so good about it. I remember thinking that it all sounded totally stupid, at least at the start. But once many of the government departments had to downsize or shut down because tax revenues imploded and there was less for them to do, it all started making more sense. And once I heard that small towns were running their own show, and not abiding by Federal and State legislation, I really started to pay attention to what was going on".

"How good are we when we work together", injected Gary. "Local communities just started building their houses and gardens wherever the fuck they wanted. It was boss. They were mostly smart about it though, and made sure they were safe to not invite any legitimate criticism. Eventually properties began to merge with each other and shared spaces just got bigger and bigger".

Rex handed Gary the joint for a second time, which Real-Gary had only just noticed. He was so enthralled by the conversation that he didn't recognise the first time Gary had smoked it. As he took some more puffs, Real-Gary realised how stoned he already was. "It feels more like a body-stone", he said to himself, before acknowledging the irony of the statement.

"Speak to me, Gary", said the Voice out of nowhere, startling him a little.

"You're back", he replied, sounding a little disappointed.

And suddenly, Gary was gone.

CHAPTER 15

Teacher

"Are you serious?", Gary said in a fiery tone. "That was just starting to get interesting!"

"Why do you assume it was me?", countered the Voice.

"Because you interrupted the conversation!", he barked.

"Whose experience is this?", the Voice laughed.

Gary felt a bit silly upon reflection, but he still had a burning question. "Why didn't you let me make changes to the choices I made?"

"Who said I'm stopping you?", he countered again, with escalating sincerity.

"Oh shit", Gary smirked, privately to himself. "This is my experience, Gary. The Voice is probably part of my subconscious or something. After all, I'm stuck in a video game or I'm dreaming or whatever the fuck this is, but it's not really real. Well, I don't think it is".

Gary deliberated for a few moments. "So where do I go from here? I need to figure out the next step. I'm on the right track, but more needs to be done". He recalled when Gary had said to Apollo that many people felt lost and confused and had fallen back into poor habits.

"They need to learn to rediscover themselves!", he shouted to the Voice.

Wheels. Lights. Action.

He woke up in a bed, like he had just been dreaming. "Not this again", he thought. As he threw off the sheets and put on the trackies and boots that were next to the bed, it was clear that he didn't know where he was. "I hope I'm back in the previous incarnation".

He realised he was once again a version of himself, so he took a backseat and let Gary take the reins whilst he tried to make sense of his experience. After the standard shit, shower and shave, he got dressed in some causal clothes and headed into the kitchen.

Whilst he made a coffee Real-Gary admired the rustic nature of his home. It was made of wood and concrete just like the other building. It made him wonder if it was the hempcrete that Adam had spoken of. It had an earthy vibe with greens, browns and creams dominating the design, and various ornaments, artworks and sculptures were in abundance. Beautifully patterned blankets covered the back of the lounges, which looked very artistic.

The living area was relatively large, just like the bedroom. There were two other bedrooms, but he hadn't seen in them. The kitchen was simple, but practical. Through the window he could see a huge water-tank with a passionfruit vine covering it. There were lots of bees and butterflies and birds doing their thing, especially because of the flowers that seemed to be purposely placed. The deep green foliage was also stunningly intense, making him a little jealous after growing up in what now seemed a stale suburbia.

Gary went out to a small garden to pick some herbs in the early morning light. He cooked up some vegetables, then ate whilst reading a local newspaper. They both read an article which centred on a community education day that was planned the following week. What drew Real-Gary's attention was the mention of a new educator that had just moved to town.

His name was Aaron Mack. He was determined to meet him, but couldn't see how given it was a week till the event. "Let's see if I can randomly run into him", he thought to himself, before realising the paradoxical nature of his word choice. "I'll set my intention to bump into him when I go into centre street".

Gary finished his breakfast and washed up his dishes. He then grabbed his bag and headed to his car parked in the dirt driveway. On the journey through thick forest, Real-Gary could see greenhouses of various sizes in the neighbouring properties. As he was trying to see into one out of the corner of Gary's eye, the car brakes were engaged with a jolt, with the car slightly skidding on the dirt road as it came to a stop.

"Hello", said Gary. "Need some help?"

"I'm almost done", said a fit-looking man in his fifties. "I could do with some water, though", he continued as he wiped his sweat from his brow. "Dry as".

As he sprung out of the car, Real-Gary watched the man do up the remaining nuts on the wheel he had just changed. Gary reached into the back of his vehicle and pulled out a large bottle of water.

"Here ya go", he said, as the man stood up after tightening the last nut.

"Cheers", he replied, before taking a long skull. He wiped his mouth with his sleeve, which removed the remaining water and gunk on his lips from building up a thirst. "I'm Aaron. Just moved here a few days ago".

"Gary", he responded, as he held out his hand for a handshake.

"Fucking hilarious. Had to be a smartass!", Real-Gary laughed to himself, believing that he had manifested Aaron in a cheeky way. This was another deeply empowering moment for him, though. He felt a profound magical feeling, like he was wrapped in reverence.

"I was just reading about you in the paper. I live a k up the road".

"I'm about three k's out. Just heading for a bit of exploration", Aaron said with enthusiasm.

Real-Gary quickly capitalised on the opportunity. "I'd be happy to show you around and introduce you to some people if you don't have any specific plans?"

"Sure, why not. I've been looking forward to meeting new people".

"There's so much to do, but how about we start with a walk up Mount Voice", Gary suggested, stepping back into the driver's seat of his own body.

"Mount Voice", Real-Gary chuckled to himself. "Nothing surprises me anymore".

"It's beautiful this early in the morning", Gary continued. "It's only half an hour there and back once we drive up to the top".

"You read my mind", agreed Aaron. "It was on the to-do list today".

"Excellent. Do you want to follow me back to my house so I can get some proper shoes?"

"Yeah, sure. After you", Aaron said eagerly.

Doing a U-turn, Gary headed back home with Aaron following closely behind. In a flash they were back in the driveway. "Come in, check out my pad", invited Gary.

As they entered the front door, Aaron was more than impressed with the energy of it. "Very nice. Great vibrations. Did you decorate it yourself?"

"Yep. Healthy home, healthy mind. Can I get you some more water, or a tea?"

"No, I'm fine thanks. I'm just going to duck into your bathroom".

"Door on the right", said Gary, pointing down the hallway.

Gary got together some additional items for the trip and packed it into his bag. As he finished putting on his hiking boots, Aaron walked out of the bathroom. "Let's hit it".

As they got into Aaron's car and drove towards Mount Voice, they talked about their past lives before the relocation began. Gary admired how down to earth and intelligent he was. He had a swagger about him too.

Around five minutes later, they had reached the foot of the mountain. "A few minutes and we'll be at the walking track", he informed Aaron.

"Great. So what occupies your days here?"

"I'm a mentor for some of the kids, I work in the garden regularly, and I just help out with various projects.

For example, I helped build a new property a couple of weeks ago".

"Sounds great. Diverse work. And I love the mentoring gig", he responded.

"Yeah, it's actually fun. I wouldn't even call it work. I've got a lot of free time to do what I want as well. We're encouraged to be creative and artistic here".

Real-Gary realised an opportunity had gone by, but tried to recover it. "There's a big challenge when it comes to helping people though. It's like we need to rediscover ourselves. Re-educate ourselves properly. We were so poorly educated in the materialist slash consumerist paradigm that we had ignored so much stuff about who we really are. And we lack so many life skills, it's almost unbelievable. Many people who relocated are still very unhealthy in the mind too. They've fallen into old programs instead facing themselves and evolving accordingly".

"Your finger is on the button Gary", Aaron replied supportively. "This is exactly what I have been trying to do in my work. I have been helping individuals and communities to empower themselves. For the last three years I've been travelling to various locations all over the world and teaching a program I created, called 'Illumity'. It's a combination of illuminate and community. It's specifically designed to liberate individuals from their internal conflict and connect them better to themselves, so they personally thrive. This helps the community ecosystem to do the same. It's great that many people have expanded their own consciousness in many ways, but it needs to be done on more of a widespread scale. Otherwise the collective consciousness on both local and planetary levels struggles to expand with efficiency".

This information was just what Real-Gary was hoping to hear. "What are the key principles?"

The car winded around to the left and they reached the end of the road. "A conversation for the mountain", Aaron noted, with a spiritual tone.

They exited the vehicle and put on their jackets, given how cool it was. Aaron grabbed their water bottles and put them in his backpack. "You ready?", he asked eagerly.

Gary nodded his head and led them towards the walking track. They couldn't see the top of the mountain from where they were, because a lavish canopy hung high overhead. They were completely surrounded with tropical rainforest that was rich in bird and other life. The forest floor was layered with rebellious seedlings pushing through fungi and decomposing plant material, symbolising the cycle of death and rebirth.

"Illumity is a simple map towards self-realisation and community vitality, Gary", Aaron reinitiated the conversation, as they began to take on a steep incline. "It's interesting that you asked what the key principles are, because there are five values that drive the entire program. They are Health, Abundance, Creativity, Sovereignty and Unity, or HACSU for short. Each one has its own subcategories, but they essentially cover the entire process".

"HAC-SU", Real-Gary repeated to Aaron. "Sounds like 'Hacks You'. Was that on purpose?"

"No, actually. I've never said it like that before. Excellent pick up. That's what the program does in a way. It hacks the 'conditioned you' to free the 'real you' for your own benefit, and the benefit of your human family".

"How do you know who the real version is?"

"The principles do it in two ways", Aaron began to explain. "First they identify commonalities between all of us. It doesn't matter your age, place of birth, religion, any of that, we all share some very basic stuff. The other way is that it guides how to find and create the real you, not define it for you".

"I like it. So an example of a common thread might be that we all have an innate right to be free, and an example of our unique qualities is how we choose to be free?", Real-Gary said, with mix of certainty and apprehension.

"You've pretty much just summed up the core of the syllabus", chuckled Aaron, slightly out of breath. "We're going to work well together".

The track had funnelled into a single lane by this point, where Gary took the lead. The air had a sweet fragrance in it, which balanced out a mildewy smell. It was damp and foggy, but the sun managed to break through the foliage at various places. The gaps through the trees also gave them slight glimpses of the valley.

"Have a look at that", exclaimed Gary, pointing towards the best view of the walk so far. "Just wait, too. It's even more magnificent up top".

"Enchanting", Aaron responded.

They continued the ascent after they'd caught their breath for a few seconds. "Okay, so let's start with health. Why is it so important that it gets its own category?"

"Health is the foundation for change", commenced Aaron. "It's one of the biggest barriers that we face in creating the next level for humanity. The reality is understanding our health leads to understanding ourselves. It's pretty fucking simple, really. Just take good care of yourself. The complex part is that there is so much to our health. It's not just physical, but mental and spiritual health too. Actually, it can be broken into many layers, which I'll unpack in a sec. But an important aspect to remember is that when we aim to increase our health and vitality, which effectively means 'to grow', we need to address the conscious and subconscious layers otherwise it's not a holistic approach".

He took a couple of deep breaths, and then continued. "These all interrelate, but physical health is the base level. We don't need to be super fit or anything, but at the least we need to eat well and engage in some stretching and exercise. Then there's psychological health, which means thinking in functional and productive ways. Philosophical health deals with our beliefs and dogmas, and emotional health deals with stress, trauma, anxiety and all that other not-so-fun stuff. Then there's spiritual health, which doesn't mean we need to believe in God or even a higher power, but we do need to honour our connection to ourselves, each other and reality at large".

At that moment a magpie swooped from the trees and captured what looked like a blue beetle, about five metres in front of them.

"The circle of life", chuckled Real-Gary.

"Magic timing. A representation of interdependence, of connection", remarked Aaron.

He thought to himself for a moment and then continued his spiel. "What I just described are the internal aspects, in a sense. We need to connect with ourselves, including delving into our subconscious to reprogram unhealthy pathways. But there's the practical stuff too. Are we honouring our creative side? Do we have healthy relationships with family and friends, and if not, what can we personally change to make them more functional? That includes our sexual health too, especially men who are lost in a pornographic conception of sex and women who use it for some sort of gain, including feeling good about themselves".

"You're definitely right. There's so much to our health that we haven't been taught that well. So what was the next one? Abundance, right?"

"Yep, this is a tricky one. When some people think of abundance, they only think through a material frame. Like an abundance of food or money or whatever. Whilst access to abundant food and medicine and community support are all very important, so are the intangible things too".

"Like love and a healthy state of mind?", asked Real-Gary.

"Spot on. And the other facet is that it's also a method of thinking and feeling".

"I think I understand. Like thinking abundantly puts out those electromagnetic vibrations into the energetic grid which helps to attract abundance in return", Real-Gary added.

"Wow, summed up perfectly again. So once people begin to look after their health better, they should also think and act more abundantly too, which naturally removes inhibitors like selfishness and greed. That's because it's also about building abundance for each other, because we're connected to each other. It's not just about creating it for the individual, but the community at large too".

"Alright", Real-Gary said, whilst spelling out HACSU in his mind. "Creativity".

"A well overlooked quality of being human", stated Aaron. "We really need to care for ourselves and our world, operate abundantly, and then activate our collective artist! Humanity is ingenious, in so many ways. But the old system stifled our innovation on so many levels because of the way money guided scientific and technological endeavour. Don't misunderstand me though, we did some amazing work, but if it wasn't profitable, it was put on the backseat. Plus, we were all so busy spending two thirds of our lives working and sleeping, so our creative energy was nowhere near unleashed to reach its potential. So creativity needs to be encouraged on both individual and collective scales, without the influence of money. If so, the possibilities are endless!"

The climb had just reached its most difficult point because it was the steepest part and there were huge boulders to navigate between. Accordingly, they both stopped for a quick rest and a drink of water.

"This is great stuff, Aaron. I'm really happy I ran into you, it was exactly what I needed".

"Ditto Gary".

To their right was another gap in the trees, showing off a big portion of the valley. There were small towns built all the way through it, with various pockets utilised for agricultural and other purposes. The difference that really stood out for Real-Gary is that it still looked very natural, like humans and nature were working in unison with each other.

"So, Sovereignty. Let me take a stab at this one", Real-Gary continued, as they began to venture through bolder city. "If a person honours the Sovereignty in themselves, such as what it means to be truly free, then they will naturally honour it everyone else too. Simply, all interactions with each other need to be based on this mutual recognition and respect".

"You got it", Aaron approved. "The Pope's speech really was eye-opening, wasn't it?"

Real-Gary nodded, without saying a word. He was a little embarrassed and proud at the same time.

They climbed over a rock that was hiding the next phase of the climb. "We're very close", Gary advised him, accompanied by a large smile.

"And the last one is Unity. As you could probably tell, health sort of permeates all the principles, including the health of our cooperation. We are really close to accomplishing this, especially in places like The Web", segued Aaron. "Whilst it's fundamentally important to respect each other's Sovereignty, it's equally important to respect the fact that without each other, we wouldn't be here. It takes more than one person to experience being in love. It takes more than one person to have a baby. It takes more than one person to form a community. And it takes more than one person to evolve a species. Plus, on top of that, we are interdependent with all life on earth. Our ecological connection, our Unity with nature, is vital. So as much as we need to celebrate Sovereignty, we need to do the same with Unity".

"Here here", Gary proclaimed.

They had just approached a massive rock that was half embedded into the earth. There was a small cliff that seemed to encircle the entire peak of the mountain, so the rock appeared as the most efficient way to reach the top. It was rough, not smooth, so there were plenty of areas to grip onto.

Gary took the lead in climbing, just after giving Aaron a look that said, "wait till you see this".

"Hacks You", Aaron laughed out loud, as that memory came back into focus. "That's a good one, can't believe I never noticed it".

He followed Gary up the rock which was around five metres high, whilst still continuing the discussion. "We need to open our minds and hearts so that we not just learn from others, but empower ourselves to be our own teacher", he said, with a huff and a puff.

After inhaling deeply, he continued. "We need to be able to change anything about ourselves that does not serve us, or others, regardless if it's so deeply wired that it's a massive challenge to do so", he stated, as he climbed a difficult part of the rock.

He looked up to see what the best way was to climb, then proceeded. "And we need to ensure our values and principles are a primary focus in each of our lives, so humanity can take the next step in its evolution".

As he finished his sentence he pulled himself over the edge and raised himself to stand next to Gary. The sun had just penetrated though a white fluffy cloud and was shining spectacularly onto both of them, like a beam from a lighthouse. The sky was saturated with an abundance of rich colours that were just beginning to fade, as the dawn became day. The valley was laced with a foggy haze that was illuminated as a deep orange from the angle of the sun. Smoke from littered chimneys swirled in the light breeze. Birds raced across the valley chasing and playing with each other. It was a picture of reverence.

"Well, you're right again Gary", Aaron celebrated. "This is amazing. Thank you for bringing me here".

"Believe me, the pleasure is all mine", Real-Gary replied.

After sitting for a while soaking in the serenity, they headed back to the car. They chatted about various topics, including unpacking the 'Illumity' package further. Not long after they had arrived at the bottom of the mountain, Gary's phone rang. He looked at his screen and it was Al, so he answered it.

"Fuck, this is crazy", Al said with deep concern.

"What are you talking about, mate?", he replied.

"Oh shit man, don't you know? It's all over the news. There's a group that call themselves 'The Skulls'. They've hacked into government computers from all over the world and are holding us at ransom. If their demands are not met they say they'll start dropping nukes".

At that moment a deer ran across the road in front of the car, which shocked Aaron into swerving away from it. The car veered off the road at speed, which resulted in him hitting the breaks as hard as he could. Real-Gary's experience of time slowed right down, but it was too late for him to do anything. They were headed straight for a tree that looked strikingly familiar, like the one he had climbed in his brother's body.

And suddenly, Gary was gone.

CHAPTER 16

Healer

"Fuck, where am I?", Gary asked himself, hazily. As he lifted his head he realised it had been cushioned from the collision by an air bag. "Shit, I'm still here".

He looked next to him and Aaron was making some sounds, like he was in pain. "Aaron? Aaron? You okay?"

"Arr, fuck. I'm not sure. I think so", he murmured, as he regained consciousness.

Gary exited the car and circled around the back to the driver's seat. Before he opened the door he could hear his phone ringing again, which he assumed it would be Al. He pulled strongly on the door, which took a bit of work to open, and helped Aaron to sit up. "Is there anything broken?"

"It doesn't feel like it". Gary helped him to stand on his feet as he guided him out of the car. "Yeah, I think I'm fine. Just a bit woozy. I'm so sorry Gary, I shouldn't have swerved".

"It's okay mate. We're okay".

At that moment Gary felt more like himself than he ever

had. He tried to let Gary back into control but he wasn't there. "Does that mean I'm just me?", he asked himself.

The two of them drank some water and sat down to recover. "I'm feeling okay. Do you need to go to the hospital?", he asked Aaron.

"No, I'll be fine. Can't say the same about the car, though", he answered with a smirk.

"You can replace a car, but you can't replace a body", Gary replied, before realising the irony of what he had said.

Gary thought about the conversation with Al, realising he better inform Aaron about it. He quickly explained what Al had told him, but before either of them could comment the sound of a vehicle startled them as it came from around a corner, sneaking up behind them. It came to a swift stop and a lady of about sixty years of age opened the door.

"You guys okay?", she asked with alarm.

"Yeah, we're not hurt, just a little shaken", replied Gary, as he heard his phone ring again.

"Let me take a look at you two", she said warmly. "I'm an energy worker".

"This should be interesting", Gary thought to himself.

She walked over to them and closed her eyes. After half a minute she began talking. "The accident has left no serious issues, but there's something I need to explore further in you", she said, whilst opening her eyes to look directly into Gary's. "My home is a few minutes away. Can I take you both there for some herbal tea and to rest for a while?"

Aaron looked at Gary who nodded in approval. "That would be great", confirmed Aaron. "I'll call the Service to let them know we've had an accident, but that everyone is okay".

Gary grabbed their belongings from the car, including his phone which was on the dashboard, and made his way to her vehicle. "What's your name?", he asked the woman.

"I'm Valentine, Val for short", she replied. "And yours?"

"Gary. And this is Aaron. He's new to town".

"Nice to meet you both. I'm new too. I've been here for two months now. Absolutely love it".

"Me too", agreed Aaron, in a slightly unsteady way. "Need to work out the roads a bit better, though", he continued in a light-hearted manner.

They all entered the car and put on their seatbelts. Aaron pulled his phone from his bag and dialled a number, whilst Gary texted Al to let him know what happened and that he'll call him later.

After he sent the message, he began racking his brain about what was happening. "I'm now stuck in a world that I created", he thought to himself. He then thought about Elle, which made him feel sick. He got really scared that he was never going to see her again.

"Voice? Are you there?", he asked, internally. No answer.

"Exit Game". No change.

"Reset". Nothing.

"I want to go back to the island!", he pleaded, with no result.

This sent him into a spin. He contemplated if the whole experience was a dream, which seemed more and more plausible as he navigated the memories of Gary. "I can remember all of his experience. I can remember his childhood, his first kiss. I can remember so much of his life. But I can also remember Elle and my previous life. What the fuck is going on with me? Am I crazy? Was all that a dream?"

"They're going to send a pick-up truck out to take it back to the mechanics. This integrated community thing really is top notch", said Aaron, interrupting Gary's thoughts.

"Yes it is, or at least what I've experienced so far", agreed Val. "My husband and I lived in the city our whole lives, up until recently. We were going to move sooner but we felt we had some healing and clearing work to do. Finally we felt the timing was right, so we just packed up and left. He's already out for the day, but our two cats and two dogs are holding the fort for us", she said with a smile.

Val slowed down to a near stop to take a bumpy exit to the left. It was a dirt driveway which winded through thick bush. There was no house in sight for the first two hundred metres, but then it appeared along with an opening in the trees. "Welcome to my castle", Val said with soft pride.

Two dogs that looked like small wolves came racing out to greet them. "No jumping!", directed Val.

Once they entered inside Val pointed to the lounges, indicating them to sit. "I'll make us some tea. It still should be hot".

Gary looked around and was struck by the artistry that saturated her home. It felt really sacred, like it was alive. He noticed the geometric shapes that dominated the paintings. They were also woven into blankets and other fabrics too. It reminded him of the symbols that materialised in the portal when the Voice spoke, some which looked very much the same.

"Here you go", Val said, handing them each a cup of tea. "Have you heard the news about The Skulls?"

"Yes, Gary told me briefly", replied Aaron. "What's wrong with people?", he continued, with disdain.

"I wouldn't worry", she said confidently. "It's most likely another false flag designed to inject fear into the masses so they re-enter the toxic relationship with the power centre. They're really pissed that we don't want to participate in their little game of control. After all, if we don't play, they don't get paid", she said, with a chuckle.

"What if it's not?", asked Gary, referring to the false flag.

"Well, there's nothing we can do about it", she replied. "Except of course summon and emit the right energy in our own lives. Just stay positive and send out good vibes into the greater grid".

"That's not going to help if they pull the trigger", Gary replied sceptically.

"If that's the future of this timeline, then it is what it is", she countered. "I get it, we need to be realistic. But, what is reality? I know it's much more than just this little experience. So I don't see anything wrong with people putting out good energy, regardless of how dire it might seem. We know it works, too. There's been so many experiments where groups of people have meditated for a specific purpose, and it helped to create it. If enough of us do that then it might actually manifest what we desire".

"Fuck I miss Elle", Gary thought to himself, after hearing the word desire.

"The world needs to heal in so many ways", Val continued. "Humanity needs to heal. We've got so much collective trauma wired deep into our DNA and energetic fields. We've been corrupted on so many levels, and I wouldn't doubt if this is partly why many of us have incarnated here, to help heal it".

"What do you mean, corrupted?", asked Aaron.

"The story of humanity is much more rich than what we've been taught. And I'm not just talking about the unknown history of civilisation on this planet, either. It's really difficult to understand the truth, but it's very much possible that we are not exactly from this earth. For starters, the chance of life evolving here randomly in the time that it has, is phenomenally large. The mathematics just doesn't add up, indicating at the very least non-random processes are very much part of evolution itself, which might be facilitated by the conscious and subconscious 'intentions' of all lifeforms. But let's put that to the side and consider the irrefutable links not just between different animal kinds, but also between humans and their so-called ancestors as well. Simply, there are little to none".

Val looked at the boys who had strange looks on their faces. She took a sip of her tea, and then continued.

"I know that's hard to hear for some people, but the supporting evidence is nowhere to be found. It's simply guesswork. So there might be something else we're missing, like an intervention or a creative force. There are competing theories about it, which generally fall into several camps. I don't pretend to know the absolute truth, because I don't believe any of us really do know. Not the scientists, nor the meta-physicists or spiritualists. Not even the ancient cultures, who all had their unique take on it. So what I'm about to say are merely the competing views about it. The first is that this 3rd dimensional construct is a holographic computer simulation. You'd be surprised at how many academics, scientists and people in general believe this too. And considering we're very close to developing the computing power necessary to create a virtual reality that resembles this exact experience, the likelihood that it has already happened is so much higher than this being the moment before it happens. That and a specific type of computer code is naturally embedded in certain equations too".

Gary's mind started spinning, which led to an image of Elle.

"The second", she persisted, "is that extra-terrestrials or multidimensional beings came here and tampered with life on our planet, including mixing our DNA with theirs. That would mean we're literally aliens ourselves. Some people believe these entities are benevolent, some believe they're malevolent, and others believe there's many that visit us and they're a mixture of both good and bad".

An image of the Voice occupied Gary's mind.

"And the third is that we were created as humans from the start. Like an experiment. We could have been placed on this planet to be studied, or for another purpose. This could be orchestrated by other beings in this universe, or by a being or beings outside of this universe. It could also be that something of a divine nature just decided to create us, which also manifested the so-called history of the universe at the same time".

Gary and Aaron looked at each in a mix of amazement and scepticism.

"Or all of them could be true as their own frequency", laughed Val, with a witchy, but friendly cackle.

"What do you mean?", Aaron asked bewilderedly.

"There are some key ingredients to this reality", she

replied swiftly. "Consciousness appears as fundamental, but then so does information and energy. Or put another way, spirit. They could all be the same thing but just a different way of describing it, or just different levels of the same thing. Regardless, there are all types of fields pulsing around us. There are also various states of energy such as light and sound, which are energetic waveforms. They have their own frequencies too. Think about how musical notes are different vibrations or sounds on a spectrum. Each sound has its own frequency, which means it is different than others on one level and the same on another. That's like reality at large. For example, the frequency of visible light is an extremely small aspect on the electromagnetic spectrum. I can't remember the exact percentage, but it's zero point zero zero something. Essentially this means we see so little of what's really out there".

She took another sip of her tea, which seemed like a peculiarly long time to Gary.

"So the same can be applied on a grander scale", Val continued, giving off a powerful feel. "Think about yourself as a radio or TV. You're tuned into a particular channel, which is co-manifested by your core force and your body-brain. That channel is consciously in a third dimensional construct where you were born in a particular location with a particular body, where you've had particular experiences and you're in this particular moment. That's your channel. But just because you're experiencing your own unique frequency, that doesn't mean there aren't an infinite amount of other frequencies, or channels, existing all around you. Sometimes we can tune in differently, like when we meditate or consume psychedelics, but generally our frequency is pretty consistent".

"Well, that's a headfuck", responded Gary with a cheeky smile, whilst thinking about the double frequency he was experiencing in that moment.

"Tell me about it", she said with a burst of laughter. "So when it comes to whether we are aliens or Gods or an extension of a cosmic or divine mind, they all could be true on their own frequency, regardless if they contradict each other when compared on the same level. Or put another way, there might be objective or absolute truths in each construct or frequency of reality, but they might not apply in other layers of existence. In fact, each individual filter of consciousness might be sharing certain frequencies with other perspectives, but have different ones as well, meaning we all have a unique collection of absolute and relative truths. That's the 'Many Truths Theory'. And given that a lot of our beliefs are guesswork, I don't invest too much time and energy in just one aspect, I just do what I can in my moment to live as authentically as I can by embodying all of it the best I can".

"Well, I'd like to bloody know", Gary thought privately.

Val, Aaron and Gary drank some more of their tea, sitting in silence for a moment. Gary had the feeling that it must be important to tell Val about his experience, so he worked up the courage.

"I think I need to tell you something", he began. "You probably won't believe this, but here it goes anyway. I'm from a different timeline, or frequency as you put it. At least I think I am. I was with my girlfriend and we started playing a virtual reality game. I got lost in the game and ended up in this body, which is another version of myself. After the crash this morning I was no longer experiencing this version of Gary, I was this version. I can remember both lives right now, this one and my other one".

Val had a look on her face like she had just seen a ghost, but then started laughing. "You little terror, you almost had me for a sec".

"Yeah, good one", smirked Aaron.

"I'm not joking, guys". Gary started to explain his experience, beginning from the start. It took him over half an hour just to describe the basic storyline.

"And so after you showed up, I've been trying to work out if it was all a dream or if I'm really both Gary's and stuck in this reality".

"I believe you, Gary", Val said supportively. "No one could make that story up. The blockage I saw in you must be related to it all".

"What blockage?", Gary asked, with a curious tone.

"My focus rests primarily in healing. Healing myself, and helping others to heal themselves. Before, when I closed my eyes and looked at you two, I saw a misty haze of various colours. It sort of looks like an aura. I've been seeing it since I was child so I knew part of my life purpose from very early on. I've been doing it in a professional capacity for over three decades, so I thought I'd more or less seen it all. But when I saw the blockage in you, it took me by surprise".

"What did you see?", Gary asked.

"I saw a blockage near your head and heart. There were two separate components, but they were connected somehow. Their shapes, their behaviour, was nothing like I've seen. I'm not sure what it means".

"Can you help me?", Gary enquired, in a hopeful pitch.

"I don't know. I can try to free it. What I usually do is clear it in my mind's eye, which in effect clears it in a person's energetic or etheric field. I hum too, to find the frequency that will heal it. But that's not the full process. If the person doesn't change their diet or undertake psychotherapy, regardless if it's self-administered or guided by a professional, then the blockage sometimes returns. What I've realised over the years is that sometimes they stem from a person's DNA or genetics, or even a parallel life, but most of the time it is driven from their subconscious programming. It's like only treating the wounds of someone who self-mutilates. If you don't help remedy the part that drives them to do it, then no amount of tending to the wounds will stop future mutilation from occurring".

"Exactly", agreed Aaron. "That's basically the process I've been encouraging in people. Work out what the fuck is causing the problem and restructure yourself in response".

"Pretty simple when you put it like that", noted Gary. "Okay, so if the blockage manifests from something deeper, it potentially can be treated by someone life yourself, Val. But if it's because of a person's neurological wiring or psychological design, what's the point of clearing the blockage at all if it's just going to come back?"

"Think about it in these terms", Val began her answer. "Sometimes certain medications, preferably herbal and non-toxic, can help balance out the neurotransmitter production in the body and brain of someone who has a mental dysfunction, such as depression or anxiety. But if they don't get to the core of the issue, the trauma or whatever it is which is causing the problem, then no amount of these substances are going to cure it. If the chemicals are balanced out a bit though, then their depression or anxiety isn't as extreme, meaning they're in a better state to actually deal with the issues. So, it's the same with clearing blockages. If their energy field is being disrupted by their wiring somehow, then clearing those blockages can help them to be in a better energy state, which will help them to actually deal with the real issues".

Gary's awareness was suddenly focused on something the Voice had said to him: "Programming is really difficult to overcome, Gary. The power of the subconscious and its neurological wiring is phenomenal. It takes so much introspection and a repetitive shift in behaviours to actually create sustained change".

"Okay, before we do it, I want to understand something", Gary said, redirecting his attention back to Val. "What is self-administered psychotherapy and how is it done?"

"Ah, I'll take that one if you don't mind Val?", interjected Aaron, with Val nodding at him with a smile. "That's an easy one. Psychotherapy is simply treating dysfunctions or disorders of the mind without using any drugs or substances. Self-administered is doing that yourself, instead of engaging a so-called professional to do it. So for example, if you realise you're too angry, like you trigger really easy or something like that, then once you change it that's self-administered psychotherapy in action".

Aaron drank some water that Val had placed on the coffee table whilst Gary was telling them his story.

"To change it is easy in theory, but much harder to do in practice", he continued. "The conscious part of our mind is tiny compared to the subconscious. Yet, when we remember something, that is the subconscious becoming conscious.

The subconscious isn't always in the dark, but most of it is, most of the time. The analogy I like to use is visualising yourself outside on a dark night with a little torch. Where you shine the light, that is what you're conscious of".

He closed his eyes in unison with a deep breath, like he was centering himself. "So when we want to heal ourselves we need to shine that light into places that need to be healed. Not only do we need to be conscious of the actual issues, but we also need to bring into resonance our brain and heart fields. That's why meditation is so effective, as are certain psychedelics. They help bring to light areas that need healing, as well as bring the body into a healthy harmony. And when I say healing, I mean two things: first is attaching more healthy emotions and philosophies to traumatic and dysfunctional memories, and the second is identifying and resolving poorly designed neurological and philosophical infrastructure".

"Sounds hard in theory too", grinned Gary.

"Let me put it more simply", Aaron continued. "If we want to heal, we need to figure out what the problem is and then change it. When we do find it, we need to implement the change and then keep repeating it, otherwise we're likely to go back to the old pattern or behaviour. So when it comes to the anger example, once I decide I want to be less angry I need to maintain it. Sometimes I will get angry, and that's okay, but I'll need to remind myself that I need to be less angry, and then do it. Then I'll need to repeat over and over again until I'm wired to be less angry in general".

Aaron took another sip of his water and continued. "I can't emphasise how important it is to continually repeat over a long period of time. Of course we'll go back to old pathways sometimes, but all we need to do is recognise it and then shift back to our desired direction. Let me frame it within another analogy. Just say the old pathway of poorly managed anger is a well-worn walking track through the forest. It's easy to walk, because the track is well cleared. So when we want to create a new path, we need to use a machete to slash away at the branches and shrubs. The first time we walk it will be a serious effort, but the more we keep doing it the more the path becomes cleared and easier to navigate. Eventually it will become our primary path, whilst the old path is being reclaimed by the forest at the same time. This is exactly how the body-brain can be permanently changed, by forging new behavioural pathways and then maintaining them.

"That's called neuroplasticity, right?"

"Yes, our neurological pathways can change if repetitively forced to do so. When we're younger, our brain naturally grows which is why it's easy for kids to learn new stuff. They're like a sponge, absorbing new information. But when it stops growing, it's much harder, which is why most adults are very slow to change their ways. You can teach an old dog new tricks, but it's much harder to do. As an example, when someone who has been overweight for a long time suddenly loses a lot of weight really quickly because of a lot of exercise, they'll most likely put it on just as quick once they stop, even if they're still eating pretty good. Put simply, the programming is still designed to store the fat, so until ongoing exercise and proper eating has been sustained for at least a year or two, the program or pathways are the same. That's why I say to repeat and keep repeating; that's the only way that real change gets programmed into us neurologically and philosophically".

"An exception are certain psychedelics, such as Magic Mushrooms", added Val. "Oh, and definitely Ayahuasca".

She stopped and thought for a moment, looking behind Gary's shoulder in a way which seemed like she was penetrating through the wall.

"It's a shamanic healing plant, well, two plants actually", she continued. "It stems from South America, but there are other similar examples from all over the planet. Many people who have several ceremonies with shamans are able to cure some of their diseases or addictions pretty quickly, because it is a reset or rebirth on so many levels. Energetic. Psychological. Philosophical. Emotional. It gets right to the core and right to the surface. It doesn't always work, but it has a very impressive strike rate. But once again, even if some deep healing does occur, if a person returns to their unhealthy habits and behaviours then similar issues will arise".

"Wildfire said that healing begins with a smile", Gary said in reflection.

"Makes perfect sense", Val agreed. "Turning a frown into a smile is a metaphor for turning a negative into a positive. It's a metaphor for constructive change. They really had it going on, the traditional peoples of this earth. We really need to return to it, in certain ways. In places like The Web we are, because we're rebuilding our tribes and our connection to each other and the earth. Plus, neoshamanic practices are on the rise too".

"Neoshamanic?", questioned Gary.

"Yes, neoshamanism. There are many definitions of it, but the way I like to explain it is that there are many people who either consciously or unconsciously help to heal or transmute the energy of our human tribe, or collective unconscious. They do it within themselves first and foremost, but ultimately it reflects the development needed on a macro scale. Do you remember the 'Power Rangers' cartoon?"

Both Gary and Aaron nodded.

"Well, it's like how the Power Rangers combined to make the big one. No one shaman can accommodate the needs of the planetary tribe, so it takes many thousands of individuals to contribute to the collective shaman. So whilst we unfortunately lost our connection to our clan for many generations, resulting with a lack of initiations for the youth and guidance by the elders, we have been simultaneously building a human culture, a human tribe. And there are people who are working within themselves to make it healthier for the whole".

This reminded Gary of when the Voice had said something very similar, making him feel safe to proceed with Val's clearing. "Well, given all that has happened to me recently, I don't doubt any possibilities anymore. So, let's do it. Let's see if you can unblock me".

"Okay, let's head to the studio. Aaron, are you right to occupy yourself for a little while?"

"I've been eying off your bookcase anyway", he replied, with a grin.

Gary followed Val out the back door to a little room disconnected from the house. Inside were more of the same symbols in various artwork. "What are these symbols?", Gary asked.

"It's called sacred geometry", clarified Val. "They're mathematical or geometric patterns which symbolise how the universe came into creation, as well as how it is structured. It's fractal and magical. I meditate on some of them when I do my work, especially the 'Flower of Life' and 'Metatrons Cube'. I sometimes breathe according to the phi ratio too".

"I really don't know what you just said, but you can tell me about it later", Gary remarked, as he laid down on the massage table, face up. "What do you want me to do?"

"I just want you to try and clear your mind. If you start thinking, try to clear it again. If you have visions that's okay, just let your experience wash over you".

Gary closed his eyes and followed Val's orders. It was dark to begin with, but after a minute or so it exploded with an array of colours. They danced and played like they were alive and showing off to him. He felt like some entered into his body and then exited a different colour. A few minutes later an image of Wildfire emerged through a collage of images from his recent adventure. His face looked concerned, like he was unhappy with him. Then out of his mouth appeared a picture of the Voice, which began to spin anti-clockwise with increasing velocity.

The image moved so quickly that Gary started to feel dizzy. Once it had hit what felt like light speed, it converted into the wheels and colours associated with his journey with the Voice. Slowly it deaccelerated to a less nauseating pace and finished in a tantalising tango with his mind.

And suddenly, Gary was gone.

CHAPTER 17

Craver

"Gary? You there?"

He woke up on the massage table to Val touching him on the shoulder. He felt good, like he had just had a refreshing sleep. "How long was I out?"

"Not long, just over ten minutes. Listen, Gary. I wasn't able to release the blockage. As soon as I would, it would come back. It's too strong. Stronger than anything I have seen before".

His first thought was Elle. "How long will this go on? Am I gonna be stuck here forever?", he thought secretly.

He stood up and gave Val a hug. "Thank you for trying, Val. It means a lot. We might try again some other time if that's okay but for now, there is probably a purpose behind it all", he said, with increasing conviction.

"My pleasure, darl. We can try again whenever you like".

"Thank you. I appreciate it".

They walked back inside, just as Gary's phone rang. "It's already rung twice", informed Aaron. "How'd it go?"

Val answered Aaron's question, whilst Gary raced to pick up his phone. "Hi, Al".

"How's the head, mate?"

"Yeah, I'm all good", he replied, positively. "Not sure if you know her but I just had a session with Valentine. She does work with the energy layers".

"No, I don't think so. Listen Gary, we need your help mate", he said with urgency. "We've got to lock down some of the stuff and make some preparations, in case there's any issues. I'm just picking up Hugh, Rocko and Diana now, but can you pick up Rex and his sister?"

"Yeah sure mate. Where are they?"

"Rex has moved down Archetype Drive. You know, opposite the field?"

"Yeah I think so. Remind me again?"

"Fuck mate, you sure you're head's okay?", he said with a light-hearted laugh. "The road that is adjacent to your place of work", he said, with increasing sarcasm.

"Yeah, gotcha", Gary replied with a fake, but convincing giggle. Gary's memory had just resurfaced, like it was hiding to not overload him. "I'll be there in fifteen".

"Alright, cheers. Its number 1116. See you soon".

"Oh wait, you still there Al?"

"Yeah mate".

"Where are we meeting you after I pick them up?"

"My joint".

"Okay, catch ya".

He hung up the phone and motioned to speak to Aaron and Val, but Val got in first. "All good darling, I'll drive you home now".

Gary and Aaron grabbed their belongings and headed

out the front door and over to Val's car. They strapped in and left quickly, but Gary wasn't paying too much attention because he was lost in deep thought about Elle. Val noticed that he looked a little sad so she sparked up a conversation with him about sacred geometry, explaining some of the fundamentals of the field of study. Just over five minutes later, which felt like a flash, they were pulling in Gary's driveway and parking behind his car.

"Thank you Val. And a big thanks to you too Aaron. I know this all might seem seriously fucking strange to you guys, but believe me, it's even crazier to me. I don't know where this is going to lead, but if I never see you again I just want to say that I'm absolutely stoked I got to meet both of you. Come here, can I get a group hug?", he said, extending his arms.

"Aww", they both replied at once. They reached out their arms and embraced each other for close to ten seconds. "Just a little bit longer", smirked Aaron. "The oxytocin from this hug is just about to be released", he continued, with a slight chuckle.

"You guys are awesome", Gary stated, as they rounded off the embrace. "And if I don't ever leave, then it looks like I've already made some lifelong friends", he continued, whilst straightening out his shirt.

Val teared up a little and reached in for another hug. "Promise me you'll come back tomorrow if you're still here?", she pleaded.

"I sure will", he agreed.

They got back into their car and reversed out, whilst waving goodbye. Gary went inside and picked up a few additional items. Not long after he was in his car, heading towards his destination. It took him a short time to reach it, where he had to make a sharp left turn. The road was dirt but well graded, so he was able to reach good speeds. He rounded a long left turn and to his northeast saw a house with a man and a woman out the front carrying some boxes towards a small pile of them.

He turned into the driveway, which was about fifty metres long. As he pulled up Rex was stacking boxes and his sister had returned inside to retrieve some more.

"Hey Gary, thanks for picking us up, mate", Rex said sincerely. "We're right to pack this into your ute, yeah?"

"No worries at all, mate. What is it?"

"Food supplies, seeds and other equipment. I brought so much with me I figured that I should add some to the prep pile. Pretty freaky what's going on with The Skulls, hey?"

"A friend suggests it's probably just another false flag, but better to be safe, than sorry".

"You've got that right. So stoked I'm here. Wouldn't want to be in a city if some UE's were unleashed. Who knows where they'd hit. Anyway, Al just called and he asked me to come in now to help with the heavy lifting. I'll take my bike in, so are you right to help my sis to sort out the rest of the boxes?"

"Yeah, no problem".

At that moment Rex's sister walked out through the front door with a large box, which she was struggling to carry. Gary jogged over to take it out of her hands. As he took its weight, she appeared from behind it.

"Elle?", he said in a surprised manner, half dropping the box, but catching it before it hit the ground.

"Yes, I'm Elle. Gary, right?"

Gary's heart shed a thousand tears in that split second. His eyes welled up at the same time, which he tried to hide from her. "Yes, Gary. Nice to meet you".

"You too. I think I've seen you around before, actually. You've been here for a while, haven't you?"

"Sure have", Gary replied, trying to disguise his collapsing emotional state. "You look familiar too", he continued, but with a greater sense of poise.

"I'm gonna take off guys. You going to be okay?"

"All over it", Elle replied.

"Okay, see ya's soon".

Rex walked around the side of the house, out of sight. "There's some still inside", Elle indicated to Gary. As he followed her towards the house, Gary's eyes immediately travelled towards her rear end, as if it was an automatic response. She was wearing tight jeans that showed off her waste and curves, with a tank top that exposed a little skin above her hips. He almost felt hypnotised, watching that waste swing side to side.

Gary heard the bike start as he walked through the front door. Rex revved it a few times and then departed, leaving behind the loud sounds of the muffler. "How long have you been in The Web?", asked Gary.

"Few years now", she replied, whilst picking up another box.

Gary followed suit and picked up a box next to her, which was stacked against another dozen or so. They both walked outside and placed them on the ground with the others and then repeated until they were all outside.

"Is that it?", Gary asked.

"That's it,", Elle replied, looking straight into his eyes.

Once again, Gary was blown away by how beautiful she was. She wore very little makeup and had her hair tied back in a simple ponytail, but she still looked like she was a glamour model. "Fuck, just phenomenally sexy in every reality", Gary thought to himself. She was slightly sweating all over her body, which reminded him of the copious massage oil that he had rubbed into her skin throughout their relationship. It gave him some tingles in his groin, making him feel a little awkward and horny at the same time. But it was her deep brown eyes which glistened in the sun that dominated his attention, because gazing into them prompted him to imagine all the lives that he had stared into them.

"Straight in the back then", he said, trying to snap himself out of the comatose. He picked up a box, put it in the back of the ute, and slid it up against the front wall. Elle grabbed a box, handed it to him and then repeated until it was fully packed.

"Alright, ready to roll?", she asked him, with a slight huff in her breath.

"Wouldn't mind a glass of water?", he asked, deliberately intending to extend his time alone with her.

"Oh shit, of course. Sorry", she apologised, almost excessively.

Gary and Elle spent the next twenty minutes refreshing themselves and talking casually. Gary asked her about her life and she did the same. It was a great feeling for Gary to get to know this version of her, and it inspired him with a little hope. "Well, if I can't get back to my old world for whatever reason, then at least you're here with me", he said to himself, happily.

"Shit, we better get going", she reacted, once she realised how long they'd been talking.

"Ready when you are", Gary reluctantly concurred.

They got in his ute and headed down the driveway. As Gary put his indicator on to turn left Elle suggested that he take a right as she knew a shortcut around the back. He followed her direction and travelled two to three kilometres before she pointed to a dirt track. "That's it".

Gary turned onto it and moved at a much slower pace, due to the potholes and narrowness of the track. They were in the thick of the bush when it came to a clearing, where they saw a green ute, a red sedan, a couple of tents and a fire.

A man and a woman in their late twenties walked out in front of them, waving them to stop. Gary pulled up a few metres ahead of them, as he noticed several more men and women at the camp. "Have you seen them before?", he asked Elle.

"No, I don't think so. I don't like the feel of this, Gary. Apparently robberies and looting have spiked since The Skulls went live. Let's see what they want and get the fuck out of here".

Gary wound down his window as the man walked up to it. "Hey fella, how's it going?", he said, with a thick, ocker accent. "What you got in the back there?"

"Just some old clothing for the community centre", Gary replied, quick-wittily. "Can we help you at all?"

"Nah, not really", the man responded, in an increasingly distrustful manner. In a swift move he reached through the window in attempt to grab Gary's keys from his ignition. Gary grabbed his forearm with both of his hands, and bent his elbow over the door with extreme force. The cracking sound it made almost matched the look of pain on his face.

"Fuck off cunt!", Gary screamed in rage, whilst pushing him away from the vehicle via his face. He hit the accelerator which shocked the woman who was still standing not far in front of the car, but she was able to jump out of the way before it hit her. They sped past the camp site where two men were jumping into their ute to give chase. He looked in the rear vision and saw them reverse out whilst the other man hopped into the back passenger seat.

"I wish I didn't take us this way", screeched Elle, in a panic.

"Don't fret baby, we'll be fine", Gary replied. "We just need to get off this track. How far is it?"

"Two k's, maybe three", she answered. "I'll call Rex and the boys now and let them know what's happening and where we are".

He took on the trail like a rally driver, whilst Elle called Rex. He swerved around potholes and fallen branches, narrowly missing trees and shrubbery. The adrenaline hit flowing through his veins was making him feel highly receptive, like his senses had been sent into hyper-drive.

After two or three minutes, which felt more like a lifetime, he had lost them from sight, as the last few times he had checked his side and rear mirrors he wasn't able to see them. "They won't catch us now", he reassured her.

They came to an end of a long left hand bend where Gary was forced to slam on his brakes. In front of them was a tree blocking their path. "Fuck, they've trapped us", Elle exclaimed. "The boys are coming. They know where the track hits the mains road".

Without saying a word, Gary reversed whilst looking for an opening in the bush to get around the tree. As he swung into a bushy section that contained no large trees, the green ute pulled up next to them and cut them off. "What are we going to do? Should we run?", questioned Elle.

Gary had a calm wave of energy wash over him. He felt more powerful than he ever had before. "No Elle, let me handle this".

He exited the car and told Elle to lock the doors. "Trust me, everything's gonna be okay", he said to her, with a smile that made her believe him. She followed his direction and watched him walk towards their vehicle.

"We don't need to do this", Gary said to them calmly.

"You've fucked my arm, you're gonna pay", said the man, holding his elbow.

"You brought it on yourself, mate. Look, I'll give ya's one more chance. Leave, or get hurt".

The men standing in front of him broke out in laughter. They outnumbered him three to one. They were all of a decent size and one of them held a thick log that resembled a baseball bat. "You think you can take us", said the man with the bat. "You must be a little bit loco", he continued, in a crazy sounding voice.

He ran towards him and took a hard swing at Gary's head, but he smoothly moved out of the way like he was a Matador teasing a bull. As he came back towards him Gary leapt forward and plunged his right hand finger-knuckles deep into the front of his throat. The man dropped his bat and reached for his neck with his hands, sounding like he was being choked by a rope. As he dropped to his knees

Gary met his jaw with his right knee, which sent his eyes rolling backwards and his body crashing to the forest floor.

The second man had run up behind Gary by this point and crash tackled him with force, ensuring they both fell to the ground. He was at least one hundred kilograms, so his strength was a challenge for Gary. He still managed to wrestle himself free, however, and in a fluent movement picked up the bat and cracked it across the back of his head, behind his left ear.

Both of them lied motionless as Gary directed his attention to the man who had tried to steal his keys. By this point he was running towards the vehicle, so Gary sprinted to stop him. As the man tried to start the car, Gary sent his right fist through the open window to connect with his mouth. The man fell to a slump, and Gary discharged the keys from the ignition.

"Irony's a bitch", Gary said with a smirk, like he was reciting a line from an action movie. He turned to see Elle running towards him, with her arms held out.

She jumped up onto him and wrapped her arms and legs around him, and kissed him on the forehead. "Thank you, thank you, thank you", she said with pure gratitude. After hugging him for a few seconds she jumped off and thanked him again. "Oh my god, you were amazing, Gary. Thank you so much. Thank you for fixing my fuck up".

"You didn't fuck up, how were you to know?", Gary reminded her.

One of the men was starting to stir, so Gary walked over and sent a forceful blow to his chin with his left foot. "We can't let these fuckers go free, they'll just hurt others", Gary said to her. At that moment two cars appeared on the other side of the log, with at least one being Al's. Seven men hopped out and ran towards them, but pulled up to slow jog once they witnessed the carnage around them.

"Holy fuck, you loose cannon!", yelled Al, as he ran up to Gary to jump on him. "Get this man a fucking beer!"

Rex walked up to Elle to see if she was okay, whilst the boys gave Gary a hug and some high fives. Rex then walked up to Gary and without saying a word, hugged him strongly.

"Get the rope and the chainsaw Hugh", commanded Al. "You right to take Hugh's car with Elle, Gary? We can take it from here".

Gary looked at Elle, who agreed. "Let's go", she said, with a flirty smile.

"Do you want me to come with?", Rex asked Elle.

"You stay with the fellas, Rex. I'll be fine", she said comfortingly.

Hugh closed the boot after he pulled out the rope and chainsaw, and then handed Gary the keys. "Well done mate," he said, with a male-bonding pride.

"What are they going to do with them?", Elle asked on the way back to Gary's house.

"Take them for processing and then trial them publicly, I assume. We'll have to provide our statement by tomorrow, but for the meantime, we can relax".

After they arrived back to his house, Gary offered her a tea. "Would rather something a little stronger", she said cheekily. "If you've got some vodka, that'll be perfect".

"Orange, lime or lemon with it?", he queried.

"I'll have lime and lemon, but let me make it. You go have a shower and wash that energy off you", she said, whilst looking at his knuckles which had splashes of blood on them.

The water was hot and steam had filled the entire room. As Gary washed himself, he thought about how grateful he was that no one got seriously hurt. As he rested his head against the wall with the water running down his back, he heard the bathroom door open. Straightening himself to investigate, he wiped the condensation off the shower door. Standing there was Elle, completely naked.

He opened the door and without saying a word, she stepped into the shower with him. Their hands ran all over their bodies, leading them to embrace in hot, passionate kissing. They felt each other. They pressed against each other. They exposed themselves to each other.

"You called me baby, do you remember?", Elle asked inquisitively.

He had forgotten about it, but she had jolted his memory. "I do remember, now. Sorry, slip of the tongue".

"No, don't apologise. You protected me. You cared for me. You saved me. You can call me baby whenever you want", she replied, in a tone that felt both sensual and sexual in nature.

They locked into another deep kiss. After the shower they immediately fell onto the bed and made love like they had done it in a thousand other lives. For the rest of the day they fucked some more, in between talking and laughing and behaving silly, especially the more they drank. They learned so much about each other in such a short period of time, igniting their fire once more.

Elle had already called Rex to let him know she was

staying the night with Gary. As they laid wrapped in each other's arms in front of a warming fireplace, the exhaustion of the day finally got the better of them.

And suddenly, Gary was gone.

CHAPTER 18

Leader

"Look what you did, Gary", the Voice said, with a chuckle.

"Oh fuck, not you again", Gary responded, with an explicit dose of disappointment.

"You can't get rid of me that easy".

"I was beginning to think this was all one big dream, like I'd dreamt another life with Elle before I met her in that one".

"You created that experience with your love for her, with your desire for her. It was powerful, Gary. You illustrated how powerful love really is".

Gary reflected to himself how beautiful the previous encounter was with Elle. "It's like our love is beyond us, beyond space and time. I will make it back to you baby".

"Alright", Gary said, diverting his attention back to the Voice. "Where do I go from here?"

"Well, why do you think you are here?", the Voice responded.

"To learn, to heal, to grow", Gary replied confidently.

"Okay, then you tell me. Where do you go from here?"

Gary focused his attention on his body-less consciousness floating majestically through space. He looked deep into his mind to uncover his next steps. Suddenly he could see an outline of his body, like it was materialising in front of him. It swirled with lines of energy, some which had colours and others that were transparent. It then began to build itself, drawing in blocks of energy and matter from the stars in the cosmos. He could see himself from an internal perspective, as well as an external one, as his body took shape.

As it neared completion, a light brighter than the sun engulfed him, blinding him momentarily. It faded enough for him to open his eyes, which gave him a surprise. He was back on earth.

"What are we going to do now, Sir", said a friendly, female voice. "They're definitely planning something".

Gary recognised who it was immediately and looked at her with delight. It was Elle. "Alright, I'm liking this manifestation so far", he thought happily. "This must be my own creation, though. I mean, why the fuck would Elle be hanging out with the Pope?", he said to himself, after realising he once again wearing the Pope's attire.

"Give me an overview of our current situation", he said to her, almost overly professionally.

"An overview?", she said in a baffled tenor.

"Yes. Listen, we're at an unprecedented crossroads. We will either go in the direction they want us to head, which is a totalitarian and centralised control system on a planetary scale, or we will go the other way, which is mainly decentralisation, the re-empowerment of the people and a high regard held towards Sovereignty. So, I want to know what your views are. How we got here and where we are. I need your advice".

"Okay, Sir. But might I include something else that is important to coincide with Sovereignty?"

"Yes, of course", he agreed curiously.

"Natural-law", Elle said assertively.

"Natural-law? What do you mean?"

Elle looked at him in a way that said "you're the pope and you don't know what Natural-law is?" Her face quickly wiped the expression though, as she must have realised she was wearing it. "That's a long discussion but let me at least say this. Natural-law has many definitions depending on who you speak to, but there's a very simple way of summarising it. Treat others like you should treat yourself".

"Ah, the Golden Rule. Of course, of course", Gary agreed, trying to sound like he knew all along.

"Yes, the Golden Rule. That includes do no harm unless in self-defence, honour your word, stand in unwavering morality and pretty much respect other people's Sovereignty just like you should your own".

"Well said, I completely agree", he said, whilst thinking about when Wildfire had mentioned it. "Okay, now for the overview", he stated, authoritatively.

"Well, after 'The Great Relocation' government institutions all over the world lost the immense power and influence they had, right? The same happened with the military-industrial complex, as well as the banking and other corporate monopolies. Their demise left a power vacuum though, giving them an opportunity to regroup and restrengthen the corporatocracy".

"Corporatocracy?", he replied.

"You know, Sir. The 'Scam'. The alliance between big money and the governmental machine. The shadow groups and multinational institutions that controlled macro policy design for decades. This is why the people felt that the system wasn't working for them, because it wasn't. It was being used to further enrich and empower those at the top of the power pyramid, at the expense of the people and the environment".

Gary got lost for a moment in how sexy Elle looked when she demonstrated her intelligence.

"Sir?", Elle interjected.

"Yes, yes. I understand", Gary replied, once he regained his perspective. "Go on".

"Many people decided not to consent to the system which brought it crashing to its knees in some ways, but it didn't make all those corrupt and greedy people go away. There are many psychopaths and sociopaths, Sir. More than what we like to think. They've hurt so many people, including children, and they don't care at all. They relish in it, actually. It's a real problem, especially because they amassed all that technology and weaponry. They also have so many people doing their bidding too because they lure them in with their bribes and gifts. We just don't know what to do about it".

"What are their primary methods of control?", asked Gary.

"Banking and energy. We're close to releasing the Universal-Energy technologies they suppressed, but they still mostly control the creation of money, even though community banks made a massive comeback and cryptoservices are decentralising not just the money supply, but how people trade with each other".

"Give me a moment to think", Gary said to Elle.

He began deliberating on the money issue. He thought back to when John was explaining to James about the situation they were facing: "When you control the money especially, you control everything else. That's what the transnational banking institutions are designed to do for the ruling class".

"How can we take full control of the money supply?", he continued in thought. A memory of Gary talking with Al and Rex abruptly collided with his consciousness: "There is something big missing though, like it could be done so much better".

"What is missing?", he then asked himself. This led to remembering something that Aaron had said: "So creativity needs to be encouraged on both individual and collective scales, without the influence of money. If so, the possibilities are endless!"

"That's it!", Gary exclaimed to Elle. "It's not that something is missing, it's that something needs to be removed. Money! Its very existence amplifies all this toxicity, division and suffering".

"How are you going to do that?", Elle responded, with a perplexed look on her face.

"I think I know", Gary thought to himself.

He looked at Elle with an air of conviction. "We'll see, but it's clear that it creates a massive imbalance in our societal structure. If you don't have enough of it, you suffer. If you have too much of it, it can easily corrupt you. If groups have too much of it, they can influence others and the course of humanity, potentially for the bad, exactly like some have. But if you take that mechanism away and design the system so that everybody's needs are met – including food, water, medicine, shelter and a healthy community spirit – then it frees everybody to explore their creative potential, if they so choose. Instead of competing with each other to survive, people will cooperate with each other to thrive".

"Yes, I have heard these theories before", Elle added. "Money is obviously used as a method of control, but it also fosters toxic levels of greed, addiction to power, selfishness, worship of materiality, vanity and an abusive rivalry with each other on both individual and collective levels. The crazy thing is that we've got the technology and prowess right now to automate much of the work that needs to be done, such as factory robotics and self-operating vehicles, including trucks and tractors. We've also got 3D printing technology that could use hemp and other environmentally responsible ingredients to build whatever we need. It's definitely worth a shot".

"Elle", Gary said through the Pope, "I want you to know that I love you. You're the bomb, baby".

At that moment Gary stood up and opened up the doors to the veranda. He took a deep breath and thought to himself: "Fuck, I hope I know what I'm doing". Then he hopped over the railing and jumped.

The light was so immense that Gary tried to put his transparent hands over his eyes, but as soon as it appeared, it dissipated too. Before his energetic body had completely dispersed and he became a body-less consciousness again, he already had decided to take his next action.

"Alright, Voice. Where are you? I know our next step", Gary said with pure excitement.

"And what would that be, Gary?", the Voice replied, as Gary's face materialised in the starry background.

"Before 'The Great Relocation' begins, I want there to be a split between the rich. I know there are many people with money and influence that condemn pedophilia and the enslavement of their fellow men and women. There has to be! The psychopaths are few, and the good are many. So I want these people to organise together and lead humanity to its salvation. I want them to invest in Universal-Energy and automation technologies and then spread it across the world".

Gary thought to himself for a moment, and then continued. "I want their agenda to be pure. I want them to help society become self-organising and self-reliant, so that there is eventually no need for money at all. I want them to infiltrate the governments with their own people, so that it can be converted into a managerial system that honours individual liberty first and foremost, but also helps build the infrastructure required to transition into a world that will actually qualify humanity as a developed species".

"Anything else?", responded the Voice.

"Yes. I want to return to my family, friends and Elle. I want to wake up".

"I'm sorry, you can't".

"Why?"

"You were murdered, Gary".

And suddenly, Gary was gone.

CHAPTER 19

Embracer

Gary awoke next to a gathering of people in a cemetery. He could see his parents, family, friends, and Elle. They were all standing around a casket being slowly lowered into a grave. They were holding each other and weeping, some silently and others uncontrollably.

"The Voice was right. I did die".

He could see his body but it was transparent, like he was a ghost. It reminded him of the energy body he witnessed in the cosmos. Undeterred, he made his way closer to Elle, who was standing in silence with tears running down her face. "I'm so sorry Elle", he said to her. "I don't know what happened".

Gary tried to remember how he died, but couldn't. He wondered if he passed whilst in the game, but then remembered what the Voice had said to him, "You were murdered, Gary". As he contemplated what might have transpired, he realised that he still felt like his good old self, like a human without a physical body.

It catalysed him into the memories of his life. How

he grew up feeling supported by his parents, how he'd had a great time partying with his friends, and how his relationship with Elle had flourished.

He mentally walked through his experience with Elle, reminiscing of fond memories. After they had attended that festival with each other, they were nearly inseparable. The next few weeks were filled with raunchy sex sessions and whatever adventures they could create. Within the first few days they had even decided to take a week off work and travel up the coast camping and surfing.

Gary recalled how they both liked to keep fit, which quickly developed into a ritual where they walked on the beach each morning. They would also run and do exercise circuits together. Their love for staying healthy ended up one the biggest drivers that connected them.

After only six months together, they decided to rent a house on the beach where they ended up living their entire relationship. It had a spectacular view they adored waking up to and the privacy ensured they were never devoid of having their naughty fun. He remembered just after they moved in. Elle was wearing an apron without any other clothing. She woke him up the first morning together and served him a lavish breakfast.

"For my amazing man", he remembered her saying.

He begun eating the food but was distracted by Elle's hot ass as she walked back into the kitchen. He quietly followed and snuck up behind her as she tended to the mess she'd made. He surprised her by kissing her softly on the back of her neck whilst he ran his right fingers up her left thigh and in between her legs. She squirmed in delight by the way he touched her, with her juices soon running down her legs.

The next thing he remembered was taking off his pants and entering her from behind. He fucked her until she came. "It was so loud", Gary thought. "That was the great thing about that house. The neighbours were far enough away that they could scream in ecstasy without worrying about how much noise they were making".

After she shuddered in orgasm, she led him to the lounge, sat him down and climbed on top of him. She ripped off her apron, exposing her firm breasts and bulging nipples, which Gary promptly placed in his hands and mouth. She rode him for the next five minutes, until he came deep inside of her.

Six weeks later Gary arrived home from work to see Elle with a concerned look on her face. "I'm pregnant", she said to him softly. "But I don't think I'm ready for a baby".

It was an easy decision for Gary too, as he didn't feel prepared enough to bring a child into the world. "It's okay Elle, the timing isn't right. One day though I can't wait to have a big, badass family with you so we can make our love last forever".

A couple of weeks later they had an abortion. They were both okay about it, especially because it was generally accepted as normal by the society they grew up in. But as Gary reflected on this experience, he felt a wave of sadness wash over him. "I never got to start a family with her. If only we had that baby everything would be different. We'd still be together".

He directed his attention back to Elle who was standing next to his mother and father. The casket had been lowered and someone who looked like a Priest was talking to the gathering. His younger brother Simon then approached the podium where the Priest stood, indicating that he was about to do a eulogy.

For such a young age, he really held his composure well. He pulled out some paper from inside of his jacket pocket, looked into the soul of the audience and then began to talk. "Thank you all for attending today. Gary was one of the greatest people I have ever met. He really looked after me as my big brother. Even though he was so much older than me he would still come and visit us all the time because he told me that he didn't want to miss out on me growing up".

Gary felt good about that choice.

"He was one of the most intelligent people I'd met too. He was always teaching me stuff I didn't know".

This made Gary reflect on his after-death experience where he'd realised he'd learned so little through his life.

"He would play games with me that I knew he didn't like, just to spend some time with me", Simon continued. "But he would also talk to me about all the things he was learning, helping me to become smarter. He showed me things about this world that only he could, because he saw it differently to me. Gary was my role model. He made me want to be a good person".

The sounds of Sophia involuntarily letting out a cry echoed throughout the cemetery. Gerald was already hugging her with his right arm, but leant in to fully embrace her. Elle did the same and hugged Sophia from behind, and they all wept together. Gerald then pulled away and motioned for them to direct their attention back to Simon, who had stopped in the middle of his speech.

Gerald looked at Simon and nodded his head in encouragement to continue his talk. Simon cleared his throat, before recommencing. "My relationship with my brother was a blessing in my life, but I know he made many others feel the same too. Mum and Dad were so proud of him, they loved him with all of their hearts. And Gary loved them the same. It was so obvious he was grateful for them. He would always turn up at home with surprises for all of us, usually just little gifts he got from the charity shop. He loved spending his money there because he was always so disappointed that people could actually be homeless or living in poverty. He just didn't understand how that could happen, so he felt he had to do at least something".

"Hmmm, I never even thought about that since this situation started", Gary reflected. "Maybe that's why I had these specific experiences, because I was so disgusted that we could let people live like that with all the wealth that existed in the world".

Simon turned over the next page and continued. "His relationship with Elle was inspiring too. They were exactly like Mum and Dad. So in love. They were so happy together, always laughing and mucking around with each other. I wish they didn't kiss as much as they did in front of us though", he joked, with a smirk.

A gentle laugh swept through the crowd, which even saw a smile cross Elle's lips.

"I always looked up to them. Like Mum and Dad, they showed me what love is. Ever since I can remember I wanted to have what Gary had one day. I wanted to find my Elle, my love".

Elle wept into her hands, covering her mouth at the same time to muffle the sound.

"There was so much else that Gary has brought to my life!", he continued upliftingly. "I know I'm only eight years old, but I'm pretty sure I'm wiser than my mates because of him", he joked again.

Another surge of giggling made its way through his audience.

"And he taught me how to mentally destroy anyone that decides to bully me too", he continued in cheek, which was followed by another laugh in the assembly.

Simon stood there in silence for a moment. A tear began rolling down his left cheek, followed by one on his right. He took a deep breath, put his head to his chest and then looked back at the audience. "We still don't know why Gary took his own life, and we'll probably never know. It just doesn't make sense, none of it does. I miss him every day, every time I wake up he's the first thing I think of. I ask him if he can hear me, but I never hear him back. I just wish I could say to him that I'm sorry I wasn't there for him like he was there for me".

Sophia and Elle began crying again, sending waves of tears and emotions through the gathering.

"No, that's not true, Simon," yelled Gary, to no avail. "I didn't kill myself. I was murdered! I need to find my killer. That must be why I'm still here".

"I'm sorry Mum, I'm sorry Elle. I didn't mean to make you cry", Simon continued. "I think it's time for me to finish, but before I do, I just want to say to Gary if he's listening that I'll never forget you. I love you, bro".

This blew out Gary's heart, which made his consciousness

fade. As it got weaker and weaker, he had a strong feeling to keep it together. "I love you too, bro", he responded to Simon. This grounded him a little which brought better clarity to his awareness. "I need to be strong", he said to himself. As his perspective cleared its foggy haze, he had an extraordinary sense that something wasn't right.

He could remember his past from this life, as well as the past of his other one in The Web. The memory of his after-death experience was still vivid in his mind too. "Why can't I remember how I died? The last thing I remember when I was alive was being in the float tank. It just doesn't add up".

He walked over to Elle and stood next to her. He waved his right hand through her body to see if he could touch her. It went straight through, making Elle jump a little because of it. She looked bewildered by the experience.

Gary walked right into her to see if he could connect with her. To feel her. As his head met with hers, a flash of light stunned his awareness, which immediately created a journey through a wormhole that was filled with various images that flashed at him as he hit the speed of light. Before he knew it he was within Elle's consciousness, experiencing one of her memories.

She had just finished walking along the beach on a cool afternoon. Just ahead of her was the ramp which steered her off the sand. She was singing a little tune to herself, one that Gary knew well. As she walked up the ramp and along the path that led to their house, she was thinking about something emotional, because he could feel her heart beating faster.

"How should I break it to Gary?", he heard her say to

herself. "I'm so excited, he will be too. I know we're ready to have this baby".

Gary almost lost consciousness. As soon as he heard she was pregnant again he was so overwhelmed with emotion that his awareness started to fade. "No! Be strong Gary. You need to see this!", he said convincingly to himself, which brought his perception back into focus.

He thought about the decision they made several months before. They had decided to be less careful whilst they had sex, without pushing to become pregnant at any specific time. They were simply happy for a baby to be conceived when it was ready, so they were both open to it occurring at any stage.

"This is exactly why there's no way I would kill myself", Gary reflected, trying to convince himself.

Elle walked past his car in the driveway and opened the front door, which was already slightly ajar. "Gaz, where are you?", she yelled out. There was no answer, so she went into the bedroom to see if he was there. His bag was on the bed, but nothing else had been disturbed. She went back into the lounge room and then headed towards the garage. "Probably playing with his toys", she thought to herself.

She opened the side door to the garage and immediately let out a bloodcurdling scream. Before her hung Gary, from a noose around his neck. He wasn't moving and appeared lifeless, urging her to run to him, lift him up and take the strain off his jugular. He was too heavy for her to make any significant difference, so she rushed over to where his tools were. She grabbed the closest sharp object she could find, which was a hacksaw. Then she dragged a stool from his makeshift bar, climbed up and cut him loose.

"I don't remember any of this", Gary thought, with utter contempt for himself.

His body fell to the ground with a cracking thump. She fell on him and hugged him, screaming for him to wake up. "How fucking dare you Gary!", she bawled in tortuous pain. She put her ear to his chest to determine if he was breathing. After not hearing any signs of life, she rolled him flat onto his back and began pumping his chest. She pressed it at least fifteen times and then opened his mouth, breathing into it five times. Then she pumped his heart again with two hands, crying for him to regain consciousness.

"What have I done?", Gary tormented himself. "Why?"

Elle stood up and ran back into the lounge room where she had placed her handbag. She pulled out her phone and dialled emergency, whilst running back into the garage. She pressed the speaker button as it rang and then placed it next her on the ground so she could continue trying to revive him. As she thrusted her hands into his chest a voice answered the phone.

"Gary, you need to come back. It's your time".

And suddenly, Gary was gone.

He recuperated his perspective almost in reverse to how he left the Voice last time. The building blocks of his body broke apart one by one and rocketed into the infinite, like a puzzle unravelling itself. He was once again awareness, without a physical body.

"You said I was murdered, Voice. You lied to me!"

"Did I?", the Voice countered.

"Yes, you did!"

"You WERE murdered Gary. You murdered yourself".

Gary was projecting his anger at the Voice because he

didn't want to accept that he'd killed himself. "It just doesn't make sense. I was happy. Elle and I were even keen to start a family".

"Gary, I know it must hurt. But you needed to know, so that you didn't get stuck in the in-between. You needed to face the truth, so you could move on. It's been too long already, Gary".

"Why didn't you tell me from the start?"

"You chose your experiences Gary, you always have. And you've got another choice to make now".

"What do you mean?", he asked inquisitively.

"You need to decide now if you want to reincarnate into your baby. There is no energetic frequency ascribed to it yet, except for a combination of you and Elle".

"So I'll forget this entire experience?"

The Voice let out a loud laugh, which petered off into the distance. "Yes, that's part of the recycle. It's facilitates the process of learning and growing".

"But I feel like I've still got unfinished business. Why do I need to decide now if time is illusory?"

"I'll make this simple for you, Gary. You either want to go back to Elle, or you don't", the Voice replied, with a slight hint of aggression.

Gary thought privately about the ultimatum that the Voice was giving him. He then thought about the weird tone it just spoke to him with. "It just doesn't make sense", he said to himself again.

"Listen Voice, I appreciate the offer but I'm gonna have to decline. I need to finish something, I just don't know what yet".

And suddenly, Gary was gone.

CHAPTER 20

Server

Gary begun to stir from his slumber. He was feeling warm and cosy wrapped up in his blankets so he didn't want to wake up yet, but then the memory of his discussion with the Voice snapped back into his awareness.

He sat up really quickly, like he was running late for work. "You okay, Gary?", asked Elle, from in between the inviting sheets.

"Yeah, I'm good, just had a strange dream", he replied. He was back in The Web, the morning after meeting Elle.

Once again this tested Gary's sanity. "What's real?", he thought to himself, as he made his way to the bathroom to rehydrate. He drank two large glasses of water and then stared in the mirror whilst touching his face with his hand. "I need to get a grip", he said out loud.

"Get a grip on what?", Elle enquired, as she walked into the bathroom.

"Get a grip on you", he diverted, whilst grabbing her around the waste and leaning in to kiss her neck.

She giggled, pushed him away and walked to the sink. "I need some water too".

Gary walked towards the kitchen and out the front door to a very early morning sunrise. He had a quick stretch and then picked up the local newspaper, unrolling it as he walked inside. When he saw the front cover, it pleasantly surprised him. The headline read:

"MONEY OFFICIALLY A TOOL OF THE PAST".

Under it the subtitle stated:

"World Services Agree that Money is No Longer Necessary for Human Development".

"Hey Elle, did you hear this? Money is being wiped from the system".

Elle was walking out from the hallway and said with a chuckle, "No shit, Gary", as she switched on the kettle. "You know the majority of places haven't had money since it was sociologically established that it created an uneven playing field, resulting with too much scarcity and suffering, and not enough abundance and freedom".

The memory of his recent embodiment as the Pope overshadowed his awareness. "Okay, I must have a tonne to catch up on", he thought to himself.

From inside his bedroom, he heard the sound from an incoming text message. He hurried in to investigate and saw that it was Al. It read: "I'll be there in ten minutes".

"Damn, Al will be here in ten", he shouted to Elle. "I need to get organised".

"I'm coming too", Elle responded. "I'll be quick".

They rushed having a shower and getting dressed for the day. They packed some fruit and other snacks for lunch and quickly drank a lukewarm coffee that Elle had made for them. Biting into an apple, Gary heard a noise in the driveway, followed by a soft beep of the horn. "You ready? He's here", Gary said to Elle, who was in the bathroom fixing her hair.

She walked out with her bag over her shoulder. "Let's go", she said, whilst grabbing him by the arms and looking straight into his eyes. "But first, yesterday was amazing. Well, not the first part, but getting to meet you. Our time together. You are an enigma, Gary. I can't wait to see where this leads".

Gary leaned in and kissed her lips, which she reciprocated by lifting her hands onto his head and kissing even deeper. As they pulled away from each other, Gary said, "You have no idea how powerful we are together".

"Exactly what I'm talking about", she said with a slight giggle. "Alright, come on. Let's go".

Gary grabbed his bag and the paper and headed out to meet Al. "Take the front seat", Elle guided him.

Gary was blown away from what he saw. His own vehicle was exactly the same, but the vehicle Al had pulled up in was hovering about a foot above the ground. There were no wheels, and only a light fizzing sound was coming from what seemed an engine.

They both hopped in the car and greeted Al. "Hey lovers", Al said with a smirk. "Ready for an adventure?"

They simultaneously answered by saying, "Sure am".

This went unnoticed by Elle and Al, although it didn't escape Gary's acknowledgement. "Even in this life we're synchronised", he thought happily to himself.

"What's the plan?", Gary asked.

Al pressed some buttons and the vehicle did a one

hundred and eighty degree turn where it hovered, and then proceeded along the road which was made of a brownish coloured cement. "We're heading up Mount Voice for some meditation, remember? I've just got to drop into the Café and get a coffee first", Al informed them.

As he advanced towards the store, Gary went through the article in the paper. It stated that close to five years ago the word 'Government' was replaced by the word 'Service' to rebrand and redesign the role that this mechanism played. These institutions were so distrusted and condemned by the public that they vowed to hold them accountable for the philosophical and practical carnage they had not just facilitated, but generated for all those years before.

The article then listed some of the original changes the public demanded that led to the shift, which included electoral reform to dissolve two party duopolies so that independents ethically represent their communities and external money is removed from the political process, replacing entire tax systems with a transaction tax to ensure all individuals and corporations were contributing fairly, the transparent nationalisation of central banking systems to create sovereign money supplies, the abolishment of any plans for a cashless society, unplugging surveillance violations, demilitarising police, eliminating forced medications, purifying food and water supplies from harmful toxins, intelligent reforms to educational platforms for both adults and children, decriminalising drugs and funding medical research into psychedelics and other natural medicines, de-corporatising scientific endeavour, widespread creation of open-source platforms, huge funding of community media for honest societal and systemic debate and finally a modern debt jubilee to cleanse the system from its unpayable debt and somewhat rectify the extreme economic imbalances that existed.

It then went on to say that tens of thousands of communities all over the planet were already operating as money-free, because the technological infrastructure was already in place providing their core needs. It stated how important the 'Frenergy' technology was for facilitating this transition, which Gary assumed was the Universal-Energy devices. It also pointed out that 'The World Agreement' was fundamental to it as well.

Gary contemplated what 'The World Agreement' was. "It has to relate to Sovereignty and Natural-law", he thought to himself.

"So when are you going to design your Hover, mate?", asked Al, interrupting his internal dialogue. "I know you love the old school cars mate, but these things really are amazing. No emissions, little chance of accidents, just smooth sailing. Plus, you get to design it exactly how you want!", he continued, with an excitement that reminded Gary of a kid in a candy store.

"I'll get round to it", Gary replied. "There's just something about being connected to the ground that I don't want to give up yet", he elaborated, intuitively.

"Fair enough", Al said, supportively. "Now, about yesterday. You'll have to provide your statement this afternoon, but they've already agreed to ten sessions with Shrooms at the Clinic. The women too. Apparently they broke down in utter despair after they were taken in. One of the guys said that he'd been dying for intervention for a very long time. It's so awesome. Slowly but surely, all these lost souls are finding their freedom and connection again. There's just been so much trauma and bad wiring and suffering for so many years, it takes a while to flush it out for some people".

"That's great news", Elle interjected. "You probably beat some sense into them", she said with a satisfied smirk, looking at Gary.

"I'm just glad they're standing up to be counted", Gary answered. "Pride can be such a damaging force, especially when it gets in the way of facing the harm that you've caused not just others, but yourself too".

Al steered to the left and pulled into a lively street, with people walking in every direction. The buildings looked fairly new and strikingly unique. They were surrounded by trees and gardens, with birds and other animals soaring through the air. Everything looked refreshed, like it had been through its own rebirth.

"You want anything?", Al asked them.

"Nah, I'm good", both Elle and Gary responded concurrently. Gary turned around and this time they both smiled at each other and laughed.

"I'm just gonna take a quick look around", Gary said, interrupting his own laugh. "You okay here or you want to come with?"

"I'm good, you strange man", Elle answered, with a cute smile.

He opened the vehicle door and jumped out. He watched Al walk into a Café and begin pressing buttons on one of at least ten self-serving coffee machines. He continued walking along the pavement, almost aimlessly. That was until he saw a sign that said, 'Books'.

He walked into the shop and navigated around several people standing in front of various shelves, some with books in their hands. Thinking back to the article, he was determined to find a copy of 'The World Agreement'. He had his head turned to his right, scanning one of the bookcases, when he accidently bumped into an elderly lady.

"Oh, I'm so sorry", Gary declared with innocence.

"No problem, son", she replied with sincerity.

Gary recognised her immediately. It was the woman from the elevator, when he was Buzz talking with Warwick. And ironically enough, she was holding a book in her hands that was titled, 'The Shift – A Concise History of The World Agreement'.

"I am after something like that, actually", Gary said to her. "Where did you find it?"

"Right here", she said, whilst pointing at a shelf just above her head. "There's plenty there".

"Great. Thank you", he said appreciatively, whilst reaching up to grab a copy. "Have an awesome day".

He turned it over to look at the back, whilst moving slowly towards the door. He had noticed many people walking in and out with books without a cashier of any type, so he had already made the assumption it was free. He meandered out onto the path in the direction of the Hover, and read the back cover. It stated:

> *"Humanity has evolved. This transformation wasn't of a biological disposition, but of a philosophical and practical nature. It was an evolution of consciousness. Humanity was a species that created so much*

suffering for itself throughout its history, but all of it eventuated as a guiding example of how not to exist. The People of Earth in the 21st Century had reached their limits with conflict and scarcity, which invigorated their thirst for designing a world where cooperation and abundance were highly valued.

When large parts of the population began to take their future into their own hands, it resulted with a mass expansion of humanity's collective consciousness. First came 'The Great Relocation', followed closely by the spread of technology that freed them from mundane labour. Then the Services of the world developed a life-changing covenant, called 'The World Agreement'. It is an unprecedented manuscript in the history of humanity because it reflects the shared desire for a just future for the human family.

Enter 'The Shift'; the transition to a world which uses the principles of Sovereignty, Unity and Natural-law to create a planetary ecosystem characterised by Health, Abundance and Creativity.

Gary had just finished reading it as he reached Al's Hover. "Well done, Aaron", he thought to himself, acknowledging that his key values were integrated into the Agreement.

He raised his head to see Elle quietly sitting in the back, playing with a touchscreen computer on the back of Al's seat. She was sparkling with sexiness, as per usual. It made

Gary want to take her up to Mount Voice alone to explore their tantric connection.

Al was already in the driver's seat, ready to go. Gary hopped in and put on his double seatbelt, which reminded him of the ones in a racing car. "What ya got there?", Al asked, looking at the book.

"It's called 'The Shift – A Concise History of The World Agreement'. Just want to tune up my understanding of it all", Gary replied.

"How many times do you want to read it?", chuckled Al. "I've still got the copy you gave me, actually. It is a great read, though. Really puts into context how 'The Shift' unfolded".

Al began to operate his Hover and then proceeded towards Mount Voice. Gary took the opportunity to flick through the book. He went straight to the contents page and read through the chapters, in an effort to find where 'The World Agreement' was outlined in full.

He turned to page thirty three and started to read through the agreement. He skimmed through the few pages that detailed it, which he noticed was relatively short for such an important document. "Makes sense, though", he thought to himself. "No need to get lost in too much information, just keep it short and sharp".

It was soon obvious that the key principles were the foundation to it. There were some other major concepts that stood out to him too. The first one was '*Decentralising the Social System*', reminding him of when Elle had said something similar to the Pope. Others were '*Localising Resources*', '*The Pursuit of Truth and Justice*', '*Restoring Human Vitality*', '*Healing through Vibration*', '*Redesigning Education*',

'*Replacing Surveillance with Community*', '*Ending the War on Drugs*', '*Managing Artificial Intelligence*', '*Repairing Natural Systems*', '*Celebrating Diversity of Culture*', '*Expanding Individual and Collective Consciousness*', '*Decommissioning Nuclear and Universal-Energy Weaponry*', '*Neutralising Electromagnetic Pollution*' and '*A Future Without Money*'.

It was about ten minutes later when Al stopped his Hover to engage the wheel-based system. "They reckon the machines will be sorting this out in the next few weeks", he stated, referring to the dirt road that led up the hill.

They made their way up the mountain road whilst Gary continued his reading. He stumbled on a chapter titled 'The Bee Economy'. It described the transition humanity was making from a 'Scavenger Economy' to a 'Bee Economy'. It defined the Scavenger model as a scarcity-based economy where each individual had to compete for their piece of the resource pie just to survive, whilst the Bee Economy was a model where everybody worked together in an interdependent way to build a 'Resources Hive' that supported the life of the Queen, which was defined as the principles outlined on the back cover.

The chapter went on to describe the incredible change of thinking that was required for this to occur, including that generating an abundance of needs helped to reprioritise what was important in people's lives. It also illustrated how the natural strengths of each individual were utilised for the benefit of everyone, and that the creative principle also helps to manifest new strengths according to the desires of each person.

"It's definitely a totally different mind and heart space", thought Gary.

The Hover took the last winding left before the road reached its end. "Alright, everyone ready?", Al asked, with an air of passion and excitement.

"Yep", Elle and Gary responded in unison again, prompting Gary to smile into Elle's eyes.

They all gathered their gear and set up to the top. Al was a little more eager than Gary and Elle, so he pulled away from them pretty quickly. Now alone, they talked and laughed whilst absorbing the natural surroundings, pointing out different plants and animals that they knew to each other.

When Gary saw the gap in the trees that first showed off the valley to Aaron and himself, he stopped and grabbed Elle from in front, slid behind her and hugged her, with his head resting on her shoulder. "Look at that view", he whispered into her ear. "It gets even better up top, but while we have some privacy I thought we should take it in together. It's magic, right?"

"Yes, it's beautiful, Gary. Like you. I don't know what's going on, but everything has felt so strange since I met you. You make me feel a little bit crazy, but in a good way".

"Crazy between your legs, you mean?", Gary said, cheekily.

"My pussy is a little loco over you, yes, you fucking dick", she said whilst giggling. "But there's something about you, about us, which seems … I don't know. Sorry, probably just the adrenaline from all that sex yesterday", she continued, slightly embarrassed.

"It's okay Elle, no need to apologise. I hear you", Gary said comfortingly. "You wouldn't believe me if I told you what I was experiencing either".

"I'll listen to you though, crazy man", she said with a smirk.

"Maybe one day", Gary replied, "but right now we've got a view that wants to corefuck our eyes".

They both laughed whilst Gary slid back in front of her. He looked right into her eyes, put his left hand on her neck and pulled her mouth towards his. First they kissed each other in a sensual way, but it soon developed a fiery, sexual energy. They grinded their bodies against each other and kissed like wild humans, whilst their hands begun to explore each other at the same time.

"Okay you mountainous man", Elle said, whilst pulling herself off him. "Keep this up and I'll be too energised to relax into the meditation".

"I don't fucking care", Gary said with a little grin.

"We've got plenty of time for that", she responded, in a flirty way.

"If only you knew", Gary thought to himself.

They proceeded through boulder city, with surprising ease. Gary helped Elle through the tough sections, especially to take the opportunity to touch her body. The entire experience was a tease for them both, as they relished in each other's sexual drive but knew they'd have to wait a while to release it.

Gary climbed the embedded rock first to help Elle if she needed it, but as she reached the edge of the cliff she pulled herself up like she'd done a million times before. She stood next to Gary and took his hand into hers, whilst they both gazed down the valley in awe of its majesty.

Two eagles flew in circles directly in front of them.

"It's stunning, isn't it?", Elle said with a luscious smile. "I haven't been here in at least a couple of years, actually. The first and last time was with Rex, but it wasn't as beautiful as this moment. I'm glad we get to share it together, Gary".

"Me too", he replied softly.

Around twenty metres to their left, Al sat cross-legged with his eyes shut. He was already lost in his meditation that it appeared that he hadn't even noticed they'd arrived. Gary pulled out a small blanket which was in his backpack and walked over to the cliff edge. He placed it on the ground, wide enough for both of them to sit on it.

Gary had a gut feeling that once he entered into a meditative state that his perception was going to shift again, so he wanted to make the most out of the opportunity. "Come here", he motioned to Elle, almost at a whisper. "I want another kiss".

She strolled over, swinging her hips as a tease. She grabbed him by the shirt and kissed him so hard that he almost fell to his knees. "Anytime you want", she said sexily.

They both sat down and made themselves comfortable. Elle grabbed his hand and kissed the back of it, before settling into a resting position and shutting her eyes. Gary felt compelled to sneak a quick look at her whilst she sat still, in silence and with her eyes closed.

"A goddess", he thought to himself. "My goddess".

He took one last look at the rising sun and inhaled a deep breath of the fresh, crisp air. He then shut his eyes, which flooded him with a torrent of nervousness from what was to come. His visual experience initiated with a blanket of darkness, but not long after an explosion of colours and symbols began to dominate his consciousness.

And suddenly, Gary was gone.

CHAPTER 21

Communicator

"Welcome back, Gary", said the Voice, in a slightly different tone than usual.

"Do you really mean that?", Gary replied, with an obvious attack of cynicism.

"What's wrong, Gary? Have you not liked your choices?", the Voice responded, ignoring his question.

"My choices have been fine", Gary countered, "it's just that I don't trust the boundaries you have placed on me".

"You still have the choice to return as your baby's consciousness, if you so choose".

"See, this is exactly my issue. You told me last time it was my final chance, but here you are now telling me that I still have the opportunity. You're lying to me Voice, I can feel it. I don't trust what you say anymore".

"Listen Gary, you're ready", interjected the Voice. "There's something I've wanted to tell you, but you haven't been ready before now. You don't have to hear it if you don't want, yet it is important that you do. But beware, it's going

followed shortly by crystallised chunks of the cosmos, all of which he embodied. As his body was in the process of materialisation, he noticed it looked very different but he couldn't quite figure out how. As it came to completion he wasn't exactly sure what sex he was, but he felt more male than female. Then the bright light returned, shifting his perspective once more.

As his surroundings became apparent, Gary realised it was nothing like anything he had seen before, at least that he could remember. His previous life appeared to be one that existed on a future timeline.

He was in a giant city with buildings, lighting and technology that was unbelievable at first sight. Everything had a strange glow to it, like it had an energetic field of some kind. As he experienced his body running down a well-lit street, Gary could see numbers and other information in his view, which he assumed was from a futuristic helmet that he was wearing. There was also a name in the top right-hand corner, which was 'Apollo'.

"So that's why I keep manifesting people called Apollo?", Gary speculated.

He also noticed that there was a bizarre lack of people. As he took a sharp left turn into a dark alley, he realised he hadn't seen one person or vehicle. Something didn't feel right to him, at all.

Apollo came to an abrupt stop at a large metal door, which prompted Gary to notice the solid attire he was wearing. "Military gear?", Gary contemplated.

He then experienced his consciousness drift through the door and into the room on the other side. It looked around, seemingly checking for signs of life. After finding none, it shifted back into Apollo's body. He then pulled out a little device from his jacket pocket, pointed it towards the door and pressed a button that sent a laser towards the lock, melting it in front of Gary's eyes.

The entire section of the door liquefied onto the ground. Apollo kicked it in and advanced inside. As he proceeded through the building with secrecy and stealth, Gary could feel the super strength that Apollo's body had.

As he rounded a corner, a woman in her early twenties surprised Gary, but Apollo behaved like he knew she was there. He immediately grabbed her by the throat and pressed his gloved finger into her heart which sent an electrical pulse into her body. She dropped dead in front of him, with steam fizzling out of her orifices.

"What the fuck?", Gary yelled, disgusted with himself. "I'm a killer!"

Without showing any signs of regret, Apollo continued the trip through the building. Another female of similar age exited through a door in the hallway, and Apollo engaged her with a similar technique. He then darted through the entrance and stood in silence whilst his consciousness explored the building.

The experience for Gary was like looking through the premises with a birds eye view, but all the walls were transparent, even though he could make out their shape and location. There were many people scattered all over the place, with huge clusters of them in certain areas. Apollo focused on where these bunches were and then zoned in on a specific individual in a particular group. He then mapped out the most efficient route to get there whilst avoiding as many people as he could, with one slight detour.

As Apollo left through the same door, it felt like a video game for Gary. The route was displayed in the vision provided by the helmet, which Apollo followed meticulously. He came to another door, but this one was already slightly open. Inside the room were four men busy working with what appeared as chemistry equipment. Apollo pointed a different device towards them which shot out four laser beams, hitting them all directly in the heart.

Gary was impressed by the accuracy of it, even though he was devastated that he was heartlessly murdering innocent civilians.

Apollo moved over to the wall and pulled a vent cover off. He then crawled inside and followed the map that was showing on his screen. After inching about twenty metres, he did something with another device which dematerialised the panel from beneath him.

He dropped four metres to the ground, in amongst ten or so people. What happened from that point felt so surreal to Gary. His consciousness slowed down to at least half of its usual time-processing speed, as he watched Apollo shoot two beams to his right, dropping two people instantly.

He then ran three steps towards a wall and took two large steps up it, then flicked himself into a backflip as five thick laser beams hit the wall beneath him. "Weird", thought Gary. "The beams didn't do any damage to the wall when they hit it".

Apollo twisted to land face-on to the remaining nine people, and with the same device he sent out a forceful charge of energy that seemed to vibrate the room as it made its way through the air. It hit the people with a strong impact, which resulted in them shaking violently where they stood. Whilst they were immobilised, Apollo did an incredible series of manoeuvres that was like watching a Kung Fu movie.

Whilst still in slow motion, he forward-rolled towards the closest person on his right and punched directly into their chest as it he stood up. This sent the man backwards with steam coming out of his cavities whilst still flying through the air. Apollo then rolled and moved to every other person to undertake a similar action, whilst they all stood there with blank stares on their faces as they vibrated from the force.

Gary assumed that the laser weapon didn't work whilst they were in that shuddering state.

As much as Gary was repulsed by the vile treatment of these people, he was more than captivated by the experience. It was hard for him to watch all these lives be slaughtered, but at the same time he admired the skill and professionalism that Apollo employed.

Apollo then walked over to one of the men lying crippled on the ground. He took out another device and sent a blue laser directly into the man's arm. The laser sliced it open like a scalpel, cutting out a square part. As he rummaged through the layers of skin and muscle, he pulled out a small metal electronic device that resembled a large computer chip. Apollo then rolled up his right sleeve, unfused a similar looking chip from his arm and then re-fused the new chip with another laser, this time yellow.

Gary could initially feel a burning sensation, but a subsequent green beam activated by Apollo made the pain instantly disappear. "This is beyond any sci-fi movie I've ever seen", thought Gary.

Apollo then headed towards the door. He stopped and once again projected his consciousness into the hallway, which swiftly returned to his body once he realised the coast was clear. He exited the room, turned to his right and ran towards his destination.

In the process he murdered another three people who were casually strolling out of rooms to the side. "This is a nightmare", Gary thought. "I'm a cold-hearted killer. I don't feel any guilt or shame from Apollo, only passion and desire. Even if I have a worthy mission, why did all these people need to die? Surely there could have been another way?"

Apollo was running at the same time as he projected his consciousness into the space around him. The perspective from Apollo's body was always in focus, but it coincided with a floating, navigating viewpoint. To Gary it felt like he had two perspectives, the normal one coming from the body and another one from something like a video camera on a drone. It reminded him of when he was split into twelve layers when he visited the Voice in the other dimension.

The entire experience became fluid, like there were less boundaries to his consciousness. It was once again progressing in slow motion, but it unfolded really quickly at the same time. "It feels like a living paradox", Gary thought, with growing interest.

Apollo was focused solely on his mission. He would run and murder and slide and maim, all with a smooth energy that radiated poise and strength. It was clearly building to a climax as he had increased the velocity by which he was behaving.

As he projected his consciousness into the large room ahead, Gary saw a group of several hundred people all standing in white, oval-shaped pods, which reminded him of the dryers that would be placed over heads in a hair salon. They had no bottom, but were close to touching the ground. There were also hundreds of little blue lights on the inside that were shining into each person's body.

Apollo's consciousness scanned the environment, apparently looking for the individual who he had discovered in his prior assessment. He located them, charted their exact position and then quickly absorbed back into his body. He then shot out a transparent film with a gun that he unstrapped from his back, which completely dissolved a large part of the wall that he was running towards.

As he jumped through the hole he pressed a button on his left wrist which coated his body with a light-blue energy that looked to Gary like a force field. He was immediately met with a firecracker of lasers and other beams of light. They hit his field but were absorbed into it, like it was gaining strength because of it.

He weaved and ducked through the heavy fire coming from dozens of angles, which seemed odd to Gary because none of the beams that were hitting his field seemed to have any negative effect. Gary looked to see where the shots were coming from, noticing they were located on the roof and looked like huge Gatling guns.

Apollo's consciousness was again split into two, one of which was hovering over him in an effort to guide him towards his target. He piloted through dozens of rows of people who were in their pods face-first, hiding what they looked like.

A huge explosion suddenly rocked Gary's awareness. Bodies and pods went flying from all around where Apollo was situated. As Apollo stood up after being flung through the air, Gary noticed that his force field was flickering. It then completely disappeared, making him vulnerable to any incoming fire.

But no beams of light came. Instead, Apollo stood motionless as he slowly began to levitate into the air. His arms and legs were spread out, like a starfish. "NOOOO!", Apollo screamed.

Gary still had both perspectives operating, which meant he witnessed Apollo's arms and legs being torn from his body. Blood was sprayed in all directions as Apollo's heart continued pumping indiscriminately. Gary was somewhat traumatised, as it was complete carnage. "It's like a sci-fi horror movie on steroids", he thought.

Gary watched the rest of Apollo's battered body expand, with cracks developing all over it which were filled with a lava like substance. "No wonder I didn't want to remember it", Gary reflected.

"You failed", Gary heard someone say, followed by a slow, sinister laugh. Apollo's body then exploded in every possible direction. Gary's two perspectives immediately merged into the one floating above, and then he began to fade.

"Fuck no!", yelled Gary to himself. "I'm not leaving here until I see who the target was".

His awareness stabilised a little, which helped Gary feel stronger and in greater control. But then he heard the Voice casually say, "You need to come back now, Gary".

"Absolutely not!", he screamed back. Gary focused his attention on maintaining his consciousness in this realm. It flickered and faded, but Gary held on. "I haven't failed, I won't fail!", he said, almost organically.

His consciousness snapped back to full clarity. He detected where the target was and travelled immediately in its direction. As he floated towards the floor, he noticed tattoos on the necks of all the people in the pods. The closer he got to his target, the clearer the tattoo became.

"7G-3311429V", Gary read to himself. "That's the code from the factory. From Lez's world".

"You need to come back", the Voice repeated, resulting in Gary's consciousness once again flicking and fading.

"Fuck you Voice, this is my choice!", Gary shouted, as his consciousness diminished towards complete darkness. He zoomed into the pod to at least get one look at the face of the target. As his awareness weakened to almost shifting point, he was just able to move in front of them to get a glimpse.

"Elle?", Gary said in utter shock, as his viewpoint completely dissolved into a black void.

Light quickly erupted into his consciousness and his energy body quickly unravelled itself, soon leaving Gary's consciousness free-floating in the cosmos. "I fucking knew it", Gary thought to himself.

Gary's face once again manifested from the starry strikes, indicating that the Voice was about to reappear. "You should have just done what I suggested", echoed the Voice, with a clear bout of rage.

"You almost had me, Voice. But I do not consent. I don't consent to your suggestions, to your boundaries or your version of reality. You're done, Voice. I want you to get out of my way. I choose to go beyond you".

Gary's starry image instantly exploded into an infinite number of parts, which then quickly blended into Gary's view of the cosmos. The entire picture, which looked like a giant hologram, immediately begun to fold in on itself, heading towards Gary at light speed. The entire structure was interconnected by a sticky-looking web of squares that were beginning to catch on fire. The closer it all got, the more the web melted.

In a flash, the building blocks of the hologram had reached Gary's point of view. It entered into his mind's eye and then exploded in a blaze of white.

"Where the hell am I now?", was Gary's first thought.

"You've reached the next level", said another voice, which sounded exactly the same as Gary's.

"Who the fuck are you?", he replied.

It let out what seemed as an involuntary laugh. "I appreciate your scepticism", it responded. "After all, you wouldn't be here without it. You did well, Gary".

"You didn't answer the question", Gary continued, in a tone that indicated he wasn't going to take any shit.

"Now you probably won't believe this, but I am you. I am a different level of you, speaking to yourself. Yet you are not just you, because different levels of energy, frequency and spirits flow through you. Everything is alive, Gary. Everything is in you but you are not everything. You are becoming aware that you are an individual instrument in the orchestra of reality, folding finer dimensions of life into your perspective. You are growing strong. You are becoming aware that you are your own master".

"Okay, enough of this bullshit, I'm going back to Elle", Gary replied, rudely.

"Excellent choice, I'm so proud of myself", it laughed again. "Listen, before you go Gary, you need to hear this. The Voice you were talking to was a spirit you created, but it was slowly taken over by a dark force that has infected your world. It uses your collective energy as its own to fuel the spiritual war. The only way it can achieve this is because life gives consent for the battle to rage internally, so it uses trickery to persuade humanity to maintain this toxic exchange of energy".

"Or it was me playing tricks on myself", Gary countered.

"Or it was both", it double-countered, followed by a deep chuckle.

"I don't believe anything that I hear or see anymore, except the love I feel for Elle and my family".

"That's completely understandable, Gary. However, if you think back, you've already tried to show yourself this layer of truth".

An image instantly formed in Gary's mind. He was the Pope, sitting in front of the controllers of the Church. The following mans' words echoed through his mind: "We know you don't want to serve your real ruler, but you have no choice. As above, so below".

"Alright, so let's just assume for a moment that on some level it's true", Gary stated, redirecting his attention back to his present. "Does that means if I go back to Elle then I'm consenting to its control?"

And suddenly, Gary was gone.

CHAPTER 22

Master

Gary's eyes opened really slowly as his self-awareness breathed into life. It soon became clear that he was in a hospital bed with tubes coming out of his arms. He was stiff and sore, like he'd been laying there for quite some time. He moved his head to look around the room and was more than elated to see Elle sitting in the corner on an uncomfortable looking chair, sleeping with her head rested on her chest.

"Elle?", Gary muttered.

She stirred from her sleep slowly too, but then quickly snapped back to reality once she realised Gary had spoken to her. "Oh my God, Gary! You're back, baby", she exclaimed with great excitement, as she leapt over to hug him. "Bout' fucking time", she said, after delivering a deluge of kisses.

"Just playing hard to get", Gary replied, with a smirk.

"Biggest 'treat me mean to keep me keen' play ever!", she responded, whilst laughing. "God it's been so long you fool, you don't know what I've been through!"

A flood of memories collapsed into Gary's consciousness. "You have no idea what I've been through", he replied, whilst feeling a bit rattled by having to instantly process so much information.

"What do you mean?", she queried.

"I was conscious the entire time, I think", he answered.

"No way. You couldn't have been. You've been in a coma for four days".

"Four days?", he questioned, in a puzzled pitch.

"As soon as you entered the game, we lost you", Elle began explaining. "Apollo woke me up after five minutes because he was concerned with your vitals. The ambulance arrived fifteen minutes later. They removed you from the tank and brought you straight here, where you've been since. If it wasn't for them, you'd be dead, baby. They had you on life support for the first two days but then you showed good signs of improvement, so they took you off the machinery. It was like you were slowly coming out of a deep sleep, little by little. I knew from then on that you'd make it back".

She climbed on top of him and gave him more kisses all over his face.

"Alright, that's enough you stalker", Gary said cheekily. "Where's my parents?"

"They're at the hotel. Your brother too. So, how the fuck are you feeling my sexy warrior?"

"Pretty bloody good, considering. I'm so fucking hungry though. Anything to eat?"

"Hold for one moment, I'll go and tell the doctors you're back. I'll text your oldies too. So freaking happy you're awake, honey!"

Elle jumped off him and walked quickly out the door. Gary slid himself backwards and sat more upright, which took a fair bit of effort. He flicked the sheets off his legs and slowly crunched them back and forth, trying to increase the blood circulation through them. He was weak and found it hard to move, but the more he tried the stronger he got.

Next to him was a cup of water, which he reached over to grab. As he picked it up it fell to the floor because his hand wasn't strong enough to keep it gripped. "Got some recovery to do", he thought to himself.

"Okay, they'll be in soon", Elle said, as she walked back into the room. "Can't eat yet though. They need to do some tests".

"Alright, can you get me some water though?"

"Yes, they said water is okay". Elle made her way around the other side of the bed to retrieve him some. "Oh fuck, what have you done here?", she said jokingly. "Making yourself comfortable I see, already making a mess".

She picked up the cup and placed a towel on the ground, wiping up the water with her feet. Then she grabbed another cup and filled it halfway, and then proceeded to slowly pour it into his open mouth. "There you go my little baby, drinky drinky", she said with a childish grin, teasing him like they usually do to each other.

"Fuck off", he replied, with a fake pitch of anger. "Needed that though", he continued, with water dribbling down his chin.

"I haven't seen you dribble this much since you got wasted at 'The Sound' festival", she teased further.

"And I haven't seen you this cheeky since I last fucked your ass", Gary reacted, with a devilish grin.

"That's enough, you two", said a young female doctor who had just walked into the room. They both noticed the obvious smirk on her face.

"Well, he's still got his smartass attitude", Elle giggled. "That's a good sign, right?"

"We'll run some tests, but he should make a full recovery fairly quickly. I see you're already working on it?", the doctor acknowledged, referring to him stretching his legs.

"Yeah, I'll be fine", Gary replied. "I'm already feeling much stronger than I was five minutes ago".

The doctor pulled out one of the needles, went through some of the paperwork and checked the readings on the monitors. Whilst she went about her business, Gary flicked his pointy finger to get Elle to come closer to him.

"I am so fucking happy to see you, baby. It was you who kept me alive", he confessed, whispering into her ear.

"Is that because you couldn't bear the thought of not fucking me again?", she whispered back, seductively.

"I heard that", the doctor interrupted, whilst wearing another grin.

"Shit, sorry doc. It's been a crazy ride", Elle replied.

As the doctor went about her duties and Elle started to do some tidying up, Gary thought about how his sex life with Elle had always been really active, but healthy. They had always stayed connected on that level, especially because it was a natural way of expressing their attraction to each other. But as much as they played with their lust through each other, they always played with their love through each other too. "We've struck a beautiful balance between the physical and mental attraction in our relationship", he acknowledged to himself.

"Listen, I've done what I need to do for the time being. I'll be back in half an hour", the doctor said with a smile, as she closed the door behind her.

Whilst Gary wondered in awe over the magical connection he had with her, he tried to sit up a bit further, which Elle noticed and helped him to achieve. They spent the next five minutes stretching his arms, legs and back, whilst she informed him what was going on with his family and friends. "Your parents will be here in halfa", she advised, after reading a text message.

Gary felt confident enough to stand on his two feet, so he gradually took his weight with Elle's help. He was still hooked up and couldn't walk anywhere, so he slowly did some squats, reaching a bit lower each time. He felt great being back to some sort of normalcy, even though he needed to rebuild his strength.

The doctor revisited, walking in as he was in mid-squat. "Someone's keen to leave", she remarked.

"Out of here as soon as I can", Gary replied.

"We'll have to keep you in at least overnight, but if all the tests show up okay we'll release you in the morning", she advised him. "It's already three so let's get to it now".

The doctor unhooked him from the rest of the gear, whilst two nurses came in to help. They brought in a stretcher with them, which they prepared. The doctor gave them the approval, so they helped Gary to move to the stretcher. "An hour, max", she told Elle.

For the rest of the afternoon Gary had his tests and then met with family and friends. They hugged and laughed, taking the opportunity to really feel grateful that he had woken up. Another doctor also later informed him that everything checked out and he would be able to leave in the morning.

After an exhausting few hours, Gary was happy for

everyone to leave, except Elle. "I'll sleep in here with you again tonight", she informed him.

"You don't have to babe, you can go back to the hotel if you want. You probably need to get a good sleep", he responded, unconvincingly.

"No fucking way", she reacted. "I'm not letting you out of my sight".

"Until you fall asleep", Gary corrected her, with a mischievous grin.

"Shut up, would you", she smiled. "Now tell me about your experience. How could you have been conscious the whole time?"

"I thought I was lost in the game. You told me I was lost in the game", he answered.

"I told you?", she responded.

"Yes, you did come back into the game to warn me didn't you?"

"No, Apollo woke me up and that was it", she resolved. "I asked to go back in but he wouldn't allow it. He was worried something was gonna happen to me too".

"Oh shit, really? We had awesome sex at one point too".

"So technically you had awesome sex with yourself?", she laughed.

Gary smiled and let out a faint chuckle. "I guess I did. I've always said I'm one of the best fucks I've ever had".

They both laughed for a short time, before Gary resumed the conversation. "So you were there at the start, right? When we manifested the beach house and the butler with the Pina Coladas? We were about to get down and dirty, remember?"

"Yeah absolutely. You did a cheers and then disappeared",

she confirmed. "I was disappointed, but the butler sorted me out", she tormented.

Gary threw a pillow at her and called her a tease, whilst laughing at the same time.

"I'm joking, I'm joking", she chuckled, as he threw another pillow at her. "No, when you disappeared, which literally occurred in front of my virtual eyes, I sort of freaked out. I called for you, but heard nothing in return. I went to the reset point, but still couldn't find you. Then I went back to the cabin and you still weren't there. Then the next minute I was waking up in the float tank with Apollo asking me what happened".

"Well, you should be spewing you missed our fuck session", Gary said seductively.

"You are a naughty man", Elle accused Gary, as she stood next to him whilst he laid on the bed. She ran her hand up his thigh, under his gown and then moved it out of the way of his now thickening cock. "Better punish you", she smiled, as she squeezed it hard.

"You're right, I deserve it", he grinned.

Elle took his cock deep into her mouth. She made it wet with her saliva and then stroked it with her hand to get it fully hard. Then she resumed licking it and sucking on it.

Gary put his left hand behind the back of his head and closed his eyes, whilst soaking in the pleasure. Images of them on the island surfaced to his awareness, which increased his satisfaction. "I can't wait to tell you everything", he said in a deep tone, whilst his body jived on the bed.

Less than two minutes later Gary began to orgasm. Elle had a firm grip on him as he twisted and turned his hips, making sure he was in her mouth the whole time. Gary grabbed her head with his hands and pumped his hips, whilst he reached climax. She took his load into her mouth, which resulted with some of it dripping out and down his shaft.

As she grabbed another towel to clean up, Gary opened his eyes. "A blow job after waking up from a coma. You're the best woman I could ever dream of", he said with a wink, whilst looking into her beautiful, brown eyes.

"Welcome back, baby. Can't hurt to ground you, to release that energetic tension. Plus, you know I don't just do it for you. I'm addicted to your sex", she said, returning the wink.

"I can't wait to return the favour", he replied, in a charming tone.

"Well, why don't you tell me about our virtual sex session", she suggested, whilst falling onto the bed next to him, making sure he watched her slide her right hand up her skirt and between her legs.

As Gary began telling her the story, he interrupted himself. "Wait, have you got your phone?", he asked her.

"Yeah, why?", she replied.

"Because I need to record the story. I should have done it earlier actually, so I can remember as much as I can".

Elle pulled her phone from her handbag, loaded the recording app and pressed record. She placed it on the table next to his bed. "Okay, I can't wait to hear this", she said with excitement.

He told her that he went back to the island and what had transpired. Whilst he recounted his experience with her in the cabin, she played with herself. Within a couple of minutes or so she was reaching her climax, but muffling out her moans so that it was not captured on the recording.

"Okay, so you won't believe what happened next", Gary continued, after licking the fingers that she had placed in his mouth.

He proceeded to tell her how he had woke up in a middle-aged man, whilst he was still in orgasm. This made her laugh, but she increasingly became quiet as he continued the story. When he got to the end of that scene, she was almost in tears.

"How traumatic", she sighed. "What the fuck are you doing creating experiences like that?"

"I don't know", Gary replied. "It still feels so real. Wait till I tell you the whole story, then you might understand why it seems like that".

Elle made herself more comfortable whilst Gary thought about what to say first. "It was a crazy ride, baby. I couldn't work out if I was still in the game, if I was having a dream or even if I was dead. I would feel confident for a little while and then I'd just have no fucking idea what was happening. I was in all these random people, including Simon. I could see through their eyes and could even control them sometimes too. Like literally move their bodies. I was learning along the way, about myself and different perspectives in the world. But it feels like I need to stay open to all of it so I don't get lost in dogma".

"Sounds like a lucid dream", Elle responded.

"Yeah, it does feel that way. Some of it was seriously fucked up, but the magic was off the charts too".

"Weird", Elle replied. "Are you okay with it?"

"Fuck yeah I am, now that I'm back here with you. I f

like a different person though, like the same, but so much more awake. It lifted a veil on so many things. I feel freer, that's for sure. I understand my freedom so much more. The whole thing was a crash course in life and consciousness and what the fuck is going on in this reality?!"

"You still love me though, yeah?", Elle asked, half sarcastically.

"Of course I do my sexy girl".

Gary lent over and gave her a sensual kiss on the lips. He then climbed onto her and they hugged each other in a sweet embrace. "Love you so much", he whispered to her.

"Me too, baby", she replied softly back.

Gary got back onto his bed and spent the next couple of hours explaining what had taken place. He was getting physically stronger so every now and again he would stand up to stretch and walk around the room. Elle was captivated with his tale the entire time, bursting out with laughter at some moments and crying in others. The story was so vivid in Gary's mind that he was able to explain it with graphic detail, which convinced Elle that there might be some validity to it.

"I'm so glad you're recording this. You should write a book about it one day", suggested Elle.

"Yeah, maybe. Would make a good TV show actually, especially if Arnold Schwarzenegger played the lead role", he replied, with a wink.

They both laughed before he finished the rest of the tale, explaining how the code was tattooed on the back of her neck and that at the end he was talking to himself after e had challenged the Voice. "And then I woke up in the hospital, and you were sitting next to me. It was the greatest relief I have ever experienced".

"Hmm, I'm sure you've had better reliefs than that", Elle replied with a tone of cheek.

Gary smiled, but he was too busy thinking about how good the adventure was, now that he had some time to reflect on it. "If only I could show you Elle. I wish you were there with me", he said, in a tired voice.

He was starting to get sleepy. While Elle organised her bed his eyes flickered open and shut till they became so heavy he couldn't keep them open. Without saying a word, Elle pulled the blankets up to his shoulders, turned off the recording and then hopped onto the bed with him. She knew she'd have to eventually settle into her couch for another unpleasant sleep, but first she wanted to feel him close to her.

She spent the next few minutes sharing her soul with him.

The next morning, Gary was awake bright and early. The sun was barely above the horizon when he woke Elle up by stroking her hair. "Ready to finish our holiday?", he asked her, as she opened her eyes.

"Yes, baby", she answered. "Thought you'd never ask".

He had already showered and dressed. His strength was pretty close to normal, although he wobbled a little on the odd occasion. He was excited about getting out of the hospital and heading back to the hotel. He planned to walk on the beach and even take a quick dip, to get a salt cleanse. He was rearing to go.

"Come on, come on, come on", he reiterated to her. "Let's blow this joint!"

Elle packed up her things and they walked out towards the internal reception at the ward. "Checking out, please", Gary said to the nurse.

The nurse followed the standard procedures and gave them their paperwork. "Now stay away from those video games", she joked.

As they walked out through the front doors of the hospital, a large Raven made its loud 'RA' sounds. Elle then began to explain the dream she had the night before. "So I was sitting in a park and there was a playground in front of me, which even in the dream reminded me of your experience. I felt like I was lucid, at least for a moment. Then one of the children ran up to me and starting talking about a new video game he just got. Bloody hell Gary, now I'm bloody dreaming about this crap", she said light-heartedly.

"Hmm, well for once I had a restful sleep", Gary responded, happily. "It feels like weeks since I blacked out like that. Can't remember a thing, actually. It was bliss".

As they walked over to the hire car Gary absorbed as much sunlight as he could, opening his arms and facing directly into it with his eyes closed. "I missed you!", he yelled to the sun.

They hopped in the car and drove to the hotel. "We'll head out for some breakfast and a swim after I get changed, yeah?", Elle suggested to Gary.

"Sounds good. Sounds perfect", he answered, whilst rubbing her forearm and then squeezing her hand tightly. Gary had never felt so in love with her, so close to her, which was an incredible feeling for him.

They entered the car park, unpacked the car and got an elevator to their floor. As they opened the door to their room, a musty odour hit them. "I'll open the curtains and windows and let some light and air in", Gary informed her. "You get changed".

Elle made her way into the room and threw her bag on the bed. She stripped completely naked and then located her swimmers. As she was putting them on, Gary walked up behind her, kissed the back of her neck and then spun her around.

"I fucking love you, Elle", he said, with pure passion.

"I fucking love you too, Gary", she replied, with the same energy.

They embraced each other in a long, fiery kiss, which got a little heated. Gary pushed her back and said, "As much as I want to make love to you right now baby, let's wait till later. I've got to get outside for a while".

"Oooo, the suspension", Elle giggled. "I can't wait", she smiled.

She finished putting on her swimmers and then rummaged through her bag to retrieve a skirt. She pulled it out but then was struck by something she saw on the hospital paperwork.

"It has to be a coincidence?", she thought to herself. "Or maybe he was able to tap in psychically somehow?"

She picked it up and turned towards Gary. "I need to show you something baby. Take a look at this".

"What is it?", he asked casually.

"Take a look at your discharge number. Does that look familiar to you?", she enquired.

Gary looked at the number that had been generated when he exited the hospital. It read:

'7G-3311429V'

"The code", both of them stated, simultaneously.

And suddenly, Gary and Elle were gone.

Printed in the United States
By Bookmasters